About the Author

The author has undertaken many roles in his working life, from mail boy to national sales manager, from underwriter to head guide of a tours company. In this capacity he wrote the company's recorded commentaries and their range of "Uncle Bob" audio downloads.

A quarter of a million people a year marvel at these recordings (perhaps marvel is too strong a word, let's settle for listen to).

He is also old enough to know better.

To S for persisting

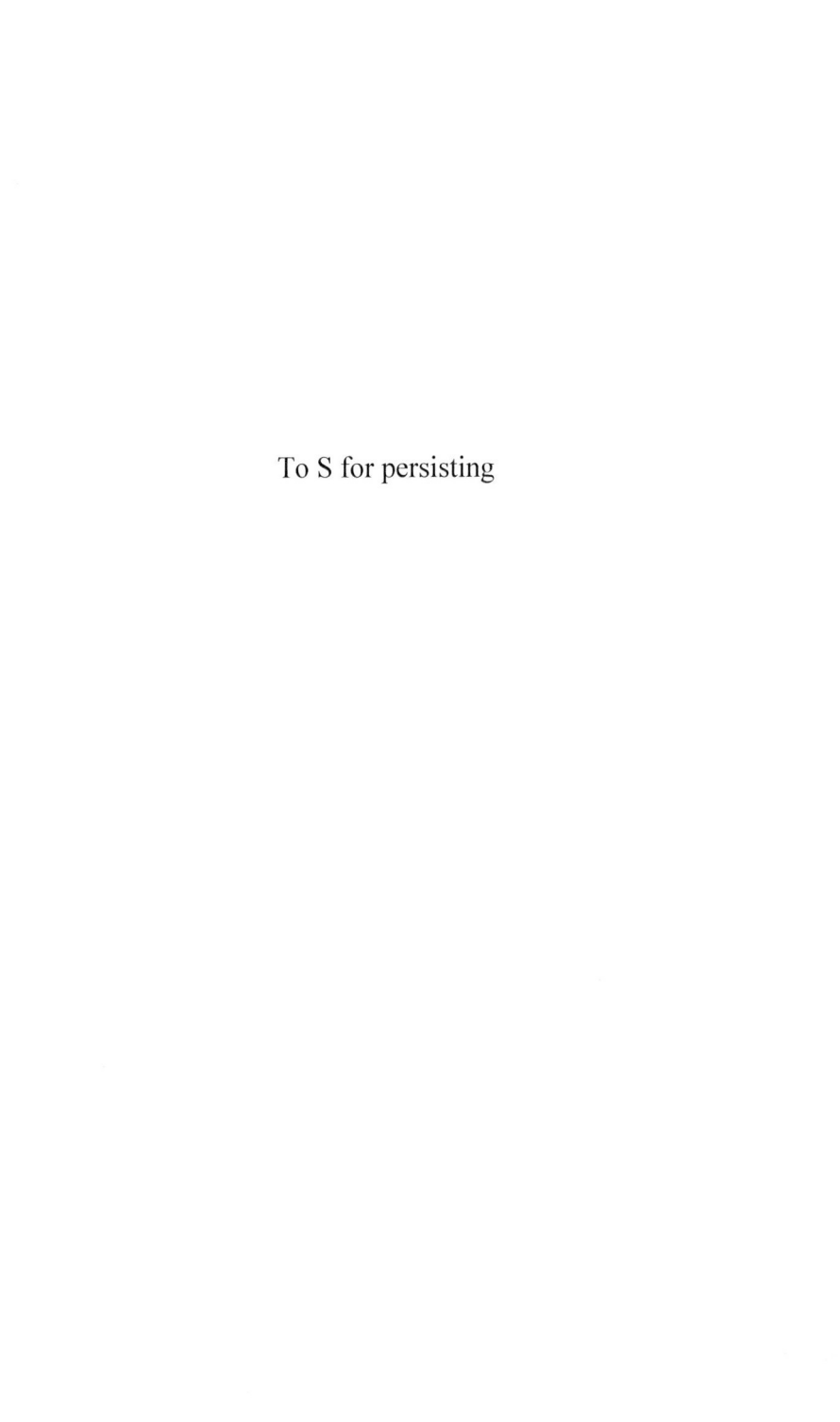

Robert Leslie

DEATH OF A GREY MAN

AUSTIN MACAULEY
PUBLISHERS LTD.

Copyright © Robert Leslie (2017)

The right of Robert Leslie to be identified as author of this work has been asserted by him in accordance with section 77 and 78 of the Copyright, Designs and Patents Act 1988.

All rights reserved. No part of this publication may be reproduced, stored in a retrieval system, or transmitted in any form or by any means, electronic, mechanical, photocopying, recording, or otherwise, without the prior permission of the publishers.

Any person who commits any unauthorized act in relation to this publication may be liable to criminal prosecution and civil claims for damages.

A CIP catalogue record for this title is available from the British Library.

ISBN 9781786294296 (Paperback)
ISBN 9781786294302 (Hardback)
ISBN 9781786294319 (E-Book)
www.austinmacauley.com

First Published (2017)
Austin Macauley Publishers Ltd.
25 Canada Square
Canary Wharf
London
E14 5LQ

Prologue

Beauty they say is in the eye of the beholder. Whether or not that is an absolute truth I cannot tell but what is an absolute truth is that grief is in the heart of the bereaved.

I sat at my father's office desk and looked at the remains of a life: a fountain pen, and as I looked at it heard his voice intoning, "There can be no other type of pen."

A calculator.

"It must have a paper roll; you cannot get proper output without checkable input."

A large book embossed in gold lettering marked the "Principals of Accounting and Actuarial Tables."

"My bible."

The impedimenta of his profession, just as a doctor with his stethoscope slung round his neck, as a badge of his professional competence, so the accountant clung to his calculator as a token of his.

"The Mysterious Death of Grey Man," the paper headline had read. A headline that had caused my mother to summon me from an audit in deepest Wiltshire; as my father before me, and as his before him, I too was a grey man, a third generation Edinburgh accountant.

I was the very epitome of respectability and moral rectitude, or crashingly boring and deeply dreary, as my wife of short acquaintance, and even briefer marriage had called me.

The marriage was almost as short as the courtship, perhaps mercifully so, as by the third month she had smashed her way through all the afternoon tea and all the morning coffee sets, and was about to start on the dinner service.

"If you marry in haste, you will repent in leisure," my mother had said and God how I hated it when she was right.

Chapter 1
An Untimely Death

My father had been found, one frosty late November night, inelegantly draped across a Crimean War Portuguese manufactured cannon, which guarded the eastern approach to Edinburgh's Calton Hill.

He had been found by a courting couple; a pair of star crossed lovers, both, however of the same sex. Calton Hill can be that kind of place after dark. Lovely, almost panoramic views by day, but when that light of day fades to the dark of night this is not a pleasant place to be. The abode of people, who have something of the night about them, inhabiting poorly light places.

Calton Hill represents the city of Edinburgh well; when the light dims so does the morality of the citizens.

The loving pair having first taken the trouble of looting the corpse, "He didnae need a bloody gold watch any mair, his time hid run oot ken," one of them had said when arrested for robbing a corpse.

Oh the profundity of the second class mind, a logic that is hard to refute.

The coroner had diagnosed that death had been caused by a small neat bullet hole in the left temple, which if it had been difficult to spot would have been given away, by finding that there remained nothing of the right temple.

Death by suicide had been mooted, until my mother pointed out that he was profoundly right-handed and had no training whatsoever in the art of contortion.

The police then somewhat reluctantly, it appeared, treated the case as murder.

The motto of the former Lothian and Borders Police Division of Scotland was "Semper Vigilo" which of course, is Latin. Presumably a language readily understood by the city's criminal classes whose fluency in this dead language is the envy of public schools the length and breadth of Britain.

Should you be puzzled, translated it reads "Always Vigilant" but fails to add "to be nowhere they're actually needed."

At my first interview with a representative of the local constabulary, much to my great disappointment he did not intone "There Has Been a Murder." It was clear that since they had ruled out my mother that I was next on their 'to do' list.

"Most people are murdered by someone they know," was the opening gambit of one of my interviewers. Whether this was a fact or something the detective had picked up from watching repeats of "The Bill," I was not entirely sure.

However, he did seem very pleased with relating this fact, so I felt it would be grudging on my part to query his assurance.

We managed, the constables and I, with a few phone calls, to remove me from the frame for the crime; since which time the trail had gone as cold and was as uninteresting as last week's fish supper.

When asked what progress, if any, was being made, the stock reply, given by an equally stock policeman and imbued with what he considered the correct amount of gravitas, was "We is proceeding with our enquiry and we wish to make no further comment at this time." He could have added 'at any other time' but didn't.

The papers, as is their way, moved on to the next sensation leaving me with the memory of lurid headlines, bad puns and dreadful alliteration. No more "Homosexual haven halted," no more "Calton courting couples questioned closely" and thankfully no more "Accountant slain facts don't add up" or "Murdered accountant's son swears to balance the books".

We were saved by the onset of Christmas, the opening of Princes Street Gardens Winter Wonderland and a collect five tokens and receive a complementary glass of mulled wine offer.

To be saved by such banality, is in its own way, a form of punishment both cruel and unusual.

Now as real spring broke through and early summer beckoned, I was sitting for the first time at his desk, *my desk*, and wondering if taking over the firm was the correct decision for me. It had, of course, been the correct decision for my mother and the correct decision for my sister and the correct decision for the firm's employees. I had simply gone along with and simply acquiesced to their version of my future.

As I sat there, 'my first day at the helm', as my mother had mentioned at breakfast, I wondered why we used so many bloody nautical terms. Maybe I thought she would like me to have the full complement turn out on deck and have them trim the sails. This first day I thought, as Henley would say, when 'I am captain of my soul and master of my fate'. God more nautical musings, it was a shame that I felt I was neither of these things.

My previous employer had been considerate and we had parted on the best of terms perhaps ensuring that if all failed I had a bolt hole to run to, a place where normality prevailed.

Routine can bring with it serenity and in such serenity, certainty and if there was one thing I lacked at that moment it was certainty.

The door opened and framed in the aperture stood Miss Wilson, coffee tray in hand. Miss Wilson was the twice daily dispenser of cheer; Arabica in the morning, and Earl Grey in the afternoon and was the unfailing, 'unstinting, uncomplaining mistress of routine.

I had known her the best part of forty years and she had not aged perceptibly; it as though she had emerged from the womb pre-greyed and bespectacled. There, I know, had been a mother but whether or not she was still on the scene I did not know and now did not seem the right time to ask. So I put on my mental to do tick list; a covert enquiry would be for the best.

"Good morning Mr. Alexander."

Touchingly respectful as always.

"Good morning to you Miss Wilson and I would really prefer if you called me simply Alexander."

She coloured slightly.

"Is that entirely appropriate? What about the junior staff?"

I smiled. I am told I have an engaging smile, but that was by mother' who could hardly be said to be a disinterested party and went on, "Well it is in keeping with the times. Even Edinburgh must embrace the fashions of the 21st Century."

She smiled back.

"Just as you say Mr. Alexander."

She turned and left.

Work in progress, I thought, work in progress.

I poured the coffee and the phone rang. I picked up the receiver and listened.

"It's the Weldon Hospice Trust on the phone for you sir."

"Thank you Agnes, please put them through."

"Mr. Gray?"

"Yes, Alexander Gray speaking how might help you Mr?"

"Macbeth, James Macbeth, can I say how sorry I am over the loss of your father. As you probably know he was finalising the accounts of the Old Hospital for the Incurables, which we have taken over to create a new palliative care day centre."

The Old Hospital for the Incurables: what odd people our Victorian ancestors were, actually calling an infirmary a Hospital for Incurables. One wondered if the words "abandon hope all ye who enter here" were emblazoned above the entry.

"Yes, I am sorry about the delay with the final accounts and the asset register and thank you for your condolences. One of my colleagues has been working on them and they will be finalised by Friday and I will personally sign them off and courier them to you."

"Well thanks that's great, but that's not the reason I phoned. The contractors were cleaning out the old matron's office, that's the one where your late father had been working and when they moved a large Victorian desk, they found a notebook that appeared to belong to your father.

I thought with something so private, rather than pop it in the post we could maybe meet and I can hand it to you personally."

"James that's extremely thoughtful of you. Where is your office?"

"It's in a basement, but the basement *is* in Charlotte Square we, of course don't advertise the exact location to prospective donors, just the image of Charlotte Square."

"Well that's not far from Ma Scotts in Rose Street how about meeting there instead and I can buy you a pint for your trouble, at say one o'clock? I'm in my early forties, six footish and mildly athletic rapidly becoming mildly overweight. Accountancy tends to the sedentary existence."

"Sounds great, I'll look out for you and the beers are on you, mind."

There was a pleasant hint of laughter in his voice. I felt I could come to like James Macbeth.

"As long as I obtain a receipt for the purpose of reclaiming the value added tax. I am not my father's son for nothing!"

I joked, "I would expect nothing less from an accountant, especially an Edinburgh accountant. I'm about the same dimensions as Poirot and about the same age but no moustache."

The last words I said in a mock French accent. I know it should be Belgian but who can tell the difference unless it's another Belgian.

"Mais oui," I replied, he laughed and rung off.

Chapter 2
A Notebook Causes a Problem

Scott's, or in my father's time, Ma Scott's, and there had actually been a real Ma Scott, was a bar with which I had a long acquaintance.

In *his* day the beer came in half pints; pints were terribly working class, not the thing for the burgeoning middle class. Unaccompanied women were refused service, owing presumably to the proximity of many brothels, and a business lunch was a pork pie with or without mustard and if you were a high roller, garnished with crisps.

Ah, those heady salad days of my late pa's life.

Nowadays Ma Scott's was, although still distinctive, slipping into the ordinary. It had the statutory outside tables not to promote a continental atmosphere but to provide a little last comfort for the modern day leper; the tobacco smoker.

As I entered there was a fair sprinkling of besuited and betied businessmen, bankers, solicitors and others of that ilk. Also a fair sprinkling of early season tourists, the casualness of their attire in some way an affront to the glory days of this drinking establishment.

As in many places in Edinburgh the predominant accent was English, rather than the native tongue. I approached the bar having caught the barman's eye. He was an unprepossessing youth with bright red acne and matching hair. I ordered a pint and sat down in a seat commanding a view of the door.

At twenty past the hour no sleuth-dimensioned person having arrived I reasoned that something had obviously turned up to detain him so I thought since this pub was but a short stagger from his place of employment, I would stroll across to his office and as it were confront him on his own territory.

I thought about having one for the road, swithered and flipped a mental coin which came down on the side of go. I thought of playing best of three but settled for acceptance of the first decision and left without, as my elderly long gone but much loved uncle used to say, further refreshment.

The air outside, when I had made my way through the smoke-laden curtain that hung round the pub, was quite warm. So I turned to the right, walked along Rose Street and turned right again along front of the Roxburghe Hotel.

What greeted my eyes was a scene only too familiar in modern cities; where speeding metal objects cohabit a space with much less robust flesh and blood beings. When these beings come into contact with the vehicles, the flesh and blood beings always come off worse.

There was the normal packed huddle of official figures and the normal ambulance with its blue light flashing, although its siren had been silenced. And the normal pathetic rag doll-like bundle of the victim strapped to a stretcher.

Then, suddenly, a not-so-normal fear gripped me; an irrational fear, a primitive fear. I stepped off the pavement and approached the group. As I did so an officialdom in the uniform of a policeman detached himself and, with all the self-assurance of his office, put out a hand out to bar my way.

"Nothing to see here, sir, just move along."

He spoke in a well-rehearsed officialese manner.

"With respect that is obviously not true, there is obviously something here to see," I replied, struggling to keep my foreboding from sounding like sarcasm. I am never at my best when dealing with officialdom.

The constable looked faintly incredulous that someone had questioned *him;* this guardian of the law.

"Do you know who the victim is?" I went on.

Another uniform peeled off from the official party. This one had stripes on his arm.

"Problem here, Williams?" enquired the newcomer.

"No Sarge, just an inquisitive member of the public I think," Williams replied.

I looked up, "No Williams, this is not an inquisitive but interested member of the public who was meant to meet somebody near here, and that somebody has failed to turn up."

The constable stiffened and the sergeant inclined his head and said in an almost conciliatory tone,

"He has no identity on him sir. Would you care to see if you recognize him? I should warn you, he's not at his best."

"Thank you, sergeant, I will see if I can help," I replied.

The officers ushered me through the cordon to the stretcher, which was now being hoisted into the ambulance.

I noticed, with mounting concern, that the blanket had been drawn over the victim's head obviously now not so much a body, now more of a corpse.

They pulled back the cover to show a face that was pale, literally deadly pale and, beneath a receding hairline and without moustaches (either French or Belgian) a remarkably round face. Whether or not he actually resembled the great detective in life, he certainly did in death.

"I think his name is James Macbeth and he has," I paused, "He had an office in a basement on the far side of the Square. He worked for a company called the Weldon Hospital Trust."

"You think."

The sergeant utilised a heavily interrogative tense.

"Well yes, you see, I've never actually met him, but the corpse corresponds with the description he gave of himself. That and the fact he was walking across the street should at least throw some light on the matter," I replied.

"Yes."

He half-turned and looked at me directly, "Yes, and perhaps you would care to accompany me?"

It was not really an invitation as invitations go, so I accepted.

"Why not?"

We moved off in uncompanionable silence and passed a couple of people, presumably witnesses to the accident, being interviewed by another policeman. As I trotted dutifully behind the sergeant I noticed one of them glance at me with more than a passing interest; he was a rat-faced individual in a chav baseball cap. After we had regained the pavement, he paused and drawing out his notebook he said,

"For the record, could I have your name and address, sir."

Back to routine then, for these people their own comfort blanket.

"Alexander Robert Armstrong Gray. I am currently residing with my mother in flat F/2 27 Morningside Road," I confirmed.

He duly noted down the details and we recommenced walking.

"You said that you had arranged to meet the deceased. Was this a business meeting?"

"Not strictly. It was more private, although our paths crossed because of business. My firm was auditing some books for his company."

He looked round sharply as if he had had a sudden revelation. His expression was now one that exhibited intensity and added interest.

"Gray, you anything to do with the accountant chappy Gray who was murdered before Christmas?"

I looked back with matching intensity and interest.

"Yes, he was my father."

"Ah was he indeed?" the sergeant said almost reflectively.

"Indeed he was."

"And the matter you arranged to see this Macbeth fellow about?"

I let my gaze soften, but picked my words carefully.

"He had come across a notebook that belonged to my father, which he presumably dropped when he was completing an onsite audit."

"And that would be where sir?"

"Not that I can see it's of any importance, but the Old Hospital on the Southside."

"On the Southside. The one that was for incurables, the one that's now in the process of being converted?"

Apparently, our sergeant was a man who liked his questions, I thought, but answered his query.

"Yes, that's the one. That's what Weldon Health do, they run private hospices, but why the interest?"

The officer was obviously unsure how much, if anything, to say. He struggled with his conscience but then he made up his mind. After all, as they say, confession is good for the soul.

"It's just that the whole thing is well, odd, very odd."

This aroused my interest, so I prompted,'
"In what way is that sergeant?"

"Well you see that accident your acquaintance had? Well according to a couple of eye witnesses, it was a run of the mill hit and run, except that the car stopped and the driver appeared to go back to check the body."

The sergeant again paused then continued.

"Only it just occurred to me that perhaps he wasn't checking the body, maybe he was robbing it."

Chapter 3
A Mystery deepens

Having had my interrogation, our next port of call was to visit the basement office which was, as the constabulary said, purely routine. This was run by a competent thirty-something woman with discreet make up, a distinctly county look and legs to die for.

She was at first doubtful, then resentful, then tearful and when she reached the last of these stages, the good sergeant felt that his enquires were at an end. He left having extracted from me a promise that I would drop into Gayfield Square Police Station within the next forty-eight hours to sign my sworn statement. With that assurance he took his leave in a peremptory fashion, leaving the world not to darkness and me, but to a sobbing PA and me.

She confirmed in an accent that could have cut crystal that Mr. Macbeth had left at twelve fifty to meet a Mr. Gray for lunch at Ma Scotts and that he had put a small package in his inside pocket and left in the normal way of things.

She further confirmed that he was a bachelor who had lived in a flat in the Corstorphine district of the city but no, she did not know of any relatives.

As the tears subsided I said, "Look you have had a bit of a shock, why don't you shut up here and we will go and grab a drink?"

She looked doubtful but the idea did seem to have its appeal.

"But I just can't leave the office I mean there's the phone and I'll have to let Mr. Weldon know. He's our principal, mind you he is away at the moment, pressing flesh in the hope of new donors so I suppose …"

Her voice tailed off, she was looking for a way out. I know an insincere objection when I hear one so I reassured by saying, "Put it on answering machine. It'll' be fine for an hour or so."

"Are you sure?"

"As your company's accountant, I insist."

"Well if you put it like that, how could a gal," and that's exactly how she pronounced it, "possibly refuse."

She started to shut down the computer whilst I phoned the office from my mobile. When I asked for Miss Wilson and was interrogated by Agnes on the switch board as to my name, I simply replied Alexander but when she put me through I was announced as *Mr.* Alexander. Having explained the reason for my call Miss Wilson, totally unmindful of my previous request, reverting to type, rang off by saying goodbye Mr. Alexander.

Forestalled again I thought, however, there was a simple way round it. In future I would address her not as Miss Wilson, but by her Christian name and, having made my plan, I felt much better.

It wasn't till later it occurred to me that I did not know her Christian name or, for that matter, if she even had one. She was bound to I reasoned, but not with any lasting conviction it has to be said.

"Well I'm ready."

The well-articulated voice broke into my thoughts.

"Right let's go, oh, and by the way my name is Alexander."

She smiled and, true to her class perception of the proper diminutive of my name, she replied, "Pleased to meet you Sandy. I'm Camilla but people all call me Cammy."

I have no doubt they do I thought. Only my mother and selected maiden aunts had ever called me Sandy; that being the contraction for Alexander favoured by the upper classes, rather than the middle class (Alec) or heaven forefend the working class (Eck).

We walked round the side of the Square, crossed the road and went down a flight of stairs to a convenient pub, Whigams Wine Cellars. I ordered a bottle of Leith Claret, robust and red. We sat in companionable silence as I looked round the room. It was close to three o'clock and I was amazed at the number of people who seem to have not only the leisure time but the money to indulge at that hour of day.

My fellow patrons ranged from the solitary scholarly type seated at the bar with beard and crossword folded paper. By the looks of him it had to be either the "Scotsman" or the "Guardian," to a couple of late-lunching businessmen clad in regulation pinstripe. Then to a group of giggling girls, possibly a hen party across several nondescript patrons, to two lovers lost in each other's eyes and possessing a barely suppressed longing for each other's bodies; all sense abandoned in the headiness of an affair, driven by lust and fuelled by mutual desire.

God, how I envied them. Even though they might, in finality crash and burn, that emotional rollercoaster ride before journey's end would be worth putting up with almost any consequence.

Again a voice intruded into to my thoughts, "Heavens I did not know you were back in town."

I looked up. The speaker was a tall gaunt man about my age and bespectacled. We had long years ago shared

Economics lectures at Heriot-Watt University, although my parents had money, his had real money so Maximillian Charles Montague-Mackenzie and I had been merely nodding acquaintances. My postgraduate existence was predestined as accountancy in my father's practice, his as merchant banking in the fleshpots of the Capital, but as is the way in polite Edinburgh society we always observed the niceties.

"Charles, how good to see you, how the hell are you?"

He smiled broadly and replied, "Dodging along, you know how it is, just dodging along. What brings you to this financial backwater? I thought you were slumming it in the Home Counties somewhere."

"Wiltshire. I came back for dad's funeral and am, at the moment, running the firm."

He looked genuinely taken aback.

"I am sorry, I didn't know. When did it happen? I mean how did it happen?"

"He was murdered late last year."

"Murdered. Your father murdered, I can hardly believe it. I am sorry to hear that news. I am just back from the States. I have been raising the finance for a dam project so I have not exactly been keeping up with the news from the old country. How's your mother taking it?"

He looked genuinely shocked. I paused then replied,

"Much as you would expect, stoical to the end and beyond. Unfortunately, since the police have not arrested anyone for it she can't even move on to some closure."

His shock had given way to embarrassment about not knowing of the death so he asked the only possible question, "Look, what are you both drinking? I'll buy a bottle and join you."

That's Charlie; ever the practical man. Life comes life goes; only alcohol is constant, only alcohol is eternal.

I introduced him to Cammy and explained the circumstances, the turn of fate, that had brought we two and, by extension, we three, together. It became immediately apparent that she was taken by Charlie and I had soon become an adjunct to the group, so it was a form of relief when my mobile went. I glanced at the screen, it was the office. Why is it never a gorgeous temptress luring me away with honeyed words? And if it was, how would I tell by sampling looking at the screen. It occurred to me that I was beginning to develop Walter Mitty-like tendencies.

"Hullo who wants me?"

"It's Agnes Mr. Gray. A party has been trying to contact you and he said it's urgent. He's' left a mobile number and asks if you could phone him as soon as possible."

"What sort of party?" I enquired.

"Dead common Mr. Grey, he says that he can do you some good, whatever that means. Do you want the number?"

I assented and she gave me the number with exaggerated slowness as if talking to some child who was hard of thinking. I wrote it down on a handy beer mat. Mind you since this was a wine bar perhaps just the generic term drinks mat would be more appropriate.

I entered the number the first time, as usual incorrectly but on re-entry I heard it ring and a pause and then a cautious voice spoke monosyllabically, "Yes."

"Who am I speaking to?"

"You rang me pal. If youse dinae ken whae I am why the chuff are ye cawing me."

I had no difficulty guessing who this was; it was Rat Face.

"My name is Alexander Gray, you've been ringing my office asking for me. Can I help you in any way?"

I tried to keep my tone neutral and curiosity out of my voice.

"Jaist the opisite pal. I can help you."

His tone was confident; caution here was needed so I said hopefully noncommittally,

"In what way would that be?"

"I got the reg nummer oh the stotter that knocked yer freend doon."

I did not correct him on that detail but went on, "I take it this is not a charitable gesture."

"You're chuffing right it's no pal."

I heard a low growl from a dog.

"Sit down you bastard before a gey ye a bloody skelp."

Whether to a mate or to the dog I did not enquire, but it did seem to have the desired effect on whomever the remark was directed.

"So how much is generosity likely to cost?" I tentatively enquired.

"Five hunner," came the immediate reply.

"That's a lot of money for a registration number."

"No fir this yin pal its no? Daes you want it or no. Dinnae piss me aboot pal."

His voice seemed to have developed a genuine menace and aggression. Perhaps it was time for the Chamberlain appeasement approach.

"Ok, ok."

My mind was racing.

"Five hundred it is. Where do you want to meet?"

He paused and appeared to be having a mumbled conversation with another.

"Dae ye ken the 'Anchor'?"

"At Granton?"

"Aye, be there at ten, and pal, bring the money and naebody else. Just you on your lonesome and a wedge, ok?"

"I'll be there. By the way how did you get my name and number?"

This question obviously amused him no end as he laughed hoarsely and replied, "Frae that nice polis sergeant, youse wis talking to whey else?"

The line went dead. I stared at the screen.

The police: what a bunch, anything you say will be taken down and spread around the town in half an hour. The police what a bloody bunch they are.

Chapter 4
An Exciting Evening Part One

I glanced over at Charlie and Cammy who were seemingly engrossed in each other's company.

I broke in on their conversation, "I am really sorry but I have to go. I hope you recover from the alarms of the day Cammy and if the firm or I can be of any help please let me know. I'll make sure that the audited books are returned to you before the weekend."

She favoured me with a toothy smile and assured me that after an early night and a good night's slumber, she would be fine in the morning.

I refrained from mentioning that if I had an early night with her I would be fine in the morning as well.

"Charlie, if you are free later in the week, why don't you ring me and we'll catch up," I said.

He agreed that would be great so we exchanged mobile numbers and shook hands. As I was leaving I noticed that he was buying another bottle of the claret, obviously settling in for secession.

I phoned the office and made up a forgotten appointment, jumped on a sixteen bus and was home in genteel Morningside in time for tea. In the Watson household that hallowed event happens with precision at half past four on the dot.

This time had been personally appointed for all posterity by my revered grandmother. It was she who had always stated, and without pretension, that was the time that the old Queen always partook of her Earl Grey or Darjeeling. In this context the old Queen was the long dead Victoria in whose reign my forbear had been born.

My mother was, as always, pleased to see her loving son and after a suitable quantity of tea to wash down the fruit cake, I made my excuses and went to my room. I lay down on the bed to ponder all that had happened on that eventful day. What with the excitement urged on by the lager and in turn brought on by the claret I dropped into a dream-filled sleep.

I awoke from a strange, but usual dream, one in which I was being pursued by unknown people and appeared to have no clothes on. One of these days I will check the significance of this recurring theme with a psychiatrist. Residing where I did this would not be difficult because Morningside houses an ageing and sprawling medical facility. This is the Royal Edinburgh Hospital, which is our central centre for the treatment of diseases of the mind, with its secure wards for those who are a little more than just eccentric.

It was dark, the mild late spring day having given way to a cold evening. The clock said seven thirty and I rose, bathed and dressed for the evening ahead. I made my appearance in the dining room at exactly G&T time, which by standard time is a little after eight and occurs at exactly the same moment as Amontillado time for my mother.

She looked up from the silver drinks tray and, as she handed me the crystal glass with its bubbling contents, looked less than favourably at my casual attire.

"Going somewhere nice dear?" she said.

"Oh you know, here and there."

Polite but vague was the correct course.

"Well you are certainly dressed for there rather than here."

The sarcasm was not lost on me; I often thought she privately despaired, not of my generation per se, but the less formal and more casual world that we had ushered in and in her heart she longed for a more elegant world. She turned to the covered chafing dishes on the buffet table, for her perhaps as much approaching an altar to the past, the dishes as some communion objects to be treated with reverence.

These were the same objects that our daily, Mrs. Watson, mother's external domestic, complained were old fashioned and difficult to clean and what was wrong with good old Pyrex anyway. It was practical and some of the dishes had very pretty patterns.

We both helped ourselves to the fare on offer and I realized as I ate that lunch, as much of my life, had passed me by without being partaken of. We ate in silence, she with her thoughts, probably at my lack of sartorial elegance, and me with mine.

I put my napkin back in its statutory silver ring and rose.

"Would you like me to make some coffee Mother?"

"No, it's already done and in the drawing room," she replied.

"Well if you are finished, can I escort you safely to that place, madam?" I enquired.

The humour broke the ice. She rose, took my arm and we made our way to the room and partook of coffee; mine black, hers with cream, but without the long-forsaken sugar.

"I have to go out for a bit but I will be back before twelve, so don't wait up."

She inclined her head and said, "You know Alexander you're behaving very suspiciously. Just like when you broke your Aunt Jean's prized Doulton jar and you tried to get away with it."

I would have gotten away with it too if a certain sister of mine hadn't, as they say, grassed me up. It is funny how the sneaky underhand acts of one's sibling cast such long shadows.

"This is nothing to do with…"

She paused, uncertainly in her voice, "to do with…" Again the pause.

"To do with dad?" I said.

I felt it was time somebody finished a sentence. She nodded and I could see the start of tears.

"No, it's just a personal matter," I lied, feeling that the truth was too complex.

I kissed her brow, put a reassuring arm round her and left the room, grabbed my jacket as I left the flat.

I walked up the hill towards Holy Corner and used a convenient hole in the wall, drawing the agreed sum from two different cards; my own personal one and helping myself to an advance from the other, my company credit card.

As I did this, I could hear myself lecturing poor clients for doing the same thing. Just look at the extra charge, I could hear myself say. However, needs must when the devil drives, and I had no doubt that Rat Face was someone who could easily fit that description.

I hailed a cruising fast black and told the driver the destination. He looked dubious but clicked the flag down and set off.

The particular area of the city of Granton, where the appointed hostelry lay, was an area of multiple deprivation. This was evidenced from the collection of shops that clustered close to the pub. I noticed there was an off license advertising a special offer on cider, a chippie, an Indian takeaway and a Chinese takeaway. In fact, the only thing that denied this area total multiple deprivation status was that it lacked a bookie. Ah but one day maybe, one day.

As we approached the boozer I sat up and said to the driver, "Could you just pull in past the door further down the street please?"

He nodded. I looked at the fare. The meter registered twenty pound odd.

The cab came to a halt and the driver made to knock the flag back up.

"Just a minute I would like you to wait for me," I said.

He looked at me with a highly doubtful expression.

I went to my pocket and drew out a bundle of notes, "Look there's fifty. Stay until it's used up and if you're still here when I come out you keep the balance and I will pay again for what's on the clock."

His eyes showed in the street light exposing a glimpse into a slow thinking mind torn between uncertainty and greed. He wrestled with the problem but came down on the side of greed, which in turn emboldened him to a greater greed.

"A hundred and you have a deal pal."

It is funny in Edinburgh that everybody seems to be my friend. I pretended to think about it and then said, "You drive a hard bargain but alright then."

He was pleased with my decision. Here was a story he could repeat in the pub to his cronies about how he had put it over some Morningside type.

I parted with the cash, opened the door as I did I committed to memory the cab number, just in case. To add to the drama for my friend the driver, I paused, looked back and said, "Remember to keep the engine running."

He nodded his head in what he obviously thought was a conspiratorial way and I walked back up the street where a harsh dirty yellow light leeched out of a half-opened door. As I approached nearer I could hear the growling noise of lower class speech patterns. These people always seemed to be arguing, when they are in reality indulging in normal conversation, just at a higher than expected decibel level.

I opened the door and stepped inside. The sight that met me was only too familiar, for all the world as a howf of my youthful student days, or rather youthful student nights, of indiscretion. When the governing motive when choosing a pub was not for its ambience but for the cost of its beer.

The place had a couple of dozen drinkers in various states of inebriation. High on a side wall was placed the statutory big screen television, showing the statutory game of football, being watched by the statutory two persons who were having the statutory dispute over whether or not a certain player had taken a statutory dive.

The overhead lights were neon and harsh. The sickly colour of the walls was mirrored in the sickly pallor of the faces of the patrons, existing in this strange netherworld. I glanced round examining the suspicious faces that eyed me. This was a tribal crowd gathered in a tribal area, in a tribal place of worship and I was not of, or known to, the tribe.

A man appeared from behind a group, or rather a dog on a thick lead attached to a studded and spiked collar did. I did not have to see the man. For as soon as I saw the dog I knew that the tattooed hand pulling on the lead would be Rat Face. I felt the menace heavy in the air.

Chapter 5
An Exciting Evening Continues

It *was* him, dog in one hand, beer glass in the other. I was obviously sticking out in this alien environment as he gave me what passed as a smile. I signalled with my head to a space at the end of the bar and moved in that direction. Man and dog or rather, dog and man followed.

The barman approached, elderly, grey-haired and bald and noticeably short on the social graces.

"Aye," was the greeting. The last customer service course he attended obviously did not live up to its aims or perhaps it did not live up to his all too limited aspirations. He was not going to be an ambassador for Edinburgh, let alone Scotland.

"You want a pint of lager?" enquired mine host.

I thought a bottle in these circumstances might be more useful, as a weapon rather than a drink.

"No, make it a bottle," I said and then added the required, "pal."

I turned to my new companion,

"For you?"

He turned to the barman, "Usual Tam and since this fella is payin', make it a double."

"Comin' up, right away Darren, pal."

So Darren it was. By their name shall ye know them?

He laughed a sort of high pitched braying donkey-like noise. Then he turned fully towards me and coming close, he said quietly.

"You got the dough?"

I nodded. The drinks arrived, I paid the bill and, as I did, he gulped from his glass and I regarded him in his full splendour. He was arrayed in the full uniform of a chav, first class.

From the baseball cap with its bowed peak, to the regulation two earrings; shiny glass studs are compulsory. A tattoo in the shape of an onrushing wave curled up his neck spilling from under the collar of his hooded sweatshirt. Right down to the obligatory white shell suit bottoms and the unmissable white gold trimmed trainers.

With the stereotypical Pit Bull Terrier in tow he had almost the full regalia almost the Full Monty. The only accessory missing from this fashion statement was a Gregg's carrier bag.

Under different circumstances I might have found the situation amusing, but this was life. This was life in the raw and this was near the edge, perhaps too near the edge. This situation was, I suddenly realised, well out of my comfort zone.

"Show me the dosh," he broke into my thoughts, then as I put my hand inside my jacket he gave a restraining hand.

"Be carefy let's no let the rest ken yiv got aw that money. They'd slit you baws off fur a tenner."

I could tell from the earnestness in his voice that this was no passing idle threat.

I paused, and then enquired in an equally low voice.

"So how you want to do this then?"

"Bend doon and pat the dug, money in yer hand I'll pit the paper wi the reg number in mine, then we dae the exchange, the money for the paper understand?"

35

I nodded. I moved off and bent towards the dog. As I did so I slipped the money from my pocket to my hand and leant down to the dog.

"What's she called?" I asked.

"Chardonnay, donnay for short."

"Chardonnay, but well she's black not white?"

"Naw, I cawed her aifter a bird I kent, and just like her, she is a bluidy stupit bitch."

Again the laugh: the high-pitched braying donkey noise.

The dog, unaware of her owner's slanderous comments seemed to like the attention and wagged what passed for a tail. Her master bent down, effectively screening us from the rest of the company. Our hands touched, met and exchanged their contents. On his part this was a manoeuvre that he had completed many times before, presumably the easiest way to pay for, and receive, a drugs score under the public gaze.

I stood up and swigged from the bottle. He had already pocketed the cash. I moved to replace the bottle on the dreg pooled bar top and said, "I think that concludes our business, so I'll be off."

However, as I finished placing my bottle on the bar, I noticed that the hand which had held a glass, now held a short-bladed commando-style stabbing knife. As to how I could identify it as such, blame the reading of too many "Battler Britain" comics. At that moment I fervently wished that I had some of that comic book hero's qualities of bravery and resource.

"Have yae nae mair cash in yir pockets? I wouldnae want you wanderin' around this kind o' neighborhood cairryin' lot of money. Somebody might hurt ye tae get it?"

I have never liked people who state the obvious, and I saw no reason to start now. However, before I could make to reply, Tam the barman had noticed the dull glint of metal and leaned across the bar, "Darren, I want nae trouble in here. If there's to be any goin ons tak it oot side."

Wherever you go in life you can always find a Good Samaritan there to help you when you least expect it. Nevertheless, it seemed that Tam's idea of how to be a Good Samaritan had somehow become lost in translation.

Darren looked angry.

"Shut yeru bluidy auld gob or I'll cut ye, ye interfering auld bastard. I've warned ye afore tae keep your filthy auld neb oot o ma business."

He accompanied the words with a scything motion with the knife towards my erstwhile saviour, the hapless barman.

Then with a speed and agility which came from nowhere and belied his general age and condition, Tam grabbed the oncoming arm by the wrist and slammed it hard down on the counter. Darren let out a wail of pain. He tried to wrench free and in so doing he stepped back and trod on the faithful hound, Chardonnay who now joined her pained master in announcing loudly to the world that she too was hurting.

Darren wrenched his arm back in an attempt to free himself; Tam let him go as far as his initial repulse took him. Then like a master angler he reeled him back in. Darren's body banged against the bar, causing him to lose his footing and as he squirmed his feet flayed. One of the feet hit the back of the legs of one of the other drinkers, causing him to lunge forward in an involuntary movement and in doing so to spill his beer over an enormous man with his back to him. The description of that particular man as being built like a brick shit house would not be overstating the case.

Unaware, or perhaps uncaring, that it had been an accident, the second man turned, his bull-like neck reddening. He had little porcine eyes, deep-set in a large porcine face, topped with a completely shaven head. As he turned he raised a fist, itself the size of a ham and smacked the unfortunate and totally innocent victim square in the face.

The unfortunate target of the attack then in turn fell back on the dog and *she* thinking she was under attack from all sides, immediately bit the already wronged man and a general mêlée appeared to be well under way.

No one's eyes being on me, I moved to the door, skirting round the fringes of the brawl. As I reached the door, I glanced back only to see Darren, his arm now freed, casting me a look of malevolence that bore me no good whatsoever.

I hurriedly moved through the door anxious to regain the relative safety of my waiting cab, grateful that I had had the foresight to have a back-up plan.

As the door clanged shut behind me I jumped the three entrance steps and looked into a completely empty street.

Chapter 6
Even More Excitement

If ever there was a marketing opportunity it was now and the product I had in mind was Tena pants for gents.

You've seen them in the adverts; they apparently allow women to laugh heartily and play ten pin bowls and even ride camels.

To my left, in relative dark, lay Granton Square, the harbour and the sea. If you were cornered there it could be a short struggle and an unwelcome but close acquaintance with the cruel sea. Whereas to my right lay bright lights and more importantly people, possible witnesses for the prosecution.

I moved swiftly, as a moth towards the light and as I passed the chip shop, I noticed there was a large queue; presumably awaiting the cooking of a fresh batch of chips. I checked, paused and doubled back into the shop, into the crowd, and hopefully into anonymity.

A woman, of the bottled blonde variety with a patchy spray tan, approached. She vouchsafed the information that, "Wir waitin fir chips pal."

Another friend. What a day this had been for new and meaningful acquaintances. Talking of which, I noticed in the mirrored back of the shop, passing the window, my other new friend, Darren complete with dog and the large man from the pub brawl.

However, as the two Pharisees in the aforementioned parable, they passed by, if not on the other side, at least without a glance. Should I now hightail it in the opposite direction or stay put? It seemed to me I'm damned if I did and damned if I didn't. Besides, the queue was moving and the blonde had been joined by her clone and they were up to their elbows in steaming, glistening, fried in lard, chips.

This was Scotland where we eschewed vegetable oil as a southern namby-pamby fad. This is a land where men are men, and particularly in the West Coast, die in their early forties with clogged arteries.

"Whet's yours?"

The enquiry came from Blondie number two.

"Steak pie supper doll."

You see, I could speak the patois as well as the rest of them.

She enquired which of the two traditional condiments I desired,

"Salt and sauce?"

"Just salt please."

She grabbed a deep fried steak pie from the hot compartment and heaped on a quantity of chips.

"Do you want it left open?"

For those of you not fluent in Scottish East Coast chip shop speak that means left open at one end. This is done in order to facilitate the instant consumption of your chosen meal, as you stagger your way home.

"Open doll," I opted.

"You wan any skoosh?"

Again a translation might prove instructive: the lady was enquiring as to whether I wished, as an accompaniment to my repast, some aerated water. The word skoosh is not a universal term for that product in Scotland and, if you were in Glasgow, the expression would be substituted for the word ginger, or in Fife, with lemonade. However, the word lemonade is not a specific term, but a generic, thus if you ask for lemonade the next question would be "aye, but what flavour?"

As the advert says, it pays to have local knowledge.

I replied in the negative and went to the exit, only to see my seeker enter the other door. He stopped momentarily then I heard him shout, "I found him! The bastard's in here."

Whether he shouted this to himself, his accomplice or the dog was not immediately clear.

His voice was loud and high-pitched betraying his barely suppressed excitement. The dog responded, taking heed of the excited tone, which obviously aroused in the beast some ancient hunting urge deep inside her and she leapt forward. Darren, momentarily caught off balance, was dragged by his now highly excited, hound across the chip shop, straight towards me.

He struggled manfully and managed to regain a modicum of control, reining back the dog some two feet from me. The dog growled, showing a fine set of yellow teeth. It was at that point, with the open end downwards, I shook my recent purchase vigorously. The golden contents cascaded onto the floor.

The animal, true to its opportunist eater genes changed her attention from her former quarry (me) to the free dinner that had miraculously appeared before her eyes. As I stepped back, the dog made a determined bid to decrease the distance between herself and her intended meal. As she made another leap forward, this time at the pie, Darren again was drawn inexorably by the lead and, in an attempt to once again regain control, the sole of one of his gold trimmed trainers encountered some stray chips.

The cooked lard on the chips ensured that the ease of movement from inertia to imbalance, was accelerated and the unfortunate Darren, now in a state of headlong movement plunged forward. This he would have continued to do for a fair distance had his head not encountered the shop wall. The sickening thud was followed by the howling of the dog, which had discovered that in attempting to consume my scattered largesse, that the temperature of the offering was greater, both than the ambient temperature of the room and the liking of the delicate parts of her mouth. She howled like a beast possessed; a beast in torment.

Time, I felt, for the second occasion in less than fifteen minutes, for a sharp exit. Taking the opportunity of the crowd's preoccupation with the felled Darren and his ailing beast, I slipped out the door leaving a babble of excited voices and the low moaning of the dog. As I regained the pavement, blocking my path was the Incredible Hulk. His face wore a perplexed look and his mind was apparently raging with indecision.

"Whit's aw this?" he intoned in a speech that was slow, drawn out and deliberate.

"Somebody fell ower I think pal."

I fell into this local dialect with practised ease. This was the sort of accent you put on to amuse your Home Counties' acquaintances who would laugh in that brittle way and say "how quaint".

His doubt grew, for obviously he had been insufficiently briefed by the hapless Darren as to whom exactly they had been seeking. He was hired muscle, not hired brain.

"Whey fell?" he enquired, obviously not a man to overtax his vocabulary.

"Sumboady wi a big dug I thought aye herd him someyin caw him Darren oor summit like that."

"Jesus Christ," was his only response and having taken the Lord's son's name in vain, he brushed past me and went into the shop, which I had just noticed rejoiced in the splendid title of the Jubilee Supper Room.

Without hesitation or overmuch haste I continued my walk towards the row of shops. I passed a Chinese Takeaway across the road, blue coloured lights shone brightly in the Masala Pot Indian restaurant, enticing you in for a special tandoori night buffet, eat as much as you like.

As I rounded the corner the shops ran out and here the street lighting was less bright. I hesitated, and then saw the sign announcing that this was the way to the Iceland car park. Now orientated, I followed the car park sign only stopping momentarily to check behind me to look for pursuers and to my great relief there were none.

I walked towards the sparsely populated car park, presumably those belonging to the company's workers on the twilight shift and I passed the former bingo hall which had become a casualty of the no smoking ban. No more 'two fat ladies' here no more 'clickety click' here; the last house had been well and truly called.

I scaled the wall and in so doing I ripped my jacket. I hesitated monetarily on the top of the wall before dropping as quietly as I could into the back garden of a house in Granton Park Ave. I then made my way through a well laid out vegetable patch, for which effort I mentally recorded a vote of thanks to the solicitous gardener. I dropped down on all fours as I passed the lit kitchen window then, following the slabbed path, I exited along a gravel driveway and into the street. The street, I noticed, was poorly lit so I made my way in a cautious fashion; the denizens of this particular road had obviously not stumped up enough for their utilities.

It is strange how odd things, in moments of relative calm after great stress, come unbidden into your mind. But as I picked my way along the street, I was aware that a spotter associate of mine had been assured by a fellow anorak that the first purpose-built car factory in the world had been built and to this very day still stood, at the far end of this very street. I felt however, that although this was the place, it certainly was not the time to check it out as I felt it incumbent on me, if for nothing else, to take account of my own safety first.

Coming to the end of the street, I peered around cautiously. Firstly I looked down the main road to the left which lead to the harbour. I had decided that, if it was deserted and clear, I would risk a stroll down to the harbour. However, before I did, I risked a check to the right. Outside the supper rooms, its light still mournfully revolving was an ambulance and a knot of interested spectators. But it was not that which caught my attention, but further down illuminated by a feeble light that leaked from the front door of the "Anchor" pub, stood in all its glory, my very own shining black cab.

Chapter 7
A New Plan is Called For

I cautiously turned the corner and walked slowly towards the cab, suspecting an ambush at every turn. However, the entire population of Granton that was awake was either back in the boozer or being willing spectators to poor Darren's injuries, which I hoped fervently, would not be too slight.

I reached the door of the cab, safely depressed the handle and entered the cab, falling back into the seat with a feeling of both weariness and relief. Perhaps the adrenaline was slowly ebbing back into its secret reservoirs, as the necessity for fight and flight had similarly abated. Before I could say anything my cabbie turned and said, "There you are. That's' another forty-five smackers you owe me pal."

I was almost dumbfounded by the offhand greeting so the only retort I could manage was,

"Where were you twenty minutes ago?"

He had the good grace to look abashed.

"Got caught short, didn't I, so I went down to the bog. There's' one in the Square."

I was about to argue the matter further when I noticed that the ambulance light was now not only revolving, but pulsing. A sure sign that things medical were under way. I also noticed the crowd break and start to drift away so it was time for another swift, sharp exit.

"Fine, I'll get your money just drive."

"Where to? Back to Morningside?"

I looked at my watch. It was just after ten thirty, God what a lot can happen in thirty minutes! Particularly if you had been following the lyrics of the late Lou Reed and taking a 'walk on the wild side'. What I needed was bright lights and people, yes, lots and lots of people. I quickly thought the matter over then instructed my driver saying,

"No, drop me in George Street, the Charlotte Square end. No, even better make it the top of North Castle Street."

As he engaged the clutch and the cab moved slowly off I saw the Incredible Hulk shambling back to the "Anchor." He looked inquisitively at the passing taxi, his little eyes reflecting the yellow neon glare of the street lamps. A sudden look of recognition flashed across his pig-like features, turning his face into contours of rage. His pendulous jowls started to shake and quiver, his mouth was open and shouting obscenities. As we continued to pull away, he made a despairing lunge for the door. He was just too late and I gave up a silent prayer that the driver would not stall the bloody cab.

I could not resist a polite wave, a polite two fingered wave and with that and a backward glance the lights of Granton faded away. We made for the Botanic Garden the New Town and hopefully relative safety.

Edinburgh's New Town whose construction commenced in 1767 with a pair of unprepossessing houses in Thistle Street, a lane that lies behind George Street. The initial plan consisted of three streets running parallel, east to west, with a square at either end. Between the two outer streets and the central boulevard, are two lanes which were originally to house the artisans required to service this New Town and the mews to stable the horses. It was to a pub in one of these lanes that I was headed.

This grandiose scheme was the work of a little-known city architect, James Craig. His prize for this feat of vision and draughtsmanship was a good medal and the freedom of the city in a silver casket. He subsequently died young, after fourteen years in penury. One can only feel that the cash might have been a better option.

We drove up Dundas Street into Queen Street and pulled up in North Castle Street in less than fifteen minutes. I paid the taxi off and checked my heavily depleted cash reserves and finding them wanting, I walked to the top of the street and topped them up from a hole in the wall machine.

The ATM was a system first introduced by The Royal Bank of Scotland forty years ago. The first machine took a plastic punched card and in return gave you a ten pound note. There was no other option apart from putting in another card.

Each person was allowed six cards which were returned to them monthly, with their bank statement. It is perhaps an interesting observation on inflation that ten pounds all these years ago was considered a significant sum of money.

I turned back down the hill and took a left turn into Young Street, which is a continuation of both Hill Street and Thistle Street, and towards a sign proclaiming that this was the Oxford bar.

This is where one can quaff a pint of ale in the pub patronised by the fictional character Inspector John Rebus. If you were lucky you might bump into Rebus's creator Ian Rankin, as well as a whole host of colourful characters both imagined and real. In particular, I hoped to find an acquaintance, Billy, a man if not for all seasons, then certainly for all tight spots.

In the fifties and sixties the owner of the Oxford Bar, a certain Wullie Ross, a man of a somewhat eccentric disposition, which was particularly exhibited in the opening and closing times of his licensed establishment which were on his own whim. At that time it had no ladies toilet, presumably he either did not want women customers, or perhaps he considered them to be the more continent of the species.

I entered the unprepossessing doorway, which led to an equally unprepossessing bar. I glanced round, but Billy was not to be seen. The barman looked at me, expectancy in his expression.

"A pint of Fosters please," I said, hoping this would satisfy his expectancy.

"Coming up right away sir."

So I was no longer a pal. Oh well.

"Billy been in?"

"Aye he must be in the gents, he is sitting over there."

I glanced round at a table with a half-consumed glass of beer. I say half-consumed to illustrate that I am not of an optimistic nature, as then I would have considered it to be half full.

"Then you'd better let me have a pint of Belhaven as well."

The barman nodded his assent, and moved glass in his hand to the designated font.

I had met Billy when we were both a great deal younger. He had been working as a delivery driver and I was a young apprentice CA.

I had been undertaking an external audit for the company he worked for at that time.

My investigation had thrown up a substantial shortage of cash and the fickle finger of fate and for that matter the equally fickle finger of guilt, pointed firmly at William's door.

Perhaps because of our youth, or because we both had a rebellious streak, mine' was much better subjugated than his, we had drifted together, sharing a lunchtime in the canteen which led to a couple of pints at a local howf on pay day.

When the theft was discovered the police were called and in due course the charges were made against Billy. By this time I had finished my allotted task and had moved on, if not to pastures new, certainly to a different set of ledgers. As a result, I knew nothing of these goings on or my erstwhile chum's legal problems.

The whole affair only came to light when my father announced one cold morning that I would be required to give evidence at Billy's forthcoming trial. Although I believed my erstwhile lunchtime companion was not above straying over the strict line of the law, I did not believe that he had, as the police said, had taken ten thousand pounds; at that time five or six times his annual wage.

To cut a long, and for me a tediously involved investigation, short I took it upon myself to re-examine the accounts and uncovered the true culprit, who turned out to be the company's finance director; a real case of gamekeeper turned poacher.

For my efforts Billy, although grateful, treated his release and his exoneration in the same stoical manner as he had his arrest in the first place. Here was a man who totally believed in fate, chance and karma, and although we never became bosom buddies, we did have this certain bond that somehow held us together.

"Sandy, good to see you and, even better, you come bearing gifts."

His voice was deep as always, his hair now running to grey and his muscles to fat, but still making a presence. He was a man to be relied in a tight corner or a fight: a man to be reckoned with. I noticed that strangely, the colour had not gone from his luxuriant ginger moustache, a vaguery of his family genetics or deliberate intervention of the dyer's brush.

"What brings you to this revered watering hole of the aged, the forlorn and the desperate?" he enquired, a smile suffusing his features.

I returned the smile.

"Which are you?"

"Both," was the succinct reply.

We both took a swallow, in my case a very large one from our glasses, mine of sparking gold, his of still brown and I brought him up to speed on my father's mysterious and violent end and my more recent adventures in the night.

He listened with increasing interest.

"I read about the death but I was in Tenerife, a quick burst of late sun, so I couldn't make the funeral. I meant to write, but, well you know how it is, you know how I am, I was sorry to hear the news though."

I thanked him and he went on.

"So where is this famous to say nothing of highly expensive bit of paper? The one you almost got yourself duffed up for; what does it say?"

What with the tension, the fight and flight, the threat of sudden violence and the Hulk almost Parthian shot, to say nothing of that bloody taxi driver the paper had gone right out of my mind. I fished in my pocket and extracted the slip of paper.

"Here it is, see for yourself."

I handed it over.

Billy unfolded the proffered offering, examined the paper and then, turning it over, examined the other side and looked across at me shaking his head slowly.

"Well Sandy old friend I'm afraid to tell you what you have bought is a real pig in a poke."

"What do you mean a bloody pig in a bloody poke?"

I leant across the table and unceremoniously snatched the paper back to find, as he had, that the paper was completely blank.

Chapter 8
An Old Confederate Makes the Running

All that hassle, all that grief, for zilch. What a damned God awful mess I had made of it, to say nothing of the missing cash.

"Well that's torn it," I intoned weakly.

I felt suddenly as though a great tiredness was washing over me. As if all of my get up and go had done exactly that and left behind an adrenaline-less shell.

"So what are we going to do about it?" enquired Billy.

I liked the 'we', I thought.

"Ah Billy, to be truthful my friend I am fresh out of ideas."

Billy looked intent as though he were making some calculation and then put a large hand into his pocket and came out with his mobile.

"The ambulance, the one that took sonny boy away, what direction did it go?"

Although puzzled by the question I thought about it for a moment and said, "Towards Crew Toll."

"Then probably heading for the Western," he interjected almost as though talking to himself.

"Well I'll give that a try first. In the meantime, Sandy another pint would help lubricate the thinking process."

Then his action was as good as his words. He picked up his glass and drained it.

I followed suit then rose went to the bar and ordered refills. Having paid, I returned to the table to overhear Billy's conversation.

"Good evening. Emergency admissions please."

This was followed by a longish pause.

"Yes, that's right, emergency admissions please."

Another pause.

"Oh good evening sister. I'm sorry to trouble you, a friend of mine was taken to hospital by ambulance this evening after a fall and I was wondering if he was with you."

I could hear, but not make out, a murmur of conversation on the other end.

"Well yes, I understand that, but I am ringing on behalf of his mother who is, I am sorry to say, bedridden."

Yet another pause.

"I do appreciate that. His first name is…"

Billy hesitated and looked at me; I mouthed to him Darren.

"Darren," he repeated.

"Not tonight thank you I will try the Royal."

He paused only long enough to take a drink, and then he repeated the performance on the Royal Infirmary. This time Darren's mother was not only bedridden but a widow; the story was growing legs with the retelling. If he had to make another phone call, the said old lady would probably be taking in ironing next. Added to that, Billy was now not only a fully paid up and trained and serving member of Lothian and Borders finest, but apparently ringing from Drylaw Police Station.

This time the good William's efforts were rewarded with success. He thanked the person on the other end profusely and switched the phone off and turned to me.

"He was taken to the Head Trauma Unit but his condition is apparently not life-threatening so he is being moved to a ward as we speak and his second name by the way is Nesbit."

"Fine, do we know which ward he is currently being moved to?"

"Indeed we do. It's number thirty."

"When's visiting time do you know?" I asked.

"It's right now so drink up and let's go to it," he said and turned to the barman.

"Tommy do us' a favour and ring your special taxi number and have them send a cab round tout de suite pal."

The barman nodded and went to the phone next to the optics, behind the bar.

Then Billy confided to me, "His brother works as a dispatcher for City Cabs, good bloke he is."

This information was apparently offered by way of explanation.

I was making manful inroads into my second pint when the door opened and a voice announced that there was a cab for Clark.

"That's us."

Billy waved in acknowledgement, "Be with you right away mate."

He grabbed his coat, signed to me, waved a goodbye to the barman and we left, into the black night and into the black taxi.

"The Royal," Billy instructed the driver tersely and we set off.

The Edinburgh Royal Infirmary, with its world famous Medical School, was originally conveniently situated in the centre of the city but around the turn of the century they built a new and apparently greatly improved version, on the outskirts of the city.

At the time this was rumoured to be part of the then target-driven government' master plan to cut waiting lists. Because the new building was so far away people just could not be bothered going or in emergencies, by the time you got there, you were dead. Mind you just in case some persistent person insisted on being treated they made parking the car horrendously expensive. Presumably on the "that'll teach them" principle.

To be scrupulously fair to the modernisers, the old Royal had grown in a haphazard way and had been a maze of corridors and stairs with miles and miles of passages. If you went from one ward to another, you had to have a map and a packed lunch. Legend had it that there were poor souls who never found their way back to their ward and were condemned, like the Flying Dutchman, to aimlessly roam the corridors till the end of time.

We duly arrived at the obviously modern building and having paid off the cab we entered through the automatic doors and into a cavernous corridor. Just think of the heating bill, I could hear my mother intoning. This hallway was like a concourse that you might expect to find in an international airport. The illusion persisted as even at this late hour the place was busy and some of the shops were still open.

I do not know why but it always surprises me to find retail outlets in hospitals. What happened to the pleasant ladies of Women's Royal Voluntary Service with their carefully pressed uniforms, well-polished pearls and ever so genteel voices dispensing sweets and solicitude in equal doses?

We arrived at what was, somewhat grandly, named main mall and having consulted the plan, we discovered our destination was on the ground floor and all we had to do was follow the colourful lines on the ground which looked like they had been painted by some talented child. We then picked up the signs to wards twenty-five to thirty but as is the way of things we duly found wards twenty-five to twenty-nine but not thirty. We stopped a passing auxiliary, who explained that yes it was a bit tricky, as the sign was in fact wrong and if we went back to the start and turned left, rather than right we would find it no problem which we did.

I did consider questioning why no one had bothered to change the signage but, as others before me, I simply let it remain as one of life's little mysteries.

"What is our reason for being here?" I asked Billy tentatively.

"There you go Sandy; always the worrier. Leave it to me, I will just wing it. We'll be fine, have a little faith."

Have a little faith, he'll wing it. If I was the worrier he thought, this was hardly the cast iron assurance that would allay my fears.

We came to the ward door and entered the corridor, which was in partial darkness. Separate room style wards for four people were ranged off to our left.

At the end of the passage was a pool of light and illumined in that pool was a blonde head topped with a white pink-edged cap sitting at a desk. As we approached, the head looked up and bespectacled eyes regarded us with a degree of suspicion and curiosity.

"Good evening sister, I rang earlier from Drylaw Police Station, my name is Driver."

God, he lied with such ease *I* almost believed him myself.

The face visibly relaxed and her hand rose in a sort of nervous gesture and pushed the glasses back onto the bridge of her nose.

"It is late you know and the patient is resting."

Officialdom kicking in, how reassuring I thought.

"Well, I promise five minutes and no longer. You know what the red tape and paperwork is like when an ambulance is called, particularly to an incident like this."

Billy's words obviously hit the right chord and our by now kindred spirit replied,

"Paper work and red tape, not medicine is my life. You will have to be quick though, the houseman will be round soon for a last check up, and then I will have to give him a sedative. He is in the last room at the end, try not to disturb the other patient."

She indicated, we muffled thanks, and went where we were bid.

As with the corridor, the room was in darkness but for a pool of light on the bed head. This one lit a bandaged head above an extremely pale face, set in its unmistakable scowl.

As we approached, some sixth sense, some animal cunning, rather than intelligence kicked in and he instinctively knew we were not the expected angels of mercy and although it hardly seemed possible, his pallor grew even paler.

I moved to the bed and drew my face close to the patient's and almost in a whisper I enquired, "Hullo Darren I hear you had a fall tonight."

As he recognised me, his face tightened and he almost spat his words back at me, "You bastard, I'll knife you for this see; I'll cut you bloody balls off pal. Dae ye hear me naebidy makes a fool oot o me and gets away with it, you bastard."

He struggled, attempting to rise but Billy's hand pushed him firmly back into the bed. As I had done, he lowered his head in a conspiratorial manner spoke in an even voice, the very evenness itself infusing the words with a chilling menace. A chilling menace, that Darren, despite all his bombast, simply failed to convey.

"From what I hear pal, no one can make a fool of you better than you can yourself. If anyone is catting balls off it's gone to be me, do you hear me pal, am I getting through to you?"

Darren's response was to make to push the emergency button, but Billy's hand shot out and grabbed his wrist.

Darren yelped with pain and Billy spoke again, still in that menace evoking even voice, "Shut your stupid mouth. We were told not to disturb the other patient so your co-operation would be appreciated."

And then over his shoulder to me he added, "Stand at the door and keep a lookout while Darren and I have a little heart to heart."

I followed his instructions and I glanced at Darren before moving to my assigned position as look-out. To be truthful he did look more than a little scared, he looked terrified. I almost felt sorry for him.

From my on-guard position I heard Billy's quiet tones continue, "You took money from my friend and gave him no information in return and that has upset him, which in turn has upset me. I don't want my friend to be upset and if you, you little piece of Council Estate shite, know what's good for you, you'll not want me to be upset."

Darren's face was transfixed; his face a mask of fear, and Billy went on, "So what I am going to do is ask you for the information that you failed to give to my friend, that he paid for and you didn't give him. Do you know how bloody angry that makes me, do you? Before you say anything pal I'm only going to ask once. Just the once mind, just the bloody once, and if I don't get the right answer it will be you pal that will be the one with no balls. Now just nod if you understand."

Darren did as he was asked.

"Right, now that we understand each other, here is the question."

Before the question could be asked or answered, I suddenly heard the murmur of voices in the corridor. I turned and signalled a silent warning to Billy.

Billy clamped one of his hands across Darren's mouth, "Not a whisper from you, not one single bloody word."

Billy rasped a warning.

I opened the door a little and the voices drifted down the passageway to me and as I listened the words filled me with alarm, perhaps Billy's judgment was right perhaps I was just a worrier. Then I heard the words that confirmed that sometimes worriers have the right of it, "More policemen. My, my, we are popular tonight," I caught the nurse say.

Then a deeper voice spoke, "More policemen did you say. You mean there is someone from the force here already?"

"Oh yes," I heard the sister tell the newcomer.

"They said they were from the Drylaw Station. I am sure one of them said his name was Rider or something like that. They are down the corridor, in a side ward, interviewing one of the patients, let me show you."

I risked a quick glance down the corridor and what I saw did not fill me with happiness and joy. For as I watched Blondie rose and, coming round her desk, she started down the corridor towards us flanked by two real uniformed policemen.

Worrier or not I felt that at this there was now something to worry about; something like clear and imminent danger.

Chapter 9
A Damned Close Run Thing

I shut the door moved to my friend's side and in a whispered tone I conveyed the situation. Billy released his grasp on the unfortunate Darren's mouth. He took two steps, grabbed the slightly open window in two hands, and wrenched. To my great surprise and astonishment the window creaked slightly and then, with a sharp cracking noise, the lock simply gave way and the window swung open.

Almost in one fluid motion, Billy was over the sill and standing outside looking in at me.

"What the hell are you waiting for, a number eleven bus? For Christ's sake, move your bloody arse."

His words roused me into action. I moved to the bottom of the bed and as I swivelled round I grabbed the bed table that lay over the unoccupied first berth and threw it on its side in the direct path of any pursers. Having accomplished my delaying gesture, I moved across the ward towards the open window and my anxious companion.

As I moved two things happened. Firstly, Darren suddenly recovered from his recent fright and started shouting about assault and generally crying for help. Secondly, the door burst open, the policeman obviously alerted by the breaking noise were, now on the case. However, just as quickly as it had opened, the door encountering the obstacle of the upturned table banged back catching the leading officer squarely on the nose. To my great satisfaction that stalwart member of the constabulary went down much as the proverbially poleaxed ox.

Before any further disaster could befall me I was over the window and following Billy through some low growing shrubs, leaving behind a screaming Darren whose moans and complaints were joined by the sounds of an enraged and hurt member of the boys in blue.

We cleared the gable end with no obvious visible sight of our hunter's pursuit. Stopping at an emergency door, which I noticed was alarmed, whilst I was whimsically wondering what it was alarmed about, Billy brought out of his jacket pocket a type of Swiss Army knife and flicking out a long slender blade, he inserted it in the door lock. He gave a twist, there was an audible click and then the door swung open. Billy was through, I followed and he swung the door shut with his foot.

He kept his foot firmly against the bottom of the door, until his free hand clicked the latch back to the shut position and then he raised a finger of his other hand to his lips. I recognised this as the universal sign for silence.

As we listened, we could hear the sounds of pursuit and part heard snatches of conversations, then the metallic voice of a radio transmission.

"No sir, they seem to have just vanished into thin air."

Then came a mumbled reply.

"No sir, they have taken Constable Wills round to the A and E. He suffered a suspected broken nose and concussion."

Again the indistinct comeback.

"Yes, I have done that, I have alerted hospital security and they are monitoring all exits until further notice. Yes, I will go round to the main entrance until the reinforcements arrive I'll wait for them there, very good sir, over and out."

I could hear by the rising and falling sound of sirens that these reinforcements were not far off.

As we listened the sound of pursuit died away. I could see Billy's face under the pallid emergency lighting and could see he was smiling broadly: the old bugger was actually enjoying all this. He caught my glance and signalled with his head down the corridor and, without a word, he set off and I, like some obedient gun dog, followed at his heels.

As we reached the end of the passage there we encountered another door, through this we could see the *real* world well-lit and pleasantly warm and incredibly beckoning. After a cursory check, Billy opened the door and stepped into a short corridor, where I obediently followed.

We negotiated a turn and, as we did we approached a further set of doors, through them stepped, walking straight towards us a hospital security guard. The words frying pan into the fire occurred to me. As I thought, God bless him, Billy was the first to recover. A childhood where dodging the law was not only a game, but a way of life had created in him some second sense, some survival instinct. Perhaps we all have it. It was just that his was better honed and more finely tuned than others.

Tuning to me he said,

"Well, I thought the old boy looked not too bad after all he has been through."

Picking up my cue I replied,

"You know, that's just what I was thinking I expected him to look a lot worse."

Billy nodded his head vigorously then, almost as though he had just thought about it, he said,

"Do you know, I think we'd better ring mum and let her know, she will be really worried by now."

Billy somewhat ostentatiously patted his pockets, "Do you know what with all the fuss I have only come out without my mobile?"

Then, addressing the guard who was by this time adjacent to us and eyeing us, if not with outright suspicion certainly with more than a little curiosity.

As if just seeing him Billy enquired of him, "Where's the nearest pay phone pal? I need to let my mother know that my dad is alright and on the mend. She will be getting concerned."

Cool very cool, I thought.

The man looked and then, as if some automaton, he snapped into officialdom mode.

"Go to the bottom of the corridor, turn right through a set of doors and that will bring you into the main concourse and there is a bank of phones on the far side."

"Thanks mate," I managed to murmur.

Then the guard replied without any apparent irony in his voice,

"You haven't see a pair of suspicious looking characters on your travels have you?"

It was Billy who answered first.

"Not unless you count a junior doctor trying to get it on with a junior nurse."

Both Billy and the guard laughed coarsely and off we set at a leisurely pace. Following the instructions we duly arrived at the central concourse. As I looked around I realised that we were on same side of the building to where we had started. On our evening ramble we seemed to have circumnavigated the hospital and returned to square one. It was still reasonably busy and several dark blue uniforms could be seen at the exits.

"Time for a coffee and a regroup I think."

Billy glanced at me as though my words had interrupted his thinking process, "good idea, white, no sugar for me and we can maybe talk about plan B."

I collected the order and took the beverages to the table that Billy had chosen as it commanded a view of the entire area. I placed his coffee in front of him and enquired, "tell me how the hell did you know that the window would just open like that and for that matter where to switch off the alarm on that door?"

"Easy, I had a job as the foreman for the company that installed them. The windows have an emergency release button in order to evacuate the room in case of fire. As to the doors, well that was a combination of a bit of knowledge and a bit of luck. The knowledge again, from the fact that we installed the door and the alarms and they have a fifteen second delay default setting, in order to allow legitimate callers time to punch in a key code," he matter-of-factly explained.

"Well thank the lord for your knowledge and luck. Talking of which, what was the element of fortune?" I enquired.

"Oh, that's easy. Well those dozy bastards have not changed the bloody code since I installed the system, the lazy, inefficient bunch."

It is strange, I reflected, how the affairs of men can turn on little matters of fate.

Just as that reflection came and went, I noticed that walking purposefully towards us was a grey-haired sergeant with an eager youthful slim and pinch-faced WPC.

Chapter 10
In Which All Becomes Clearer

Before I could respond, they were standing at the table, looking down at us: the sergeant, bluff and bemused and the WPC restless, her nose moving in a rodent-like twitching movement.

Billy put his cup down and looked up with all the appearance of a double take and said,

"That's never you, is it Clive? Christ, it bloody well is. God, you have not half beefed it on."

The policeman's' face took on a puzzled look. Then it creased and, what presumably passed for a smile lit his face. His fellow constable visibly relaxed or, at least what passed for relaxing for her and her nose stopped its perpetual movement.

"Do you know, Billy, I thought it was you. It's been what, twenty-five years since we first met?"

"No need to be coy Clive, you mean since you first nicked me, and no, it's nearer thirty." replied Billy. He continued, "and no I have not been found guilty of anything since, though it's not for the want of trying on your forces' part."

Then tuning to me, Billy said in a pastiche of a policeman's official tone,

"I was charged with underage drinking, breach of the peace, and acting in a manner likely to cause an affray. Clive, the good sergeant here, was my very own arresting officer, although at that time he was but a humble constable, patrolling the mean streets of Leith."

Then glancing back to his erstwhile captor, "What you doing here anyway Judging by the amount of you it must be on some sort official business, something really serious. Or has the Chief Constable, our whatever the holder of that post is now called come in for brain implant, and you're all just here to wish him or her well."

At that slight to her boss, the head at the top of the Lothian and Borders Force totem pole, the WPC became restless. Her nose went back to its movement and she compressed her thin lips and when she spoke it was almost a hiss, a formal hiss perhaps, but definitely a sibilant intonation.

"We are following up enquiries into an incident here at the infirmary," she said.

Totem pole was the right allusion. There is nothing more tribal than a police force, you are either one of them and in the tent, or not, then you will have to stay firmly outside the tent. Scratch one and they all bleed.

Billy paused then looked straight at her and, with an almost deceptively casual tone, said, "I was talking to the organ grinder dear not to his monkey."

Oh God, here we go. Billy's working class School Of Hard Knocks University Of Life bias that had bred an ingrained resentment of authority figures and particularly the police, was loose and was all the more dangerous as it had apparently hit the ground running. Thank God he never joined the Diplomatic Corp; it simply would not have suited him at all.

The constable's face reddened, her nose started to move at a terrific rate, and her hands moved towards her belt, where her extending baton reposed: the atmosphere was tense.

However, in an effort, if not to necessarily to ease the situation, but to ensure it did not escalate, the older and perhaps wiser head broke in, "We have had a complaint that two men, impersonating police officers, have conned their way into one of the wards and assaulted a patient and injured a policeman," he paused reflectively and went on, "and the description we have been given could match you and your friend here to a tee."

Then turning to me he said, "And your name is?"

He fished out the standard issue black notebook and laboriously found a blank page.

During Billy's spell of police baiting, I had been thinking. Maybe we could turn it into a national sport and award caps, I had been thinking. However, on reviewing the situation I thought now was about the right time for a bit of distancing, therefore putting off a bit of clear water between me and my erstwhile partner in crime.

"My name, sergeant, is Gray and shouldn't that be what is your name *sir?*"

It occurred to me, as I spoke that my middle class, public school, University of Edinburgh life had, it seemed, also bred ingrained resentment of authority figures and of the police in particular. Deep down, Billy and I were in this regard no different, we just had our own reasons for resentment.

His face betrayed no emotion, but his voice contained a tone of barely suppressed anger, he went on almost mechanically, "Can I have your full name, *sir?*"

There was I felt, an over long emphasis on the sir...

"Robert Alexander Adam Gray," I replied as tersely as I could muster.

"Robert Alexander and then is that Adam sir?"

"Yes, my father was very interested in architecture."

"Thank you, sir, and what's your address?"

"42 Morningside Road."

"And the post code there, sir?"

Four sirs in four sentences well what a good little sergeant we are. But four sirs or not, I could tell if he could 'put me in the frame' he would be overjoyed.

"Not the slightest clue officer. But I'm sure if it's of great moment you can look it up."

He suppressed his natural feelings and settled for,

"And what's your age?"

No sir, things were obviously not shaping up.

"Forty-two."

He duly wrote down everything ponderously in his little black book as though it was "his book of collective wisdom" then he said, "Can you explain why you and Mr. Clarke here are in the Infirmary this evening?"

"No," I replied.

"No?"

His voice betrayed both incredulity and caution, "And why would that be sir?"

The policeman was now becoming wary. Back to sir, but now it was tentative. As though at any time it might be withdrawn and substituted with 'sonny' or some other degrading diminutive.

"Because I did not come here with Mr. Clarke tonight, I came on my own and met the said Mr. Clarke here."

He stopped writing looked up and enquired, "And why would that be?"

"Why would what be?" I retorted.

"The reason you came here?"

"The reason would be none of your business," I replied.

The younger police officer's restlessness was now becoming apparent; her face now set in a belligerent mask; her whole body tense as a hound waiting and straining to be released to have its prey, and I had no doubt who she thought of as her prey. This was not a woman I thought who would be blessed with a forgiving nature.

"Come on Mr. Gray. It's a simple enough question. Of course, if you would prefer, we could always carry on this conversation down at the police station."

She had a thin reedy voice and had settled for the traditional well-tried and equally well-tested formulaic approach.

"Is that relevant? I do not want to seem to be rude but for me this has been a long night…"

I started but before I finish there was an outcry from the other side of the concourse and shouts of "stop them", emanating from the duly signposted, north wing.

"For heaven's sake stop them, stop them don't let them get away!"

As the voice called out, through the swing doors on the far side emerged three youths, all hooded, emerged carrying large sports bags. The sign on the wall announced that they were coming from the direction of the pharmacy, so no guessing was required as to the contents of the bags.

On seeing them, immediately our intrepid interrogators broke off and moved to confront the youths. The hoodies hesitated only momentarily before in unison they separated, two of them each peeling left and right, while the third, a squat bulky lad, like a bull on heat charged straight at sarge and co.

Taken aback as much by the ferocity of the assault as by its suddenness the defence simply, literally, fell away. As he cleaved through the centre of the pair he sent the lady constable spinning like a latter day whirling dervish causing her to collide, it has to be said, very ungainfully with two of her oncoming colleagues, who had until that time been coming to her aid. The ensuing pile up now bore a close resemblance to a collapsed scrum. 'Bulky boy' took off like the proverbial scalded cat through the swing door and disappeared into the corridor and into the South wing.

One of his partners in crime, the one that had chosen to peel to the left was not so lucky. As he made for the western exit doors he was struck by an inward opening swing door, which had been propelled open by an ingressing officer and he was now flat on his back and to all intents and purposes, hors de combat. Had he been a cartoon character, he would have had an enormous throbbing bump vibrating out of his head.

The police were now swarming all over the place, running left and right, a bit like one of Stan Kenton's Keystone Cops productions. I was brought out of my reverie by Billy's voice behind me, dragging me back to reality.

"Jump in here and let's get out the hell out of this place before this commotion all dies down."

He spoke whilst he was standing behind a large clumsy hospital issue wheelchair. Good old Billy, his natural instinct to outdo the local police was as always, at the forefront of his mind, so plan B it was.

I jumped into the chair and said, "Home James and do not on any account spare the horses."

The corridor to the Royal as I mentioned earlier is both very wide, and from my strained nerves point of view, very long. I was worried that at every step we took, we might again be required to account for our presence.

After a journey that seemed to take a lifetime, we eventually made it to the exit, and as we regained the night, there were plenty of flashing lights, but they all seemed to be flashing on empty vehicles. The only representative of the law we encountered pointed us in the direction of the taxi rank and pleasantly wished us good night.

Billy wheeled me in the direction indicated, where we picked up a vacant taxi. He solicitously helped me out of the wheelchair and into the cab, not out of concern for me, the patient, but to play the part right to the end for the benefit of any suspicious onlookers. It was right here we wanted the trail to end. He then carefully placed the wheelchair in a designated spot and joined me in the cab, as he settled I directed the cabbie to Morningside. As he pulled away the taxi driver said over his shoulder,

"I don't think I've ever seen so many police in one place, has there been a problem do you know?"

"I think there was some sort of attempted drugs robbery that went wrong," confided Billy.

The cabbie nodded his head knowingly and pulled away as he did so I said in a low voice,

"Well thank the lord for drug dealers."

Then I settled back and put on the proffered seat belt.

"All that damned trouble for nothing," I said.

I could see in reflection of street lights, Billy smile then he rejoined in an equally low voice, "Oh, I wouldn't quite say, nothing."

Chapter 11
In Which We Follow the Clues

I have to admit to some astonishment and I was momentarily taken aback at Billy's comment. I kept looking at him and then asked,

"Did you just say what I thought you did? What do you mean when you said that you wouldn't quite say nothing?"

"I mean that Darren, bless him came up with the goods. He, as they say in the pictures, spilt his guts."

"Spilt his guts; oh Billy what a dreadful phrase. So are you saying we or rather you now have the registration number?"

"Oh yes indeed we do. The question now is how we obtain an address to go with it. My contacts are not quite in that field."

Billy seemed almost apologetic.

"Don't worry, I think I know just the man for the job, in fact I bumped into him earlier today..."

I answered and glanced through the glass at the taxi's meter which showed the time to be one thirty in the morning; my lord how time flies when you are having fun.

"...or rather yesterday. I will try to get hold of him tomorrow, or rather today."

Our cab was now driving up Morningside Road and we were approaching my flat. I leant forward and said to our cabbie,

"Just over there driver on the left, just at the public library will be fine thank you."

I then said to Billy, "Do you want to come up for a night cap?"

He hesitated, then asked, "Is your dear Mother in residence?"

I smiled, "Yes, but she'll probably be asleep."

Billy returned the smile, "It's the 'probably' that worries me. Thanks, but I think it would be wise to avoid the risk of getting a lecture from your mother for leading her darling boy away from the primrose path trod by the righteous of Morningside and into the backstreets of crime, no thanks. But remember if the cops do a follow-up visit, I was taking you up for an X-ray after you had fallen leaving the Oxford, but owing to the ensuing problems we thought it best to give it a miss. I know it varies slightly from what you told them at the Royal, but you can, if pressed, put it down to bloody mindedness brought on by pain and shock.

If you could maybe limp a bit it would help. In the meantime I will fix the cabbie. It will cost, but I'll send you the bill. Oh, one other thing, since you have involved me at the start, I want like to be in at the kill so keep me in mind. After all, look at the trouble you might have got into without me." He grinned.

"And just look at the trouble I got into with you. I'll ring you this evening, oh and Billy, thanks."

I touched his shoulder, opened the taxi door and stepped out onto the pavement.

I closed the cab door and watched it pull away. I found my latch key and remembering my advice I practised a limp, I let myself into the quiet hallway of the apartment block, and I climbed the two flights of steps. I then let myself into a quiet and somehow after all that happened that night, lonely flat. I went along the hall and into a quiet and lonely bed and a fitful, unquiet sleep populated by blue flashing lights, large dogs with fearsome fangs dripping blood, and harridan women hitting me with enormous truncheons.

Chapter 12
In Which I See Though a Glass but Darkly

Despite the late and somewhat adventurous night I awoke at the usual time. If you are not aware of the environs of Morningside Road I should tell you that it has a natural alarm clock; it's called traffic noise. From just after seven in the morning there is a constant rumble of passing vehicles emanating from the street upwards. There was a knock at the door, a pause, and then my mother entered with a cup of morning tea for her beloved son.

"Good morning mother, are you well?"

"Yes, thank you, but a more apposite question would be, how are you? You were very late arriving home last night."

This was not so much an enquiry as it was a statement so I replied with what I hoped was sufficiently vague answer,

"Yes, I met Billy and we had a couple of jars together."

As soon as I had uttered the B word I immediately regretted it, and as I looked at my mother's expression, my regrets were fully realised.

She pursed her lips, in a fashion given to Morningside matrons, showing both disapproval and contempt. Billy, as he had said last night was not her favourite person. This was, if for no other reason than my championing of his legal cause all these years before. This had led to my first major adult disagreement with my father and an exchange, immediately lamented on my part, of extremely harsh words.

The old boy had taken longer to forgive me following a retort which had come out through my mouth, before my brain had a chance to engage. At the time I thought I was extremely clever when I said that if I was an interfering young fool, then that was at least, better than being a non-interfering old fart, with his head so far up his on backside that he could only see the sunlight second hand. At the time I coloured my vociferous attack with expletives now deleted. This, as you would expect, was not well received from an accountant knocking loudly on the door of middle age. However, with all the benefits of hindsight perhaps I had just been a precocious, arrogant and young man but, what burned bright was that I was correct.

God bless my father, his humour which had suddenly and from my point of view sadly deserted him, had, with the passage of time, returned and overwhelmed his justifiably righteous "father and senior partner mode" and normal relations had been duly restored. It did teach me a useful life lesson though, and that was no matter how good and just you think your cause, there may come a point when you realise that the price is one that you are not willing to pay, or a precious relationship you are not willing to sacrifice on the altar of your particular personal crusade.

Having expressed her disapproval but unlike my father without any forgiveness my mother asked,

"Will you be in for dinner tonight?"

I gave the matter some thought and answered,

"Best say no, as I am not sure what the day might bring. I bumped into Charles yesterday. He's back in town for a while and we exchanged numbers. I will give him a ring when I get to the office."

She treated me to a now smiling face, "Charles, yes that does sound much more appropriate than…"

Her voice trailed off, and then she went on, "Do remember me to him, and do give him my best regards."

Merchant banker always wins out over the artisan; cash trumps dirty hands. Charles, my mother thought, was a much, much more suitable companion for my advancing years.

I assured her I would do as she asked and she left my room reassured. I went to the en suite, shaved, showered, dressed and left the flat with a shouted but hopefully cheery goodbye.

I hopped on a crowded number sixteen bus. Edinburgh has a first-rate public transport system, which an all-knowing council did its best to sabotage by introducing an ill thought out, enormously over cost tram system. This system had during its constructional phase, brought Edinburgh's traffic flow to a stuttering halt, whilst saddling the taxpayer with an ever-increasing level of debt. As an accountant, I always hold this up as an example of allowing amateurs to interfere in matters best left to professionals.

The bus dropped me fifteen minutes later in Princes Street and within a further ten minutes, I was in the office and ready to start the day and face whatever it had to offer. To kick start the wheels of commerce I knew that Miss Wilson would bring me a china cup of the best freshly toasted, freshly ground, aromatic Arabica and, of course the almost obligatory, two digestive biscuits.

As the thought formed in my head, the said lady had knocked on the door and insinuated herself into the room, complete as predicted, with the cup that cheers and the mail that doesn't.

"Good morning…"

A decided pause whilst you could almost see her thinking and struggling with her better, her more restrained, old school Edinburgh alter ego, "Alexander."

There she had actually said it. Mind you she almost blurted it out, as though it was some distasteful morsel of food she was attempting to forcibly eject from her mouth.

"Good morning…"

My turn to pause, she had followed my repeated request: she had dropped the honorific Mr. and it was now my turn. However, as many a modernizer before me I had not, to my regret, fully thought the whole thing through. I suddenly realised with a momentary feeling of panic, that I did not know the highly estimable Miss Wilson's Christian name; did she even have one? She must have. A guess perhaps, but no. So I settled for "Good morning. Coffee, thank you very much."

And a self-promise that further research on this subject was indicated, and went on, "Anything pressing that requires immediate attention in the post? For that matter anything interesting? I'd settle for that."

She flicked through the bundle and commented, "No, just a couple of the usual progress enquiries, a letter asking for a quote for an audit and, of course the usual bills and the inevitable junk mail."

She was about to place the letters on my desk when I said,

"Fine, leave the progress letters with me and ask James to follow up the new business opportunity as soon as. I have a couple of phone calls to make, but if you would ask Tommy to come in about nine thirty. Let him know that I want to go over the monthly accounts with him."

"Thank you," she replied.

"I'll get things underway right away... Alexander."

With that she left, closed the door and I took out my mobile and rang the number Charles had given me at Whigams yesterday afternoon. It rang for a while before a sleep-laden voice announced, in the expected plummy accent that this was Charles and what's more, it was he, who was speaking.

"Charlie, it's Sandy. Good morning, where are you?"

"Ah, where am I, well that's a bit difficult. I mean I do know where I am, in as much as I am in the highly comfortable bed of the delectable Camilla, which she is currently sharing with moi. However, as to the exact location of where the bed is, well that as they say, is another matter completely."

I smiled, if there was one thing Charles was when it came to members of the opposite sex, it was that he was always a quick worker.

"And is the good lady prepared to supply said information?" I enquired tentatively.

"To be brutally frank no, she is still slumbering blissfully in the, oh so peaceful land of nod. Is it something urgent or can we meet somewhere for a hair of the dog at say one ish?" he replied.

"No and yes, there is no point shortening the dear lady's beauty sleep, lunchtime will do fine. Best make it Ma Scott's; see you there."

He assented to the arrangement and I rang off, and sipped my coffee reflectively. I then shook myself out of my thoughts and mentally prepared myself for the struggle ahead with our revered cashier Tommy. Unbeknown to him, Tommy was known to the members of staff because of his strict religious beliefs, as Saint Thomas of Leith.

Chapter 13
In Which the Glass Does Not Clear

At just after the significant, in cinematographic terms, of high noon, my unremitting battle with the sainted Thomas and the accounts over, my mind was happily turning to thoughts of luncheon; of a pint and of a puzzle. A problem that I fervently hoped Charles could with any luck, solve.

I pick up the receiver on the desk phone, and punched in Miss Wilson's number and waited, she answered it on the second ring,

"Good morning or perhaps, good afternoon would be the more correct."

"Indeed it would, I am going out shortly for luncheon. I do not expect to be all that long so I should be back for two at the latest. Before I depart, is there anything pressing that needs to be done before I go?"

There was a slight pause as though she was consulting a diary, then she said, with just the hint of a warning, "No. But bear in mind you have an appointment with the treasurer of St Mary's this afternoon. The St Mary's Cathedral treasurer will be here at three."

Was it my imagination I wondered, or was the second mention of St Mary's slightly more drawn out than the first? Whatever, the message had been duly delivered and received. I was now no longer looking forward to luncheon and a pint but luncheon and a softish drink.

"Thank you, I will ensure that the niceties and proprieties are properly observed."

I left the office walked along Rose Street and, since I had the time, walked round Charlotte Square and crossed the road at the spot where my would-be informer had come to his extremely messy end under the expensive wheels of the Porsche. Now the vehicles' registration number lay in my pocket. As I looked at the "locus" of the crime, it seemed to me as though I had lived an entire lifetime since yesterday. In the last few months, what with my poor old father's murder and the gradual unfolding of events, I seemed to have lived *many* lifetimes in that particular passage of time.

I entered the appointed hostelry just before the appointed hour to find Charles fresh-faced, his wet hair a testament to a recent shower. His hand was clutched round the stem of a large glass containing a white effervescent, opalescent liquid with a slice of lime floating gently on top. He glanced up, saw me, turned and smiled a greeting, "What you having Sandy?"

"The same as you Charles but without the large Gordon's."

He looked mockingly aghast, "Gordon's no, no it's Tanqueray, old chum. Only the full strength stuff for me."

"Tanqueray. I stand corrected then, nevertheless not for me, I have matters of a financial nature to discuss with a man whose discussions are usually more Episcopal and Evangelical."

"Poor old you, the things you accountants have to do to earn a crust to keep the wolf from the door."

Then to a loitering bar man he said, "A large tonic water with ice and a slice."

Then in response to the barman's enquiry, "Good God no bottles please; none of that draught muck."

Having given, received and paid for the order, he placed the glass on the table between us and enquired, "Well, first things first. What's the big mystery, why the summons to this lunchtime tryst?"

I sipped the purchased drink, and started, "Do you remember the events of yesterday, the happenings that led to your re-entry into my life, and your serendipitous entry into the life of what turned out to be your new paramour?"

He looked momentarily puzzled – not quick these merchant bankers. Then with a look of memory flooding back, like a spring flood tide after slack water, he said, "Ah got you, you mean the events that led to our meeting at Whigams. Which in turn led to my first having to anaesthetise and then actively and frequently console the recently bereft and grieving Camilla?"

"You have it in one. After some adventures and some misadventures, and several things that went bump in the night, I now have the registration number. This is the plate number of the car that did for Camay's boss the late James Macbeth. But what I don't know is whose vehicle it is, and I thought, or that is I wondered, what with your previous connections, you may know one of the top boys in blue. One who could perhaps help me fill in this blank."

"So what you're actually looking for is to have two particular blanks filled in."

I paused and then confessed, "You are absolutely right! What I desperately need before I can do anything, is the name and the address of the registered keeper of the vehicle that bears this registration."

I passed across to him the slip of paper that bore the number in question, the number that Billy had persuaded the somewhat reluctant Darren to part with.

He took it, looked at it, and then gave the paper back at me,

"I think we should be able to do that small thing. Can I borrow your mobile? Mine' I'm afraid, is as dead as the proverbial door knob."

I handed him my phone as requested. He put in a number, turned away from me and rose, moving away from the bar. As the number was answered he held a detailed, muttered and distant conversation, before saying in a more audible voice,

"Thanks, yes fine, just give me a second."

Then to me he said, "Sandy old man can you give me your number?"

I told him, and he in turned relayed this information to the person he had rang.

"Right and I owe you one. About half an hour. Many, many thanks."

Then again to me, "Well that's that done. My source says give him thirty minutes and he will ring back. Shall we order lunch, which incidentally is on you, agreed?"

I nodded.

"Excellent, pass me the menu, there's a good lad."

I did as I was bid and handed the bar menu to Charles with the thought that only he could get away with something so downright melodramatic as his recent statement "my source says." I found myself left with the overpowering feeling that I should be shouting down a candle stick phone to a desperate subeditor instructing him to "hold the front page."

The phone rang just as we were just about to have coffee, both of us having decided on the obligatory Ploughman's' for our lunchtime repast. I personally had, self-amusing hope that said ploughman didn't catch us with his lunch. Knowing what rough types these ploughmen can be.

As we consumed our lunch I had a passing thought that since, of the three cheeses provided, one was brie and the other was Edam. That this particular ploughman had gone much further than simply showing his gratitude for the European Common Agricultural Policy. He had in fact gone that extra cheese or, in this case, that extra two cheeses.

My phone rang. I glanced at the number which was unknown to me so I passed the mobile back to Charles.

"Right. Thank you, yes I have that. Nelson, what, oh, Thomas as in the printer and the address is one hundred and eighty, the Causeway, Duddingston Village. Yes perfect. As I said I am in your debt. What was that? No, no it's strictly for lawful purposes, no, no one will be told from whom and from whence the information came. Thank you, good bye."

He handed me back my phone.

"Duddingston Village. That does not sound a likely address for the hideaway of your mysterious hit and run merchant. They're all far too respectable by half for that sort of thing in that district."

He paused, then smiled, as though pleased with his own thought, "Mind you, I suppose, it was after all the place where Bonnie Prince Charlie, that well-known Italian Scot patriot, rested his weary head."

He chuckled to himself, obviously the thought had more than just pleased him, then he glanced back at me, "Did you get all that?"

I nodded, "Yup, many thanks I'll follow it up when I leave the office tonight. Must strike whist the iron is hot."

Charles waved away my thanks, "Good, well I'll let you settle the bill. Then I am going back to the flat for a restful afternoon, with my loins suability re-girded I'll be ready and fit for round two with my new paramour, as you so neatly put it."

We finished our coffee. I paid the bill and with a promise to keep him touch, we parted, he as indicated to rest on his virtuous couch and me for a no doubt Jesuitical discussion on the church's finances These usually centred on how they could minimise their taxable outgoings whilst maximising their legitimate income. Hoping perhaps to be granted the Wisdom of Solomon, in the words of one of Christ's own parables, to render unto God that which is God's and to render unto Caesar (or rather in these modern times the board of the Inland Revenue) that which is theirs.

As things turned out the treasurer that appeared at the appointed hour of three o'clock was not the grim-faced holder of that office that I had talked to in the past. He had been a gentleman of distinct military bearing, with staccato conversation delivered like a parade ground command and with a tendency to disbelieve and have an intolerance of the faults of others.

He had it, transpired, succumbed, not, just temporarily, but unfortunately permanently to the past winter's influenza epidemic. Now not only had he become a statistic, but I liked to think that he was also barking orders on that great parade ground in the sky.

The man ushered into my room and who was now sitting across the desk opposite me, was a rubicund-faced, dog collared young curate. He had taken his accountancy degree before being summoned by a greater calling than the serving of the God of Accuracy and Balance. He had been bidden by, and was now serving, the God of Righteousness and Retribution. As he himself succinctly put it he had swapped the balance sheet for the hymn sheet.

As luck would have it, unlike the relationship I had shared with his predecessor, we found ourselves singing from the same aforementioned hymn sheet. After a soupcon of Earl Grey' to lubricate the wheels of commerce, as practiced here in the temporal realm, he departed happy and satisfied that the Cathedral's funds were in good hands and that the balance sheet was as satisfactory as it could possibly be in this secular and God-absent world.

As the pleasant clergyman left, having concluded his business, Miss Wilson arrived, bringing with her the outgoing post. I signed it, she left with the post, and, with a cheery goodbye to Agnes on reception, so did I.

Chapter 14
In Which Limited Progress is Made

I walked up to and across George Street. Then, down Castle Street and on to Princes' Street, here I waited for the arrival of a bus. It had turned out a pleasant afternoon, which was slowly turning into what promised to be a fine evening. I therefore decided to take a bus to Newington and walk down, through the Queen's Park, to the village of Duddingston.

This was, in fact, more than just a village in name. Unlike the dozens of similar settlements that had been absorbed into the City of Edinburgh by numerous Boundary Extension Acts, this one had managed to maintain a distinct village identity. This was partly due to its topographical location being sited next to a large loch and nestling at the foot of the hills in the Queens Park and the fact that it was subscribed by a main road, thus ensuring that there was no room to expand, except into the Park and that was without a doubt, strictly against the rules. It also had the two things that any good going village needs, a church for the God-fearing, and a pub for the less devout and more thirsty. The extra ingredient that has ensured its exclusive village status is the well-heeled nature of a large quantity of its inhabitants.

A number thirty-one bus deposited me just outside the Commonwealth Pool, a box-like structure which contained an Olympic-sized swimming pool, which had obviously been designed for Olympic-size swimmers and a dedicated diving pool similarly, one could assume designed for dedicated divers.

I turned into the road that leads towards the park with, on my right the strange, yet from certain angles elegant, former Scottish Widows Fund Building. It had thin bronze lines on a brown glass curtain wall and was surrounded by a water feature. It had been designed by the legendary Sir Basil Spence and others and in its time it was cutting edge architecture, which is presumably why it is now a listed building, despite its relative modernity.

It was not, I reflected, as much the building that was strange, just the setting: jutting as did out of a sheet of water much as some ornate Cranach; much as an Inca version of an Egyptian pyramid.

This had been built on the site of Nelson's Parkside Printing Works. Here were produced a range of books that were economically priced that did much to educate and enlighten the lives of the under privileged, before and between the wars.

The Scottish Widows, as I often had to explain to many a potential investor, were not a group of modern husbandless women but an assurance company which was set up to provide a remuneration for ladies whose husbands were unlucky enough not to have survived the Napoleonic Wars. The Scots of yesteryear were God-fearing and prudent, where every penny was a prisoner. Where, oh where, you might just wonder, did it all go *so* wrong?

I walked though Queen's Park'. Now a former Royal Park administered by Historic Scotland for better or worse. Previously it had safely reposed in the hands of the Monarch protected from Edinburgh's local counsellors who were at best, well-meaning but at worst, could easily rank with some of Britain's great incompetents.

I entered the park itself, turning right towards my destination of Duddingston Village. As I strolled, along the path I noticed a road sign which warned against falling rocks. The import of the sign meant nothing because, unless you walked with your head permanently looking upwards, by the time you noticed the rapidly descending rock, it would in truth already be too late.

Should you consider walking in that fashion, think of the collision risk with fellow walkers and joggers, to say nothing of passing motorists, if we all went along gazing endlessly skywards it would seem to me to be a recipe for disaster.

Further on the left the rocks feel steeply away, to reveal a small house sheltering in a small glen. This is the called the Wells o'Wearie, where in past times the Royal shepherd, tended the Royal flock of Royal sheep, which had the right not only of grazing where they wanted but more importantly they had right of way in this Royal Park. These animals were bred to provide, presumably for their Royal owners, Royal wool for Royal jumpers and no doubt, Royal lamb for a right Royal Sunday lunch.

Beyond it and lying to its right was the mass of water, Duddingston Loch, one of three lochs or, if you are from England lakes or if you are from Ireland loughs, in the park. The others are the man-made St Margaret's Loch which was made at the command of a Consort for the delight of his wife, dear old Queen Victoria and the topmost Dunsapie Loch which is an enlarged mountain tarn.

These lochs all attract a large bird population, but this one has the largest and has been an official bird sanctuary since 1929. It had, in fact, been gifted to the city by a certain Mr. Askew, who was seemingly either municipally munificent or as the cynic in me wanted to believe, he had a found an interesting loophole in the tax legislation. Maybe a sort of early form of set aside perhaps.

Behind the former shepherd dwelling and across a wall lay the rolling green sward with manicured greens, well-cut fairways and precisely raked bunkers which was of one of the bastions of Edinburgh's rich elite. This one was Preston Field Golf Club, with the mandatory anglified architectured club house, as if it was to be found along some Surrey lane.

I crossed the road, passed through the car park and up a loan that brought me to the Causeway; this was the main internal street of the village, immediately adjacent to the entrance was one of the two claimants to be Edinburgh's oldest pub. This one was called the "Sheep Heid," the other the "White Hart" which is to be found in the Old Town in the area of the old town called the Grassmarket.

From the numbering, I quickly worked out that the address was not a property on its own. The house I was seeking was obviously built in the grounds of a larger property, perhaps a stable conversion, or an enlarged gardener's hut.

I found the gate, but as is the way of things in my life, I also found a padlock, but unlike my normal run of luck, I also found an intercom. There is a God.

I pushed where it said push and, when an answer came, I spoke where it said speak and having stated my business, I stated that I was the Honorary Treasurer of the Duddingston Village Preservation Trust, a spur of the moment fictional office post in an equally (as far as I know) fictional organization. My accent appeared pass the Duddingston Village Preservation Trust speech patterns acceptability test and I was bade to enter and informed that Mr. Nelson's abode was the former old coach house and it was to be found up the drive and the first turning on the right.

I waited; the gates first juddered, then creaked, then grated and then slowly moved open. It was just as well I was not being hotly pursued by the hounds of hell, or for that matter Darren's far-from-friendly dog, because by the time refuge beckoned, I would have already had my backside chewed big style.

I went through the growing aperture and onto a well-kept gravel path with ne'er a weed to be seen. Either weeds in this neighbourhood knew where they were not wanted or the inhabitants were fastidious and keen users of "Roundup" or some other glycol-based substance. Mind you, these people were sufficiently well up the social scale to have their own illicit stash of "agent yellow."

I followed the directions I was given and there parked in front of rather a fine example of a Victorian coach house, stood the car which bore the registration that I so dearly sought. Ah, but no elation here, no sense of the quarry run to earth, because the car that bore the plate number I was searching for was not my renegade person-slaying Porsche. It was an innocuous and anonymous Ford Fiesta. As I looked at it I had the distinct feeling that if an inanimate object *could* this one seemed to mock me.

Chapter 15
In Which a Little Light is Shed

I turned away from the house, my quest unrewarded, my progress thwarted, no longer having the heart to make up some excuse or other, so as to engage the householder or in this case the coach house holder in conversation.

Ford Fiesta's, highly reliable as they maybe are not the stuff of desperate criminal gangs and bumper to bumper, adrenaline raising, heart pumping, Top Gear featuring car chases. They were the stuff of pipe smoking, flat cap drivers with cushions, folding picnic chairs and table neatly stowed in the boot, and nodding dogs on the back shelf. All that bloody effort, all that bloody trouble, and I was no further forward than I had been before I embarked on last night's expensive nocturnal outing. Like Jesus I could have bloody wept.

I retraced my steps back down the drive finding my somewhat disconsolate way back to where I had only been a few moments ago. In this case it was certainly better to travel hopefully than to arrive.

Once again I found the gate, once again I also found a lock, but this time, unluckily I found no intercom. It became obvious to me, faced with this problem, that it was normal practice for the person you were visiting, having allowed you ingress, would on your leaving activate the lock releasing mechanism thus allowing you to egress.

My day I thought, was obviously going from bad to worse. Whilst I stood there, debating what would be my best course of action. Trying to decide whether or not to retrace my steps, and come up with a plausible explanation to whomever I meet and plea to be released. Or to take, for me, the less embarrassing but more daunting choice of making a Herculean effort and try to scale the damned gate.

I was saved from either course of action. I was neatly removed from the possibly tricky horns of that particular dilemma by a large powder blue Mercedes which was such a particularly inappropriate colour for a Mercedes that you could almost feel the car whining with embarrassment. It came to a halt stopping in front of the outer face of the gate.

The occupant did not disembark from the vehicle but merely waited patiently whilst the gate machinery once more wheezed and spluttered its way into motion. The car was obviously equipped with an internal gadget to trigger the barrier mechanism. Perish the thought that this particular Duddingston resident may have to alight from his luxurious private car, especially when the weather took a turn to cold and inclement weather, just to open the private gates that lead to his very own private driveway, that in turn lead to his very own private house.

The car swept past me and the driver, an elderly head-scarved lady, favoured me with an almost regal wave as she passed. Observing that the gates had reached the maximum point of their opening and were now starting to make their closing manoeuvre I decided to betake myself, and betake I think was the entirely apposite word to fit these grand surroundings, out and onto the pavement.

I stood for a moment pondering the possibilities of my future course of action. Should I perhaps call up Billy and see if we could huckle a different answer from

Darren which seemed a possibly hazardous course of action, or perhaps have Charles re-contact his "source". So what to do first. I glanced up and the answer came to me loud and clear. The pub door was immediately adjacent to where I regained the pavement, so the order of the day was the Sheip Heid Inn first, the rest of the problems could wait their turn till later.

I pushed open the door and entered these highly revered licensed premises. The bar inside was a low beamed room and was relatively quiet for that time of the evening. There exists a time in the mid-evening in Edinburgh when there is a lull in the business of hostelries. This occurs after the homebound office workers, having consumed their proscribed units of alcohol, or in many cases more than their duly proscribed allotment often with lingering regret, leave to continue their journey for a reunion with their loved ones. After their departure there occurs a hiatus before they are in due course, replaced by a more restrained type of drinker. These individuals arrive prior to dining, having taken their evening constitutional, or exercised their pedigreed hounds on her Majesty's former green and pleasant land.

The main differences between this pub and the "Anchor" of last night, of not quite blessed memory, were like night and day. The barman was well dressed and amenable and addressed me not as mate or pal, but with the more upmarket "Sir", conveyed in the greeting, "Good evening sir. What can I get you?"

I opted for a pint of Stella Artois and conveyed this request to the barkeep. This he duly poured, I duly paid, and looking round me, I took in more fully my surroundings.

I knew the pub's claim to its "oldest pub in Edinburgh's status" was that there had been some form of licensed premises on the site for almost seven hundred years. It had I suspected, in its original carnation, no doubt been a low chabin, an unlicensed howf, that sold locally produced home brewed ale and locally distilled, decidedly illicit, hooch.

The very "Sheip Heid" was on display behind the bar, not as it happened to be completely accurate, a sheep's head but a tupp's head: in English a ram's head. Ram being strictly an English term for the male of the species, known in Scots as a tupp.

The whole thing was complete with highly elaborate, to say nothing of magnificent, twisted horns, with gleaming well-polished silver mountings; in reality this was nothing other than a rather grand snuff box. These types of thing are to be seen on the dining tables of the Scottish regiments on formal occasions, such as a regimental dinner when the port flows, always of course from the left, and quantities of the snuff are liberally applied to the nasal passages.

I finished my pint and ordered another and was looking deeply into my glass as though I expected to find the answer somewhere in its amber gently bubbling contents, when I noticed the door open. A large well-ordered Chocolate Labrador entered and looked around and for a moment it appeared as if it were on its own. But the door then reopened to bring in my bescarfed lady waver at the gate. Close to I saw she was probably nearer seventy than sixty confirming my initial guess. She possessed a facial skin that seemed to me, redolent of good causes, copious quantities of pulses, and long walks in all weathers.

She ordered a large gin and tonic and a large packet of roast chicken flavoured crisps; the drink for her, and the crisps for her apparently faithful and discerning canine companion. She was obviously no stranger to this establishment as she addressed the barman personally, as Jimmy. Mind you it has to be mentioned, that Jimmy can be a catchall name, a common form of greeting, in certain parts and with a certain class of people in Scotland. That said though, this was not one of these certain parts and she was self-evidently, not a member of that certain class.

She bent down and addressed the dog, "Well, Biscuit my old lad."

The dog realizing it was being spoken to, started to wag his thick tail and looked up at her expectantly as she opened the packet and placed it on the flagged floor. The dog observed its owner's actions and waited patiently on the word of command, which when duly given, he proceeded to consume the packet's contents in rapid time. She then sat back and took a long draught from her glass, in fact so long a draught that she drained the goblet dry. She looked momentarily somewhat bewildered, as though the contents had mysteriously evaporated or had been somehow magicked away, then with a positive sign of collecting her thoughts she said,

"Better have another one of these I think, one's never enough to hit the spot, eh James? Excellent."

Her glass duly replenished she allowed her gaze to wander round the room and then, having scanned from horizon to horizon, her gaze rested on yours truly. She spoke with a definite clipped tone giving her speech a certain abruptness,

"Didn't I just see you coming out of the Nelson's?"

I suddenly realised, not only was I being looked at, I was being spoken to. I glanced round at woman and dog as they both, with an apparent unity of purpose, seemed to be weighing me up as if to ascertain whether or not I might be found wanting on the scales of Duddingston Village respectability.

"Ah, if you mean the property across the street then, I am afraid to say I'm guilty as charged."

I tried to put a smile in my voice but was not sure I was entirely successful.

"Oh well, are you indeed?"

The voice had taken on that almost lazy universal upper class drawl, "It's just that no one had visited Belle Vue, that's my house, and I therefore, presumed you were at the old coach house and that's Nelson's property!"

She was half explaining whilst half interrogating, this lady had a good technique.

"Ah I see. You were the driver of the Merc. No I was looking for a car with a particular registration number and I was told that I might find it at that address, which is the Nelson's address. However, when I checked it out I realised that the Ford Fiesta parked in the driveway had a similar number, but not exactly the one I was looking for…"

I let my voice tail off, more than a little satisfied with how smoothly the lie had come from my brain and across my lips.

Both she and the dog looked at me quizzically,

"Aren't you a bit old for collecting car numbers eh, eh!!? Aren't, you eh, Mr. umm?"

Mr. umm duly replied,

"Gray Alexander; Sandy Gray."

I got to my feet feeling that some sort of ceremony was about to take place. She shot her free hand out and almost barked, "Peacock, Colonel Peacock,"

The drawl had been replaced with a tone that was commanding, the accent cut glass.

I grasped the proffered hand which was dry and firm, "Good evening Colonel Peacock, how nice it is to meet you."

As I said the words, I could not help but think, if this was Cluedo, she'd be probably be disposed of in the library with the candlestick by Miss Scarlett, but carried on, "Oh, and as to the question of car numbers, yes you're absolutely right, I am too old, and yes in my misspent youth, I used to. My interest in the car number is less by way of a leisure pursuit than a business pursuit. My reason is purely because my mother's car was the victim of a hit and run last week and a helpful, or as the case would now seem to be, a helpful but less than accurate, bystander had taken down although obviously now it transpires wrongly, the offending car's number plate."

My off-the-cuff explanation piqued the Colonel's interest and she enquired,

"Hit and run do you say? Was your mater hurt?"

"No, luckily it was not the mater that had her bodywork damaged; it was the mater's car."

She punched me gently on the shoulder with what was meant to be, I presumed, sort of sign of camaraderie and went on, "Not the mater's bodywork that was damaged, just the car's. Like your style Sandy Gray, like your style my boy."

She stopped and apparently mused before tentatively saying, "Do you know Sandy it's odd in a way because Maggie, that's the Nelson's youngest daughter and the owner of the car, had it stolen three or four weeks ago and it's just recently been returned. Believe it or not that stupid little car is her pride and joy."

This piece of intelligence certainly got my attention so I, as Oliver Twist, asked for more.

"When you say it was returned recently how recently was that?"

"Oh, last night, early evening, her father found it parked here in the Causeway, keys in the ignition, just sitting there."

Whoever these people were, they were certainly on the ball.

The Colonel continued, with some vehemence,

"The Nelsons don't know exactly how long it had been there, but, certainly long enough for one of these "Blue Meanies" to ticket it."

If you are not from Edinburgh then the expression "Blue Meanies" might prove to be an unknown term. This designation refers to a privately employed group of individuals who are considered to be a particularly virulent strain of traffic warden. These people are used to being regularly berated and to having opprobrium heaped on their only too miserable heads by assorted passing motorists.

I allowed what she obviously considered to be justifiable anger to abate, before asking,

"Was there any damage, any breakages or anything?"

The Colonel gave the matter some thought, then almost hesitatingly said,

"Well…no… not really, a couple of scratches. That said, mind you it was like a damned tip inside *and* the buggers, whoever they were had done a couple of thousand miles in it. There were seemingly no fingerprints that is, no usable fingerprints, at least according to the boys in blue. There were too many and they were too blurred to be of any use to either man or beast. My own opinion is it was in all probability one of those joy riding yobs from over there."

She indicated in the direction of Niddry; one of too many post-war ghettos in Edinburgh built to be populated by the great unwashed or perhaps, the great un-washable might be nearer the truth. Although now going through a renaissance, as were other similar areas of the city, it still suffered from the "give a dog a bad name" syndrome.

"Damned buggers, whipping is too good for them."

I had no doubt in my mind that when the whips were being handed out, she would be well to the fore, although whether it was the yobs or the wardens or both that had incurred her wrath, she did not make completely clear. I concluded with the thought, if not in her mind then in mine, that both groups richly deserved this promised flogging, both moreover for their sins of commission, rather than those of omission.

Then as though her memory had just kicked in she added,

"As I said, no real damage was done. But one really strange thing, now I come to think of it, the number plates were taken off and put in the boot. What a dammed stupid and spiteful thing to do."

Chapter 16
In Which It's the Name of the Dog

Although I knew very much to the contrary, I felt that my agreement was called for, "What a damned stupid and spiteful, thing to do indeed."

I repeated her angry words. But it took me all my time not to hug the good Colonel so I settled for the standard response,

"Can get you another one of these?" I asked whilst pointing at her by now empty glass.

God bless her, the game old soldier acquiesced. I signed to the barman, and James measured, James poured, the Colonel drank and Sandy paid.

I glanced at the dog, Biscuit, who looked aggrieved, aggrieved in that particular way that only Labradors can, so I bent down to him and said, "Sorry old chap, I seem to have forgotten you. Another packet of chicken crisps for you perhaps?"

The dog, whether acknowledging the question, or merely out of happiness at being spoken to, moved his tail in what appeared to me at least, in a meaningful manner.

The dog wagged his tail, the omnipresent James produced the crisps, Biscuit consumed the contents and again Sandy paid.

As I straightened up from having placed the crisps in the appointed fashion and in the appointed place, I glanced at the good Colonel, who bestowed on me a look of almost beatific pleasure that I had not forgotten to include in the round man's, or in this case woman's, best friend.

"What made you call him Biscuit anyway?" I enquired.

The Colonel looked by turns coy, or what in her case would pass for coy, guilty and then conspiratorial, and confided, "Well, it's a little naughty, really a little naughty; it's a sort of well private joke. The boy's full name is, in fact..."

She paused seemingly for dramatic effect, then looking around as if listening for some passing agency of the law; presumably working on the theory that many of our police force having given up the duties so manfully carried out by officers in the past, our more modern breed inclined to listen at doors for possible racial comments.

Having satisfied herself that all was well she went on,

"His full name is, well em, Chocolate Biscuit."

This admission followed by the full-on mode braying laugh, "Do you get it? Chocolate Biscuit."

This was followed by another burst of her personal brand of raucous laughter.

As admissions go, to say nothing of canine naming protocols Chocolate Biscuit sounded a little underwhelming. However, judging by the lady's expression a response was not only expected but overdue,

"Oh I see, with you now. Shades old Guy Gibson, who owned a Chocolate Lab called Nigger, just a bit more politically correct."

In my mind's eye I could see the bloody dog as he was depicted in the film, "The Dam Busters" sitting wistfully in the setting sun looking skyward for the return of his far to over-courageous Wing Commander master.

Nigger's master, Guy Gibson's role was played, as only Richard Todd could with his steadfast eye, air of steely determination and unflappable insouciance. Qualities it turned out, which were more than just acted, they were real life qualities, as Todd exhibited in Operation Overlord in the D-Day landings.

I have always considered that if you were involved in World War Two as air crew, you should at all costs make every effort to avoid any type of canine company; if the movies are to believed, such an association appeared to put the mockers on your projected life expectancy. It's as though you didn't have enough to put up with "Jerry" trying his damndest to end your life, you had also the latent curse of dear old Fido stacked against you.

My thoughts were interrupted by the sounds of dog and mistress gathering themselves for the off.

"Must be off, time for dinner don't you know, better not keep the Sahib waiting, dinner gong about to go and all that."

And do you know I believed it was about to do just that. She made to the door,

"Nice to have met you Sandy, thanks for the sharpener."

Thanks for the sharpener indeed. I was surprised she hadn't called it a Choate peg and gone the whole sub-continental hog; then thinking of the Muslim population, perhaps the whole hog was not the most apposite of expressions.

I thanked them both in the appropriate fashion, by smiling at the lady and patting the dog, although I couldn't but help feel that both these gestures, in this case, could easily be interchangeable. I looked at the clock built into the elaborate Victorian bar back. Time to go I thought and, remembering that the village is at this time of the evening not exactly awash with buses, I turned to the ever-attentive James.

"Do have the number for a cab company by any chance?"

"Yes sir. There are several useful numbers on the wall by the phone. It's on the wall, just on the right, on the way to the gents."

I thanked him and followed the direction given, picked up the receiver, heard the dialling tone and was about to dial, when I suddenly realised that I not only did not have a clue how much it now cost to make a phone call, but I also realised that even if I did know the charge, I did not have any change.

It is strange how a few years of an object that makes your life easier, in this case a mobile phone, can rob you of the basic life skills that a few years ago would have been second nature to you.

So, faced with this dilemma, I solved the situation by taking out my mobile and using it to dial one of the numbers pinned to the wall. A pleasant female voice assured me that my place of pick-up was noted, and the ETA of the cab would be ten minutes. I told the dispatcher I would wait outside the hostelry and rang off. I finished my drink, placed the glass on the bar and, with a nod of thanks to James, I walked back into a now darkened street.

Chapter 17
In Which I Take a Cab and Take a Call

Almost to the promised minute the cab arrived and having climbed in, I settled down in the back.

"Where to mate?" asked the cabby.

Where to indeed, time to think was really what I needed. If I went back to the flat at this time I risked an interrogation from mother, so I settled for,

"Oxford Bar. That'll' do fine, thank you."

He slid the glass partition back, let in the clutch and we glided out of the village and back into the park. This was a dark and poorly light space, a veritable wrongdoer's paradise. We left at the western entrance and went down the Pleasance up St Mary's Street, under North Bridge, along Market Street and onto Waverley Bridge, Sir Walter Scott's memorial monument looking for all the world like a rocket stood, as always, as some testament in stone to failed disarmament talks. On the journey I pondered the next move. What I felt I could really do with was having word or two with Charlie or, even better, have Charlie speak to his contact.

I took out my phone and tried the new number Charles had given me. It rang out and then went to voicemail. I hesitated but decided he would probably be either be too lazy, or as in my case, too mean to pay to listen to a recorded message.

I was searching the phone's internal directory for my home number; I felt it was time for a duty call when the phone rang. It was Charles.

"You rang?" the voice enquired.

"Charlie old man, sorry to trouble you, but I need a bit more help. I would like a little more information from your friend, your source in restricted, if not necessarily high places."

"More information you say. What was wrong with the last lot? Wasn't it accurate?" he enquired.

"Well yes perfectly accurate, that is, as far as it went. It's just that a situation has... well, developed and it now necessitates a further follow up."

I went on and explained, in as few words as possible, the encounters and experiences of my evening out so far.

Charles listened intently and then without further comment he said,

"What time is it?"

I looked at my watch, "Just before seven forty-five."

"Right Sandy, the person I need to talk to won't be off shift for forty-five minutes. My contact works in the regional collator's office down at the old Lothian and Borders Force HQ at Fettes. I will try to see if I can get in touch. Where are you at the moment?

"I'm in a cab halfway along George Street, heading for the Oxford Bar."

There was a slight pause as though he was turning something over in his mind, and then, "Right, okay, leave it with me and I will see what I can dig up, no promises mind you."

He again paused, I wondered if he was being overheard, and then as though having made a final and momentous decision he went on, "I'm about to have dinner. Will try you after the soup course."

Without further comment he rang off. I looked out of the cab window and noticed that we were now sweeping, if not majestically then certainly at some pace, round Charlotte Square. As we passed the Northern facade of Robert Adams' masterpiece, I waved, as usual, at the First Minister's house and he, as usual, failed to wave back. And he calls himself a man of the people I mused... Musing time abruptly ended as the taxi pulled up at the Oxford. The driver dipped the flag and stated the fare, which I duly paid and then alighted.

The Oxford was busier than the Sheep Heid. The office types in this part of the world seemingly less keen for the homeward bounding thing and more inclined and seemingly more keen to stay for the extra jar or two, or three.

There was no sign of Billy, although I hadn't really expected him to be there as it was a little early for him so I ordered a pint and sat at a table in the corner. I'll finish this and go in search of some form of dinner, I thought, perhaps pick up a carry-out and bear it manfully to the bosom of my family. This much as some hunter gatherer and then having made it to my modern cave, perhaps split a bottle with the mater, or perhaps not.

I had the feeling that I had been advised at some point, in no uncertain terms, that this was one of her bridge nights and even her loving son's presence was excess to her requirements.

As if she knew and had read my thoughts, the phone rang I glanced at the display and it said home. So I pressed the green button, put it to my ear and listened. My mother spoke without brooking any greeting and she spoke with some vehemence, "Alexander, is that you?"

And before allowing Alexander time to confirm in the positive she went on,

"It's an absolute disgrace. In all the years that your father was alive, we have never had such a disgrace and *this* on a bridge night of all nights!"

You see, I had been right about the bridge night. I gave myself, what I considered to be a well-deserved mental pat on the back. Although I was correct about the purpose of the evening, I felt I was obviously wrong about something else. I was aware that the tirade was not yet over merely the originator of the harangue was pausing in preparation for the re-girding of her loins'. These loins seemingly being well and truly re-girded she went on.

"So, what I need *you* to do, and quickly mind, I want you to sort this whole matter out this very night and ensure that this does *not* happen again. There must be no repetition do you hear me, never again."

Without waiting for any response from me she simply hung up. I could imagine her receiving plaudits and peons of praise from her fellow Morningside matrons on how well she had told off her errant and obviously wayward child and set him back on the Primrose Path to righteousness' and retribution.

That said I was left both bemused and amused, to say nothing of downright bewildered, by this verbal onslaught, the import of which I could not immediately grasp.

I sat for a while going over the words; the fact that firstly, it apparently had been a disgrace and secondly, the admonition not let it happen again. Then suddenly a vague possibility that might offer an explanation came to me, but at the same time, the phone went again. Again I looked at the display. This time it was Charles.

"That was an extremely quick soup course. Really small portions?"

"No, no there was a delay in preparing the table so since your request sounded somewhat urgent I rang up my contact."

"You don't call him "deep throat" or anything dramatic, do you?"

"No, of course not, do try not to be so juvenile," came the rather tart reply. That put me in my place. I'd forgotten that levity was by and large wasted on Charles; he went on, "right, the vehicle, the one with the number plate in question."

God, now he was beginning to sound like a policeman.

"Well there seems a little problem here," he said.

That certainly got my attention.

"What sort of problem Charles?"

"You said that the car that ran down your acquaintance was a Porsche, but that registration, now we have investigated further is for a Fiesta."

I could have told you that I thought, but before I could he went on.

"However, there has been an interesting development that might have some bearing on your little problem. That is, talking of Porsches one was recovered, significantly minus its registration plates, but plus substantial front end damage; it is currently undergoing forensic investigation by the local constabulary's experts. It was found at one of the Park and Ride sites. Incidentally when did they spring up? Park and Rides, that's almost futuristic for Edinburgh," he enquired.

I have to admit that the question caught me unawares. When Charles had uttered the words "undergoing forensic investigation" I suddenly had visions of CSI. Thus, when he abruptly changed from information giver, to information seeker, I was not quite prepared for the sudden change.

"Sandy, are you still there?" I heard him say.

"Yes, sorry Charlie, dropped the damned phone,"

I was getting quite good at these lies of convenience.

"Agreed, it is a bit forward thinking isn't it. I think their introduction was proposed by some councillor who slipped back through the space time continuum, he had been it appears, dwelling in some parallel, but slightly more advanced city. At any rate, could you be a little more specific? Which Park and Ride?"

"Do you mean there are more than one, my, that is progress; come to think of it I may have passed one on the way from the Airport? They tell me that this one is at somewhere called Straiton, wherever that is."

Local geography had never been one of his strong points. Once taken out of his precious, in every sense of the word, bloody New Town he was lost. This was of course with the one notable exception of knowing only too well, the road to Turnhouse, to Edinburgh Airport. So I attempted a touch of local orientation, "Straiton is possibly what you would have called Loanhead."

My elucidation was evidently, as they say, on the money as I heard him say, "Oh, I know where you are, out on the south side, on the Penicuik, Bilston Road."

He had geographically positioned himself spot on.

"That's exactly so. And was it just, as it were, sitting there abandoned and the police sort of happened upon it?"

"Well no, that's the thing, that's the interesting development. It was, according to my source, discovered without a tax disc when the Lothian and Borders' finest carried out a raid."

"What the boys in blue raided a Park and Ride site?" I replied, it has to be said, somewhat sceptically.

"Well no, it was not a raid on site per se. The reason for the swoop was not as much on the location, as on who was illegally occupying the location, in this case a load of Tinks."

Chapter 18
When I Make the Personal Acquaintance of the Fuzz

"Ah, I see, can I take it by a load of Tinks I take it you mean those people who call themselves Travellers or Travelling folk."

I had tried to translate, I knew vainly, into something slightly more PC but even as I spoke I knew deep down that with Charlie it was a lost cause and as if to prove my theory to be bang on the money, he retorted with, it has to be said, some feeling, "No, by Tinks I mean these buggers who roam around from place to place and think that the country owes them a living *and* they think they can camp where they bloody well want and *take* what they bloody well want and leave the place covered in shit. Then their apologists defend them on the basis it's their traditional way of life. When we were boys, we used to call them much worse things than Tinks."

That's how it goes; scratch gently on the surface of a merchant banker and you find, lingering, a fully-fledged raging xenophobe.

As is my wont I passingly wondered if they still made and sold pegs and mended pots and pans, as they had in my boyhood days, when as Charlie had said we did indeed call them much worse things than Tinks. But I interjected into his diatribe,

"Well Charlie your' colourful and totally disinterested description of our Romany friends' aside, your information seems now to raise even more questions than it provides answers."

He made no comment, so I continued, "Could I do you think, I mean well, would it be possible to have a quick face-to-face with your source, just to, as it were to dot the i's and cross a few t's?"

He hesitated. I could almost feel the hesitation coming down the phone, then he spoke, but it was not to me,

"What? Right Cammy, just coming, yes, yes two minutes promise. No, no it's not business it's personal. Well it's just Sandy, it's to do with that business I told you about earlier."

A pause as if listening to a reply then, "Yes, that's right, concerning the car that ran down your associate, that Macbeth fellow. Sandy's been to Duddingston but drawn a blank."

Then a mumbled conversation as though Charlie had covered the mouthpiece of the mobile with his hand. Terms of endearment not meant for a third party perhaps, then his voice was speaking again but still not to me,

"Ok Cammy my love, I will be with you directly. Okay, okay as soon as."

Having sorted out the dining arrangements to his companion's satisfaction, he then spoke to me, "Sorry Sandy, table ready, got to go. The trouble is old chum that I think that what you want to do is much more than simply just dot the i's and cross the t's, I would, if I were in your shoes at any rate."

A little more hesitation, then again not to me, "Excellent, excellent yes champagne is fine by me, but make it the "Veuve Clicquot Yellow" label and yes, I am coming."

Then back to me, "Quite frankly I have my doubts about this but dinner awaits. Oh alright look, I will give you my person's number. See what you can arrange, but don't on any account bugger it up. Am I making myself clear, do not bugger it up."

As if to add emphasis, he pronounced the last words in an attenuated manner.

"Message understood; I hear you loud and clear. I shall be polite and the very model of a law-abiding citizen."

He duly gave the number which I noted down and he added to ask for Sam. Despite Charles's admonition about my juvenile behaviour, I was mildly disappointed there was no code to be exchanged, to be delivered in a strange accent, with just the correct intonation to be followed by a breathless hush. Although time and Cammy were obviously both applying pressure, he could not resist one last rejoinder, a Parthian shot,

"You damned well better be polite and be the model of a law-abiding citizen, or whatever you just said. Oh and Sandy, one last thing, remember this is done on a favour-for-favour basis, and to be frank, God knows what a damned middle-aged accountant has to add."

Who's a little touchy then I thought, but said in my own defence, "Oh I don't know about that. I have an extremely nice set of matching tax tables, all leather bound and hand tooled with the appropriate year picked out in gold leaf, an innate ability to count and I always, always keep my pencil sharp."

"Yeah, yeah I hear what you say. I always keep my pencil sharp indeed. Just don't go blowing the thing ok. And one other thing, be careful where you stick your ever sharp pencil!"

I wished him bon appétit and rang off. It was not till then that I wondered what sort of favour-for-favour basis the local constabulary worked out, as quid pro quo, with a merchant banker. Did he discuss with them the risk versus reward balance of their portfolios perhaps, or whether or not to hold on to their gilt-edged securities or even better, when he sensed a falling market, did he phone them and shout sell, sell!!

I dialled the number and after being connected I was greeted with an official-sounding voice message. This informed me, that it was the regional headquarters of Police Scotland and that my phone call may be recorded for training purposes, more like for fitting-up purposes would have been dear old Billy's immediate reaction, I thought.

The recorded announcement was cut short as it was interrupted with another equally mechanical, but this time human or perhaps humanesque voice, which inquired in a tone which could only be described as staccato, as to the extension number that I desired, then almost as an afterthought, the voice added if I knew what it was. If not I was advised to hang on the line for a further announcement. Having punched in the extension number supplied by Charlie, I was instructed to stay on the line. This message was followed by a series of raps and clicks, followed by a ringing noise, the receiver was picked up and a pleasant voice said,

"Regional collator's office, can I help?"

"Good evening, may I speak to Sam please?"

"Sam speaking," came a crisp reply. Well, well surprise, surprise. When I had been told to ask for Sam, no gender indicator had been proffered by Charles. The old bugger had been holding out on me. Now I could imagine what sort of favour-for-favour basis this member of the local constabulary had with a merchant banker. I have to admit this development somewhat nonplussed me so I went on diffidently, "Ah right. We have never actually met, in fact we have never spoken and you must forgive my presumption. My name is Sandy and I am presuming on a mutual friend Charles..."

I paused remembering the "you might be recorded for training purposes" bit in the recorded message. I obviously did not want to land my new acquaintance Sam, in trouble for a possible dereliction of duty.

"He mentioned that you and he have had contact in the past. I know... it's a bit of a presumption... but I just wondered, if you are free tonight, maybe I could ... buy you a drink after work. Charles did mention to me you would be off work at eight thirty umm..."

I let my voice trail off in what I fervently hoped was an appealing and slightly mysterious way.

When she replied I was left in no doubt as just how appealing she found me and my trailing off voice,

"Did he indeed and you're right, it is not only a presumption, it's a *very* large and *highly* impertinent presumption, on both your parts, and when I see your friend next I will be only too pleased to let him know what I think about his giving my work number out to complete strangers!"

She obviously had not picked up the intonation of inexplicable intrigue in my tone, or perhaps, she was wrestling with and fighting against her better judgment. Or perhaps she had simply ignored the tone of my voice, deciding to ignore it on the basis of cats and the upping of their chances of popping their paws when curious.

Time for a rapid piece of fence building, was the thought which immediately occurred to me, "Oh I am sorry, really, don't take it out on old Charles, I well... I sort of put him under some duress and we really are old buddies. I am truly sorry if I have upset you, this was certainly not my intention."

Well, since she obviously hadn't picked up the air of mystery nuance first time, perhaps she might latch onto grovelling nuance, at my second attempt.

"Mr. Gray, people I have found are usually lying when they use the "sorry" word, because they rarely are."

There followed a long pause, best not to interrupt I judged. The pause continued and then she spoke again this time in a more reflective tone,

"Well, Mr. Gray…"

Again a pause, as if trying to recall to her mind something or someone, "Tell me are you Sandy Gray, the Sandy Gray of, sorry to use that terrible tabloid headline, "the Death of a Grey Man" case?"

"Yup, that's me."

"And it was your father who was the victim of the murder?"

"Yup, once again that's me."

Another pause, this time I felt the delay was Sam making up her mind, then with a brusqueness of manner,

"Okay, agreed. Where would you like to meet?"

Who would have believed it, a murder victim's son seemed to come with the right credentials, obviously much to be preferred to a random caller, even one with mutual merchant banker friend status.

"I'm a member of the Grange Club in Stockbridge; I could meet you on the corner of Port Gower Place, just along from your office, at say, about eight forty-five, if that's alright with you?"

"Do you mean round about where the old Raeburn Hotel is, or rather that new boutique hotel?" she asked.

I confirmed in the positive and we both rang off. Before replacing the mobile in my pocket I checked the display and touched the messages icon. I opened Charlie's number and sent him a text advising him of the arrangements I had made with his contact, I felt that I owed him that. I closed the screen and glanced at the time display, it showed eight sixteen, so I had almost half an hour, just the right time for a quiet evening stroll downhill through the backstreets of the New Town to our appointed tryst.

I drained my glass, placed it on the bar counter and went on a visit to the gents and I considered just how proud my mother would have been; of the effectiveness of her early years training her son had been. I was now following her dictum of my childhood days, never to go out before going.

On returning to the bar, before making my way out almost, as an afterthought I took my phone back out and gave Billy's number a try.

The number rang out and went to voicemail, so I sent a quick text asking him to give me a call on my mobile when he had a chance.

I nodded to the barman and left.

Chapter 19
Don't Look Round

Turning right I walked to the end of Young Street, then down and across Queen Street into Wemyss Place and down Gloucester Street Lane, passing as I went the birthplace of the painter and Royal Academician, David Roberts, now somewhat incongruously a restaurant, across the eponymous bridge and into Stockbridge.

For those of us, and I admit to being one of their number, who just love both word or name derivation. The word stock in Stockbridge is not, as one might think at first glance, something to do with herds of cattle being driven along this thoroughfare. On the contrary, it comes from the Anglian, meaning a timber bridge.

This is a part of Edinburgh once much favoured by the Bohemian set, but was now very upmarket and much gentrified with twee shops, delicatessens, high-class restaurants offering casual dining at far from casual prices and the statutory array of charity shops, which are always to be found clustered in Edinburgh's upmarket areas. Well-heeled Morningside and Corstorphine are similarly blessed.

I passed Cheyne Street on my left, built in the late 1820's and a narrow, fairly anonymous street constructed principally to house the lower middle classes of that period. This was, however, a street which was the scene of a terrible story of grinding poverty, a downtrodden and much put-upon woman. This was a perfect illustration of the enormous social inequalities that pervaded the late Victorian social and class systems.

The child murders of the winter of 1888 had shocked polite, gentile Edinburgh to the very centre of its two-faced, hypocritical core. At that time unmarried women who fell pregnant were socially excluded but, of course not so the man. He was often considered in certain circles to be a bit of a lad.

Abortion was strictly forbidden. It was against the law and further it was frowned upon by the church, as running contrary to the Holy Scriptures. Those pious high-minded ministers of religion who choose to ignore the words of Christ when he said, "suffer the little children to come unto me" or perhaps they squared their convenient collective consciousness, by adding to them the corollary "unless of course they are born out of wedlock." There was of course the option of a backstreet abortion; these were dangerous, with a high mortality rate, but it was either that or give up your child to the tender mercies of the orphanage. This was a crime which, if you were caught, you would most *certainly* hang for. An alternative was to pay a baby farmer to, as it were, undertake your daycare for you.

The city's most infamous baby farmer was one Jessie King. She ran a sort of playgroup, without the play, for the illegitimate issue of impoverished working class mothers. Here they deposited their precious offspring whilst they went in order to work to pay both for themselves and their bastard.

Jessie lived in another district of Edinburgh, Canonmills, prior to 1888, where she cohabited with a man, Michael Pearson as her common law husband. She had several children in her charge at this point, including one named Alexander Gunn. Alexander, (good name) seemed to be being well cared for, until one day he disappeared. The matter of the disappearance was reported to the police, who as part of their subsequent investigation took Jesse in for questioning but she was released without charge.

Following the disappearance of baby Gunn, the pair moved to Cheyne Street, in order apparently, in an attempt to muddy the waters. At the new address she continued her business as a latter-day baby minder. However, shortly after re-establishing her enterprise two babies in Jessie's care disappeared.

Following on from these children vanishing, some boys playing in the street discovered the strangled corpse of a male infant. Jessie was questioned once again about the missing child Alexander, but stuck to her story that the child had been passed on to her sister to be cared for. The police remained unconvinced and searched the house, finding in their quest that Jesse stored slumbering children in the drawers of her bedroom chest. When they re-questioned her after this search, she broke down and in an act seemingly, of contrition she took the police officers down to the cellar of the tenement block, where the corpse of a baby girl lay. The dead child that the playing boys found turned out to be young Master Gunn.

Jessie was never charged over the disappearance of the third baby, principally as no corpse was ever found, but she did admit to the strangling of Alexander in a fit, she stated, of 'drunken melancholy.' She further confessed to overdoing the whisky, which she had been using as a sort of super gripe water to quieten and settle the baby girl. 'Those who cannot remember the past are condemned to repeat it' George Santayana said, and he was absolutely right. As only recently a mother was sentenced at the Edinburgh High Court for doing exactly what Jesse King had done. This time to bring the whole thing was bang up-to-date, with a dose of methadone;

one sometimes feels that nothing changes. There, it would appear, is nothing new under the sun.

In the very unfortunate Jesse's case, although there were doubts raised as to her state of mind, she was conveniently declared fit for trial and after which she was conveniently found guilty and conveniently sentenced to death. She was held in the condemned cell of Calton Jail on Calton Hill where she was duly hanged by the neck till dead.

Nevertheless, she did have in death that which had eluded her in life, a certain lasting notoriety, a sort of fame; she was the last woman to be hanged in Edinburgh.

Had I been paying more attention to the present, to the now, rather than to the past, a fault constantly pointed out by my mother, who was given to liking me to Thurber's character 'Walter Mitty', I might just have noticed the man following me and saved myself some grief. If the truth be told had I my wits about me I would have realised that I had been 'watched' since leaving my office. When I thought earlier that these people, whoever they were, moved quickly, that was an understatement, they moved *very* quickly.

In my own defence, I did not realise until it was almost too late; that we were clasping a serpent to our bosom.

I walked along the main street, busy for that time of night, people here seeming to come and go, all with some purpose in mind. I paused to look in some of the charity shop windows, giving totally unbeknown to me, my follower palpitations, fearing as it so happened totally unjustifiably that his presence had been detected. Although as in the words of the old music hall song I had dillied and I had dallied. It was close to the appointed time when I arrived at the pre-appointed meeting point, the old Raeburn Hotel, its lights shining brightly, now fully restored to its former glory, after suffering a spectacular fall from grace.

This spectacular fall, a fall, in the literal sense came about when a visitor to the ladies' loo, created a new line in lavatorial humour. This happened when the floor under the toilet on which she was sitting collapsed. To quote the words of our local evening papers, by line, the lady in question 'had not reached her bottom till she reached the foundations'. The entire structure had it transpired, been providing open grazing, a source of nourishment for many years to assorted larvae of the dry rot beetle fraternity. Its restoration which had been stalled as the developer had run short of cash was now a thing of the past. It was at this time an up and running extremely profitable operation was rescued by a financial White Knight.

The hotel had started its life as Somerset Cottage in 1832 although the word cottage is a bit of a misnomer as the cottage in question was, in this case, a substantial two-story villa. This area had been part of the Raeburn Estates, which had erected a mixed development of tenements and villas. These had been built for, and to the cost of, the noted portrait painter, Sir Henry Raeburn, who owned the land. Which ownership, he acquired by marriage. It was he, incidentally, who painted the skating minister coincidentally, of Duddingston and whose work can be seen in the National Gallery of Scotland.

I crossed the road and looked along Raeburn Place. Running to the right of this thoroughfare are the playing fields of Edinburgh Academy, another of Edinburgh's academic institutions. This is the ground where the first rugby international between England and Scotland was played. I saw an approaching female figure so I stopped and waited. I heard the sound of heels clicking coming closer and put on what I greatly hoped, was my best welcoming face as a slim, tall figure turned the corner.

"Sam," I called out in greeting.

"Sandy," came the reply.

"Yes, how do you do? It really is very good of you to take the time to meet with me; it's greatly appreciated."

Having laid it on with a proverbial shovel, I proffered my hand in a sort of knee-jerk male response pattern and she responded in like fashion. I always get a frisson of excitement from the touch of an unknown woman; I have always put it down to something to do with my childhood, in particular with my wonderful Auntie Sally.

"The club's further along this street, just down on the right."

She followed both my directions and me and as we went we made the usual desultory conversation, of the type that is made by total strangers meeting for the first time. As we made our way through the entrance gate the grounds on our left lay in darkness, the cricket pitch illumined in the moonlight, the covers standing guard over the strip; it was starting to look as the summer game was not far away. To our right the tennis nets on the lawn tennis courts were installed, ready and waiting for another season in the sun.

Light spilled out of the windows of the Long Room, which was the club's function suite, onto the pavilion steps and I could hear the strain of music floating on the now crisp evening air. Judging by the age of the music they were playing, somebody was celebrating their big 40, or perhaps it was some recidivist old age pensioner who was reliving somebody else's disco years.

I went to a door to the right of the pavilion and used my member's key to open the door and, followed by Sam we made our way through the corridors and up the stairs to the bar.

The twin doors that separate the Long Room from the bar area were closed and as suspected the function which was in full swing was, as I had deduced, a fortieth. The celebrant was a lady who according to a banner rejoiced in the name of Lucinda, well good for her. I ascertained and ordered Sam's desired drink and decided to join her with a glass of white wine. Picking up the glasses we moved to a distant corner, almost as two illicit lovers, wanting only the company of each other.

As I laid the drinks down, Sam picked up her glass, took a long swallow of the chilled chardonnay and broached the subject of our meeting,

"So, what is it you want to know Sandy Gray and why is it so important to you?"

I followed suit with the Chardonnay and then embarked upon my narrative. I explained about the out of the blue phone call from the late James Macbeth, his unexpected and sudden death from unnatural, to say nothing of highly illegal, cause and I added, stretching the truth, the number plate that I had glimpsed. I thought it better to leave the incident with Darren and the subsequent events of last night out of the conversation. Sometimes you can be too truthful.

I then related my visit to the Hoi Ologoi of Duddingston village, the strange case of the reappearing car in the night, and my consequent phone call to Charles.

"Well, Sam that's it, the whole story in as concise a form as I can manage. Thus why I ended up phoning you, in the hope that you might be able to, or felt you could, point me in the correct direction."

She listened in silence and before answering. Sam drank again, "Right I'm with you. A group of travellers arrived on the Straiton Park and Ride site just before Easter and set up camp, actually a more accurate word would be occupied. We were asked to move them on, but, what with the Human Rights Act, test cases and professional political agitators, to say nothing of all the associated paperwork, things were not all that straightforward."

I made what I considered to be please go-on style, encouraging noises. These seemed to be effective as she continued, "So we made the command decision was to keep a watching brief on the site. Past experience tells us that eventually they can't resist doing something that will give us grounds to move them on. They had been threatening the staff at the Lothian Buses Information Kiosk because they would let them use the toilets. So faced with these intimidations the company deemed it necessary to close the kiosk; the Travellers' response was to break in the door. What with that and them generally making a nuisance of themselves, the situation was more annoying than serious, but it was all sort of low level stuff, that is until the cars started to appear. These cars appeared to be of the same make and model of the cars that had started to disappear from other parts of the city and we felt, on balance, that this was something greater than a coincidence."

"Thus the raid."

"Exactly, our sweep netted us a dozen cars and all we recovered from the site. We also made five arrests."

"Had they all have their number plates removed and swapped?"

Sam looked a little puzzled but replied, "I didn't know, to be truthful, no one has mentioned whether or not any of them had had their plates swapped or removed."

Chapter 20
In Which I Feel the Pain

I resisted the immediate thought that dropped unbidden into my mind which was, just was as well you don't work for the collator's office then, but noticing her glass was almost empty I offered her a refill which she thought about and then she said, "Just one more. It's' very pleasant here but it's been a busy day and a long soak in a hot bath reckons."

Again I resisted the immediate unbidden thought; which went along the lines of offering my services as a back, or in fact any other part of her anatomy, scrubber but departed for the bar, without comment to obtain the replenishments. Just managing to nip in before two happy-go-lucky party goers, who by the size of the list one of them was carrying, were about to ask for a shipping order.

When I returned to Sam she said, "So, let me get this right, what you're telling me is that the car that was involved in the hit and run had, according to your recollection of the number plate, the same number plate as the Fiesta?"

I nodded agreement and she took a drink of her wine and continued, "This particular Fiesta is the car that after being missing for a while, presumably stolen, suddenly reappeared outside the address of the registered owner. Do you know Sandy, I can't help but thinking that was either a coincidence or the work of someone who has a criminal, but extremely tidy mind."

"Well you could be right, or maybe a warped sense of humour?"

Sam looked thoughtful and went on,

"Yeah possibly, but if I have you right what you are saying is that the Porsche which we recovered from the Park and Ride is the Porsche that did the hitting and running. Further, it did the hitting and running with number plates 'borrowed' from the Fiesta. All of which begs the question, just how sure are you that you took the number down correctly?"

Again I felt it politic not to tell her the lengths to which I had gone to obtain said number, but simply said, "Yes I'm pretty sure I have it right, and yes it was definitely a Porsche, but not a brand new model."

It was her turn to nod her head, before the policeman in her resurfaced, "But you have not formally reported this to us yet, have you?"

Presumably this was the Royal us, I thought; she was beginning to sound as though she was on the cusp of taking more interest, taking more official-type interest.

"No, not yet, up till now it's been well, it's merely a suspicion and I am sure that the police would not want to take up a case on a mere suspicion."

As I spoke the words I just knew that would not have been Billy's take on the modus operandi of our local Bobbies.

Sam shot me what could be described as an old fashioned look, "However, you do seem to be prepared to go to some lengths on a mere suspicion Sandy."

"Ah you know how it is with accountants."

She looked a little less official, a touch less stern, as if the feeling of suspicion or annoyance she felt had come and gone, now somehow having worn off.

"To be truthful, no I don't know how it is with accountants; tell me how exactly it is?"

I smiled almost voluntarily, almost.

"Accountants have to have a tidy mind, in order to create a tidy balance sheet, we're very much bottom line people, all things must balance. We tend to carry this discipline into our private lives; we do so hate loose ends and unexplained entries, especially in the ledger of life, or in my late father's case the ledger of death."

My words seemed to have hit home, stuck a nerve. She looked as though she was struggling with her conscience and as if making up her mind then said, "So you think the accident, the disappearing car, all of it, is linked to the death of your father?"

To be honest I suddenly felt quite emotional, I could feel that prick of tears behind my eyes. Odd, how the loss of a loved parent can suddenly creep up on you and unbidden grab you by the throat. But I managed to nod my acquiescence.

"So that's how it is with accountants, or is it just this specific accountant? Give me a minute, I''ll make a quick phone call and see if I can be of any help to you."

So saying she rose, opened the door, and went into the corridor to make her call. As she did so the noise of revellers in the Long Room leaked into the bar. The matter was obviously highly confidential or perhaps she just had a highly suspicious and cautious nature that had been bred into her at her induction at Tullialan, Police College.

I took the opportunity of her absence to check for messages received by my own mobile. There was a message waiting to be read, so I opened it. It was from Billy saying that he had received my text, and he was on his way down and would be with me in half an hour. The message was timed five minutes earlier. Sam opened the door accompanied by a musical refrain and re-entered the bar; I switched my phone off and replaced it in my pocket.

"Right, I have been in touch with a colleague of mine who deals with these itinerants, these travelling people, he is by way of being our resident expert. Since the matter is, at least in your mind, urgent I have ascertained that he is on duty tomorrow morning and he is willing to talk with you and hear what you have to say. That however, is all he has promised."

Another pause, more thinking time perhaps,

"Before I tell you any more, can I just stress this, if you turn up anything, anything at all…"

She held up her hand, effectively negating my attempted, almost involuntary interruption and continued, "As I said and I cannot stress this too strictly, if you turn up anything, anything at all, no matter how trivial or insignificant you regard it, then you must come directly to us. Do not, I repeat do not go taking it on yourself to take the matter further. We do not mind, in fact we encourage, help from members of the public. That said, what we members of the police force have no time for is amateur private detectives no matter how talented, or worse vigilantes, no matter how well-meaning."

Once more I resisted expressing my immediate thought: that our local police force seemed have had no time for solving the case of murdered citizen's either. God I was getting good at this restraint, practice making perfect. So in reply I resorted to the banal. Humour with me has become a sort of defence mechanism.

"Scout's honour, besides which I do not have the requisite aristocratic credentials to be a Lord Peter Wimsey and I'm entirety the wrong age and gender for a Miss Marple. For that matter I don't have the inclination, nor, for that matter the build, to indulge in all that vigilante nonsense. What with the hoods, the burning torches and the mob baying for blood…"

She looked at me somewhat quizzically.

So I added, "Sorry I must have been watching too many horse operas."

"Horse operas," her look grew even more quizzical, or was it pitying?

"Yes, in old westerns you must have seen them. The people in the mob always wear something like a pillowcase over their heads, do you know?

With holes cut out for their eyes and some of them carry a burning brand and they all chant in unison 'lynch him, lynch him'. But when the crowd attempt to mount the steps of the jail to drag out their chosen victim, they are met with and thwarted by a steely-eyed, grim-faced, determined sheriff. Who tells them to go home and sleep it off?"

She was now looking at me as though she had begun to regret having offered to help in the first place, perhaps even also regretting having agreed to come and meet me. Then I saw the flicker in her eye and she consented to a smile as she said, "Do you know Sandy, it's really has been a very, very long day and you, well, I think you're off your trolley. It comes as no surprise to me at all that you're a great friend of Charlie's."

So Charlie, it was, not Charles, so that's how it was, well, well.

She shook her head as if in sympathy, and continued, "You do know I'm not at all sure I'm doing the right thing, however, in for a penny in for a pound. Right, the person you have to go to talk to is called McIntyre, Sergeant Ian McIntyre and he is based at our Peebles station. My advice is, if you are intent on carrying on, that you will probably get more out of him face-to-face than over the phone. He is a man that wears caution like a carapace and the nearer his steps take him to retirement the more cautious he becomes. He has, I think, really big plans for his pension. My feeling is that he will go to great lengths to ensure that said pension comes through on time and comes through at full value."

Having said that she finished her wine and placed the glass carefully and precisely on the shelf then cautioned, "Mark my words Sandy, and mark them well investigate if you must, but take no unilateral action, that's what we're paid to do."

And paid damn, well I thought, but again my forbearance kicked in.

"Righty ho officer, yours truly has been duly cautioned and duly warned as to his future behaviour, and promises to stay on the straight and narrow path. Further he will be a good boy and will make no attempt to interfere with the wheels of justice."

She smiled almost indulgently.

So I risked, "Can I escort you off the premises officer?"

Again the smile but she shook her head, "No, thank you, I am sure I will manage, I am quite a big girl now."

I had noticed was what crossed my mind, but she added, almost as an afterthought,

"Have you a business card? You never know when I might just have trouble with an income tax return, the odd capital gain or two or…something"

"Tax returns and capital gains are my forte, whereas something's are my specialty."

Another smile, this as she turned and walked out of the bar. This exit was to the accompaniment of the now-expected burst of Lucinda's chosen hits of her youth.

I stayed for a few minutes, turning over in my mind the information I had been given, whilst leisurely finishing my wine. Then, glancing at my watch, I thought it was time to take a stroll and meet Billy, for without me, or rather my key, he could not gain entry to the club house.

The night had grown colder, an almost unseasonal frost setting in, giving the grass a shimmering white sheen. My breath condensed in front of me, as I walked out through the gates and turned right into Portgower Place. I then walked up the street towards the main road, the lights of Franco's Fish and Chip Shop flickered brightly as viewed from the relative darkness of the side street.

I always wondered about the name on the sign, the owner's name perhaps, or was it as I secretly hoped, because he supplied extremely right wing mince pie suppers, wrapped in old copies of Mein Kampf. His walls festooned with signed portraits of the old generalissimo himself!!!!

My wonderings were suddenly and rudely interrupted by a gaudily uniformed delivery boy, to be truthful a delivery man would be more accurate, warning me of his intention to drive his motorcycle across the pavement in front of me. The motorcyclist, seemingly oblivious to the fact that said pavement was a space specifically designed and set aside for human foot traffic. Not for the storage and movement of motorcycles.

He was duly laden down by a large bag containing, no doubt, hot but rapidly cooling perishable products of a vaguely Italian nature. These recently cooked goods he was personally transporting with all due haste and alacrity, to some hungry Stockbridger.

The Pizza Hut Company carry-out premises, are from whence this angel of mercy to the starving masses originated, thus the vaguely Italian, or perhaps precisely American/Italian reference in the company's name. This business had the problem of having the road surrounding their premises covered with double yellow lines, a difficulty to which they applied a little lateral thinking. The answer they came up with to overcome the encircling yellow line problem, was to park their motor bikes in a railed of area, which had presumably been a small garden, directly outside the shop window. This space was accessed by simply driving their bikes across the pavement at will, to the imperilment of passing pedestrians.

As to why the local constabulary turned a blind eye to this had been a matter of some speculation amongst the residents of Stockbridge. This conjecture fell neatly in two camps. The first faction believed that in return for their non-interference, that the boys in blue received discounted or, perish the thought, free pizzas. Whilst the other group, even more firmly believed that the motorcycle delivery men were protected by some obscure clause in the European Charter of Human Rights.

As I passed the shop entrance I stopped, my attention drawn by raised voices. One of the delivery people, bag-laden was shouting from the door into the shop, and someone from the inside was shouting back, but I could not make out the words, and then the pair came out and began to look around. By the gesticulations and the air of puzzlement exhibited by the two, it seemed that the first man's bike had disappeared. I walked on leaving them searching for the missing bike but as I crossed the entrance to Dean Park Mews *I found it.*

Chapter 21
A Hospital Visit

As I stepped off the pavement I heard that particular high-pitched whining noise made by the revving of a small-engined motorbike. As I turned my head towards the source of the racket, I glimpsed the machine in question, complete with hooded rider, rocketing towards me out of the darkness of the entrance to the mews. Momentarily, I froze, rooted to the spot, whilst my brain tried to compute the information it was receiving. The next thing I felt was a thump to the right of my chest, this was followed by a squealing of tyres followed by the honking of car horns. The next sensation was of spinning round and then falling over backwards. Before I had time to react, the back of my head hit the oh, so unyielding pavement and the light started to pinpoint and then disappear, I felt and heard no more.

Gradually, as the aperture reopened and the circle of light started to widen and so did the realisation of pain, both sharp and severe, emanating from the back of my head. I could partly see Billy's face close to mine, his features, strangely distorted and somehow grotesque. He seemed to have a strange lump on the side of his face then I realised it was his mobile phone into which he was speaking, I heard his voice coming and going in a strange echoing way,

"Yes that's right just outside the Oxfam Book Shop, yes a head trauma."

Then I realised he was addressing me.

"Ok, Sandy, can you hear me? It's Billy, stay with me, you old bugger, do you hear me stay with me."

The circle started to close again, the voice still coming and going but slightly more distant; the brain trying to take me back to unconsciousness, to blessed pain-free unconsciousness. This attempt to regain peace in a hurt-free world was rudely interrupted by Billy's insistent, almost pleading, voice which even in my semi-comatose state, I was able to discern a trace of anxiety.

"No, no for God's' sake, no. Stay with me, please doesn't go wandering off on me. Stay with us I said. Come on I need you conscious. I don't want to be the one to have to face your mother and tell her that her darling son is hurt."

The small circle of vision waivered, much like the horizontal hold had gone on old-fashioned black and white tally, and then it started to open wider. I tried moving, which was not a good idea and I was rewarded by a wave of pain.

"Okay, okay take it easy. I have given you a quick check and nothing seems to be broken. I told you that first aider course would pay off, eventually. You have a lump, about the size of a duck egg, on the back of your head and you're oozing some blood. It'll probably hurt a bit for a while. Easy now, I'll try to get you sitting up."

He put both his arms under both of mine and without further consultation dragged me till he could rest my back against the Shelter shop wall. Had I been more with it, I might have commented on the appropriateness of my resting place. Gentle though Billy tried to be the movement was not without another wave of pain.

"There's no probably about it, it hurts like the devil!" I yelled.

As my eyes started to refocus, I noticed two people who were complete strangers to me, gazing down with what was either concern or out of ghoulish and prurient interest, human kind as ever fascinated by a bit of *schadenfreud*. Whilst two others, much as the priest and the Levite in the parable of the Good Samaritan, crossed on the other side of the road literally, passers-by doing exactly that, passing by.

One of my Good Samaritans was now smiling,

"Well that was too close one, too close for comfort I'd say! Been annoying the local delivery boys, have we? Or have you been complaining the last delivery you received was cold?"

He obviously considered himself a bit of a wag did my smiling Samaritan.

Any further conversation was halted by an ambulance's 'dee daw, dee daw' Doppler Effect noise.

Its lights flashing but with its siren now silenced, the ambulance came to halt at the pavement's edge, on the double yellow lines. What the hell, they must have thought; it is an emergency after all.

A green jumpsuited, white latex gloved paramedic descended from the driver's compartment and knelt beside me. Smelling my breath he remarked, I felt at the time a little unkindly, but then again, I was not at my best, it has to be said,

"Has sir had a little too much to drink? Are we, sir, not as spry as we should be on the old pins?"

Not as spry on the old pins indeed. However, before my tired and completely befuddled brain could counter his assertion by forming a well-honed apposite aphorism, Billy broke in with a firm denial of the cause of my injuries, "No indeed on the contrary! Although he may have had a drink, this poor soul was the intended victim of a hit and run."

Billy had struck the right tone for one who felt he had a genuine grievance on behalf of a wrongly accused comrade. But I thought that poor soul was taking it a shade far. Then the other bystander who up till now had said nothing, weighed in with his own confirmation, of the reason for my present plight.

"That's right, that's exactly what happened. Someone stole my motorbike without even a blooming by-your-leave and then just disappeared, *and* if it had not been for that man-"

He pointed at Billy,

"Pushing him out of the road-"

As he spoke the word 'him' he indicated graphically at me in a strangely theatrical manner and went on, "Knocking him out of the path of the bike it would have mowed him down."

So that's how I ended up flat on my back, with a blunt force trauma contusion and a cracked skull.

The ambulance man's attitude seemed to soften at that intelligence, "Do you think you could stand up and walk if we help you?" he enquired, this time with a certain degree of sympathy and solicitude.

I nodded and then straightway regretted the action as the swimming sensation reminded me that any extraneous head movement was, for the time being, not to be recommended. I pushed up against the wall and rested a moment, giving my head a chance to catch up with the progress made by the rest of my body. My knees seemed to want to give up what they obviously consider an uneven struggle and started to buckle. But, my very own male version of the ever-solicitous Miss Nightingale caught and steadied me.

"Oh, oh, easy, be careful there sir. Take it steadily, you were almost back where you started."

Our little group was joined by a second paramedic who had been talking on the radio and no doubt confirming their arrival. With a paramedic either side of me I managed to stand and after a pause to gain my balance I succeeded, albeit a little unsteadily, to enter the ambulance. Here I was joined by Billy and one of the pair of supporters, whilst the other, apparently the driver closed the door with what he considered to be reassuring words, "We're from the Western. We'll have you there in a couple of minutes mate, sit back and enjoy the ride."

It seems I had made yet another chum. I looked out through my eyes, out from my own personal misery, to see that Billy's jacket was torn and his trousers scuffed. He saw me looking, "Don't worry; it looks worse than it is. It's' just where I landed, after I pushed you out of the way."

"But, are you hurt?"

"No, it's just a bruise or two; it's purely superficial, nothing that won't mend sooner or later."

"Billy what can I say, thanks, well... Thanks seems a little ... Well not enough really."

I was not thinking as clearly as I would have liked but I was thinking clearly enough to be grateful.

Billy dismissed my thanks, "You'd have done the same for me. There will be plenty of time for talking when you're feeling a bit better. Oh and by the way, I told the ambulance driver who was seemingly concerned that a crime had been committed that I had reported the matter to the police and we would make a full report when you were up to it. I take it you would prefer that this was kept quiet. I'm sure you wish to avoid another policeman knocking on your next of kin's door tonight, it might just end her, and she, in turn, might just end you."

I nodded my silent thanks as the ambulance duly arrived at its destination. As it came to a halt the back door was flung open and I could read a sign which announced that this was the Accident and Emergency unit, meaning I suppose, that I was either, or possibly both. Hands helped me down the stairs from the ambulance. I was then thrust into a waiting wheelchair for the second time in two nights; this was becoming a habit. I was then wheeled to the reception desk for a ritual interrogation. Bureaucratic procedures and form filling are the twin prerequisites of the hospital administrator, whereas diagnosis and treatment are the twin prerequisites of the hospital user. The only fact that my interrogation failed to elicit was my inside leg measurement. An oversight which left me wondering, should I have volunteered this information?

After that I was helped into a cubicle and onto a bed, after which the curtain was pulled across. This action was followed by the statutory waiting time. The purpose of which is to impress on the injured that hospitals are busy places *and* that we the patient should be grateful for being given any treatment at all.

Suddenly and without warning the curtain was whipped back and I was confronted by an outwardly jolly and brisk-mannered nurse. She explained that the modern medical practice cautioned against taking x-rays in non-emergency cases. Well I supposed it was, at least, cheering to know that I was being considered a non-emergency case.

She performed a series of investigatory tests to assess whether or not concussion was present after which she opined not. Following this she produced a sealed bag that appeared to contain a quantity of swabs and dressings. She warned me, somewhat unnecessarily I felt, that what she was going to do would hurt and, as good as her word, it did. It hurt like the very devil.

Seemingly satisfied with her handiwork she declared that I could now be numbered among the walking wounded and this being the case I was thus ready to be discharged. She then enquired as to whether or not I needed transport home and was there anybody with me? I duly answered no and yes, and with a stern warning to stay off the demon drink and in addition to be sure to seek medical help if I felt drowsy, she wheeled me out and pushed me into the hands of my very own favourite getter-out-of-a-hole: Billy. Who at the sight of me flashed a pitying smirk, "How are you?"

"Sore, bloodied but unbowed. How about rustling up a taxi?"

Billy continued to smirk but did as he was bidden. Having dialled the number and ordered up a cab, he wheeled me to a waiting area. Here he pulled up a chair and sat down; after a longish pause, he said what I suspected was on both our minds.

"God you look awful, but seriously though Sandy, who on earth have you pissed off so much, that they would want you out of the way, either temporally or even worse permanently, and even more interesting, why?"

I thought...then grasping at a straw,

"A friend of Darren's perhaps, trying to even up the score?"

"No, no, not their style. Stealing the bike was the act of an opportunist. Whoever, did this is used to, not only thinking, but thinking on his feet, and thinking, Alexander is not the weapon of choice for the Darren's of this world. No, my hunch is that you have upset someone much higher up the food chain. Much, much higher up."

I was forced to admit that there was a lot of truth in what he said.

"So, all we have to do is work out which food chain then work our way to the highest point. Needles and haystacks come to mind. Talking of coming to mind, how did they know where I would be and at what time?" I asked, thinking aloud.

Billy was always the pragmatist,

"Who's to say they did know. You may have simply been followed. Have you noticed anything unusual lately? Someone, I don't know...someone, hanging around?"

As he spoke I realised that the truth is I had not, but then again why should I have?

"Being followed, *me!* Billy, really I think you have been reading too much Le Carre. You, my lad, are getting carried away."

He looked at me with, for Billy, a strange solemn look. Almost as though he had a feeling of foreboding,

"No, I think it's you who have the problem. My gut feeling is that you are in denial you just don't want to believe what's staring you in the face. You've just heard the beating of Death's winged charity and it came close. And I think you are bloody well scared."

Without waiting for a response he went on, "And I'll tell this if you're not, you bloody well should be scared. Just remember James Macbeth, or, rather the late James Macbeth. He wasn't as lucky as you he didn't have a second chance, but you have, so damn well make sure you live long enough to use it."

His serious frown gave way to a wry smile, "And as for reading Le Carre really, you know I hate cookbooks."

Before I could respond to Billy, an oldish looking man appeared, blinking in the harsh hospital light and announced that there was a taxi for Clarke. Billy signalled indicating that we were the party in question. He then rose, grabbed the handles of my wheelchair and trundled me out the automatic doors which opened complainingly at our approach.

Our cabbie indicated to a black cab, with it's for 'hire sign' cancelled, parked slightly further down on the right. After a bit of a struggle involving man attempting to gain supremacy over machine, Billy eventually pushed and pulled me into the rear seat. He then returned the loaned wheelchair to the area designated for these conveyances and joined me in the back seat, before leaning forward to inform our driver that the required destination was Morningside Road.

"Right Alexander I know you have had a rough night so far but…"

Billy trailed off, "I have had a rough night so far but…" I prompted.

"Well you've been discharged, look on that as the good news, now for the bad news. Think of it this way, what's happened to you is nothing compared with what *is* going to happen to you when you return to, as Sir Harry Lauder used to sing, 'your' happy abode' and your dearest mamma gets a hold of you."

A break, as though he was psyching himself up,

"As a friend in need if you like, I'll help you up the stairs to your front door but I am not, and that's a definite not, under any conditions entering your flat. I am only too aware that the dragoness is in her den and if I arrived with you in this state, particularly after what happened earlier tonight, it would just be waving the proverbial red rag, at the proverbial bull."

Well I thought that's laying it on the line. Then as if I had a divine revelation as it all came back to me, I remembered the brief unresolved conversation I had had with mother earlier. Mind you I felt that after all that had happened to me that night this sin of omission was one that might just be forgiven. That said Billy's word had reawakened my curiosity, "What did happen tonight? I did speak to her earlier on and she seemed, to say the least, somewhat upset but then she simply hung up on me without giving any details. Then before I had a chance to ring back, life as you can testify moved on fairly swiftly from that point. How come you know about it anyway?"

In reply Billy shook his head, "Well, the how I know, that's the easy bit. Prior to receiving your text I rang, I now know stupidly, your home number to find out if you were in and I received both barrels, there and then. Both barrels right between the eyes or, in this case, right between the ears, no quarter given."

I saw his face in a flicker of the passing orange neon light the smirk was back; this was obviously a matter of quiet amusement to him.

"All right, all right, I get the message loud and clear. Mother is not overly pleased with me, but what is it that I, or is it perhaps what *we*, have done that has brought on this severe attack of the vapours?"

I could feel his smirk broadening, "It's not so much what you, or perhaps we have done, but that which she thinks you and I have done. For this very evening, just before the first rubber got under way and in the presence of your mother's very own, coven-"

"Billy…" I interrupted, ever the dutiful son.

"Sorry, was my prejudice showing? Anyway, before the first rubber commenced and within earshot of your mother's bridge partners, she was questioned by a member of the local constabulary. It would appear that they called at the flat to check your alibi for last night and finding you away from home they set about, there and then, to cross examine your dear mother as to what she could tell them about your movements the previous evening."

I put my head in my hands and inwardly groaned.

Chapter 22
In Which a Prodigal Son Returns

The taxi nosed its way in as near to the kerb as you can get of an evening in Morningside Road. Billy paid him off and coming round the other side helped me out of the cab. The driver put his 'for hire' flag up and then, as he was attempting an illegal three-point turn, he was hailed by another punter so he abandoned the tricky manoeuvre, picked up the new fare and headed out of town. As the taxi disappeared, Billy positioned me with some care against a shop wall and enquired, "Right your' keys; can you remember where they are? I think a quiet entry, if possible, might be our best course of action. The girls, I am sure, are probably just finishing their bridge rolls at the bridge table, washing them down with a cheeky little Shiraz, and are getting ready to settle down for a little late night rubber."

As he broke off his diatribe I noticed that his smirk was becoming a fixture; he was self evidentially relishing my obvious discomfiture more than just a little. Almost relentlessly he went on,

"So I don't think they would be agreeable to another unwelcome, unexpected interruption even if it's from your mother's, perhaps now not so blue-eyed, boy particularly as at present you look like an extra out of the 'Mummy Returns'. I am sorry to break this to you, I am not at all sure there will be a fatted calf, slain and roasted, in Chez Gray tonight. I think you will probably be viewed as the prodigal son, to end all prodigal sons, whose return will not one be of unbounded joy and happiness for a wayward child duly returned but more an occasion of lamentations' of an Old Testament nature."

Mind you that said I had to agree with his summation of my likely reception,

"Oh hah, bloody hah, my keys…I think they are in my jacket pocket."

He fished carefully and shook his head, "Try the other side; they must be somewhere."

Again he undertook the exploratory fishing, this time though his efforts were rewarded with success and he withdrew a bunch of keys that held both those for the main door and the flat. I pointed to the stair door key which he inserted into the large keyhole in the outside door. After a certain amount of fiddling with the lock the key engaged and released the mechanism with a satisfying click. The heavy door swung open and we both admitted ourselves into the well-lit passage within.

I viewed the stairs ahead with some dismay. In my present state they looked to me as though they'd be as about as easy to scale as Arthur's Seat. The only consolation was that in Morningside the stairs are always two flight affairs. Thus in the words of Kermit the Frog's young nephew Robin 'halfway up the stairs, up the staaairs' there was a resting place. Mentally I girded my loins and grabbed Billy's arm. Acting in more or less unison, we managed to sway and stagger our way up the initial flight of stairs. Having reached the first landing, I put its window sill to use as an improvised seat to rest my extremely weary bones, where Billy joined me.

Whilst in this blessed state of recuperation, I heard the wary pad of non-human feet descending the stairs above me. Within seconds the possessor of these non-human feet appeared in the shape a large nondescript, but affable and friendly dog, called Wullie. He, as with many of his ilk, is wont to immediately recognise a friendly face. He was also of the firmly held belief that no sensible dog should ever pass up the chance of a good scratch. So, seeing me sitting there, Wullie as was his wont took time out and stopped to say hullo.

I duly scratched him in the required area, his degree of pleasure signalled by the enthusiastic wagging of his substantial tail. There's a good boy, let me introduce you,

"Wullie meet Billy."

Then turning to Billy I said, "Do you know Billy, I think this beast Wullie understands every word I say."

Then I looked back to the dag I gave him another scratch and added, "Billy meet Wullie."

Then taking the dog's head in my hands, I confided,

"Do you know Wullie I think Billy understands every word I say."

Billy's attempt at a, no doubt choice, rejoinder, was cut short as the owner of the non-human feet also appeared on the landing. She was fastidious maiden lady who went by the name of Miss Nimmo and lived with her elderly widowed mother on the second floor in, as they say, or rather as my mother says to be more accurate, reduced circumstances. I thought she always had the appearance of one to whom life was a constant disappointment.

She looked down at me and perceptibly winced. Then in tone and timbre born of both her class and the general ambience of this upmarket neighbourhood, she said or rather, a better word would be, announced, "Had a good night out, have we Mr. Gray?"

Then her imperious gaze shifted to Billy, "As for you; a man shall be known by the company he keeps."

Then to the dog,

"Come along Wullie, we don't know where Mr. Gray has been."

Then, presumably to anyone who would listen,

"It's his poor mother I feel sorry for."

Billy, who for once in his life had been completely taken aback, regained his composure and was by turns astonished, offended and then amused,

"My God, that woman could blister paint with that voice. Mind you, I will say one thing for you, you certainly know how to win friends and influence dogs, if not always their owners."

He rose to his feet, and then he made a move to pull me up as well, "Come on then Sherpa Tensing time to move of from base camp and time to make a try for the summit. You have rested long enough so let's get on up the rest of this wooden hill to dreamland."

"If anything, it's a stone hill. Come on then, Sir Edmund, give me a hand."

He pulled me to my feet and together we set off, onward and upward, or as in the motto of the Canongate 'Sic Itur Ad Astra,' 'thus we journey to the stars,' well at least in my case, to the first floor.

After another painful climb he again allowed me to rest, with my back propped against the stair wall whist he attempted to select the front door key,

"Which of these is it?" he enquired.

"It's the shiny one, the Yale."

He selected the one as described and held up his choice for my examination and final approval.

"Yeah, that's the one."

He inserted the key in the lock and then stopped, "Right, I will open the door partly. I will then hand you your keys and then, I for one, are for the offski, extremely smartski, okayski and youski are on your ownski."

"Why thank you, I'm sure I will manage from hereski"

He gave me what he evidently meant to be a reassuring look,

"Okay mate. You're on your own from here on in, but just remember, it's Saturday tomorrow, so if you need me bell me. I have made no plans, that is of course, if you survive the night and, or, the coming encounter with your very own she-dragon."

Billy opened the door and held it slightly ajar. I took a deep breath and then I launched myself from the place of relative safety on the stair wall and repositioned myself in front of the partly opened door. Billy moved aside and I stepped through the aperture and let the door close slightly, then I turned and steadied myself by placing my hand on the door edge. The hand over manoeuvre having been safely completed, he smiled, patted my shoulder and turned to go.

"Billy just…"

I paused.

"Just one thing, you know-"

Again I paused.

"Just you, know well, well thanks for you know."

He checked his progress and turned back, "No thanks, necessary you should know that."

He touched my arm.

"Goodnight old chum, stay lucky and lock the door, sleep tight and don't let those bed bugs bite. See you Sandy."

He departed, taking the steps two at a time, I watched him go and then with a mental shrug and a thought that the bed bugs biting might just prove to be the least on my worries, I quietly closed and latched the door. I was very vigilant to make my entrance with some care, only too aware that I might just confront my

Nemesis, that Goddess controller of fate, in human form: my own dear mother.

The hall was in almost total darkness, lit only by borrowed light from the outside stair, shining through the fanlight above the flat door. I turned towards my bedroom. To my right the door of the drawing room suddenly opened, spilling a gentle light from well shaded lamps, in the room beyond. I could make out a quiet buzz of polite conversation, and inside, I could see a green baize table and seated players. My attention was refocused from the general to the specific, as coming out of the opened door, was none other than my Nemesis; she looked at me and, if looks could kill this narrative would now end.

She was grim-faced with pursed lips, and a set expression. It occurred to me she looked more like a Gorgon than the goddess to whom I alluded earlier. When I glanced up, I was vaguely relieved to see that her hair was its normal neat perm and not a mass of writhing serpents. She looked as though she had much to say but she confined her comments to a terse, "Alexander, we will speak in the morning."

I said nothing, but reflected a little ruefully as I opened the door of my bedroom, that it would be her doing the speaking and me doing the listening.

I threw off my coat and lay down on the bed and considered that this was truly a time of lamentation. This was a time for the return of the dissolute, for the return of the profligate, for indeed the return of the prodigal son. One other thing Billy had been right on the money about was that fatted calf, as there was *nothing* roasting in our oven.

Chapter 23
In Which I Learn to Dress

It was another night of restless and troubled sleep: this time populated by oversized giant pizzas cartwheeling willy-nilly all over the place then pursuing me down a very steep hill. As the incline grew steeper and steeper, I ran faster and faster until I lost my footing, pitching forward, then rolling over and over until the slope evened out and I came to a halt. I tried to get up, but as I did, I was confronted by a king size, double pepperoni and ham pizza with extra chillies scything its way toward my supine body.

Before it ran over me I awoke, troubled and painfully stiff. It was still darkish. I looked at the bedside table for my watch which was nowhere to be seen. I started to search, but this proved to be of no avail, because as I was in the process of said search I noticed that the timepiece I was seeking was still on my wrist. There was just enough light in the coming pre-dawn to discern that the watch's face indicated it was nearly five forty-five.

Sleep I supposed was now behind me and the waking hours now in front so I decided that it was up and out time for me. This decision was helped along by the thought if I left the house early enough I could put off the evil hour. Thus denying the early bird my Mother, from catching the worm, yours truly. I struggled to gain an upright position only to have my head reminded of the activities of a few hours before; in Shakespeare speak, 'the alarums and excursions' of the night. I sat for some minutes on the side of my bed working myself up to some form of two-footed motion. I eventually managed to struggle to a standing position although my head was not entirely happy about it. I achieved the required upright stance for a member of the order Homo sapiens. Having achieved this, I risked movement, and started, all be it a shade stiff-legged, to progress to the en suite. I flicked the switch and the little spotlights that lit up the large mirror blinked into life. This morning they seemed as if they were twinkling which was not a property in them that I had noticed before.

I opened the shower compartment, turned the controls and waited for the water to become warm. It duly obliged and, with an effort both of bodily movement and self-will, I heaved myself into the warm stream of water. I leaned against the solidity of the wall letting the refreshing jets of warmth massage my pain-wracked body. I stood there luxuriating in the heat whilst watching the side of the cabinet turning from clear to opaque as the steam condensed on it and rivulets of water snaked down the inside surface.

I continued under the shower for a while, all the time putting off the evil hour, steeling myself for the final test of endurance. Then, screwing my courage to the sticking point, and with a feeling of some worry and foreboding to say nothing of downright fear I counted to three and positioned my head under the stream of water. God, did it bloody well hurt! I was tempted, oh so tempted, to withdraw immediately, but I hung on in there until eventually the pain started to ebb slowly, very, very slowly. The pain was blessedly replaced by a feeling of comfort that appeared to surround my whole being.

Mind you, as all frequent users of showers will know, this feeling of wellbeing abruptly stops, in all but the hottest summer months immediately the water stops flowing. I moved the controls, turning off the water staggered out from the shower cabinet and wrapped a towel round me and, complete with an additional towel, I made it back to the side of my bed.

I towelled down my body briskly, but my head with exaggerated care, and as I did so I set about reviewing the situation. The dim partial light that had earlier attempted to conqueror its perpetual age-long adversary, the darkness, now had done so. The room was now full of light and I could see by it that my suit, my suit of yesterday, would never again be my suit of the day. Its useful life was now apparently ended by a series of jagged tears in the elbows of the jacket, to say nothing of the right leg of the trousers being partially missing.

Never mind, on the plus side their replacement as 'a requirement to discharge my chosen professional duties' would be a tax-deductible amount. I'd find somewhere to make a claim along the line or else I was not the accountant I thought I was.

I relaunched myself upwards from the bedside and propelled my unwilling legs forward to the opened sliding-mirrored doors of the fitted wardrobe. From the drawer I picked out a pair of clean socks and underpants. The attempt to put on the latter could, in fact, have provided material for a sketch that would have comprised an old time music hall performer's complete first house routine. Finally, after staggering all around the room, I gave up the uneven struggle and succumbed with something less than good grace to the humiliation, as some invalid, of having to put them on whilst sitting down on the edge of the bed. This was followed by a painful, protracted and totally uneven encounter with sore ribs and a spinning head whilst struggling with my socks.

The excess energy I seemed to have expended on putting on my damned underwear required me to rest and regroup for a minute. Then once again I was wardrobe-bound I picked out a rugger shirt then discarded it in favour of a heavy denim casual shirt. I assessed at that moment that the thought of putting on anything over my head was strictly out of the question. I decided after further consideration to complete my ensemble with a pair of corduroy trousers and a pair of brown leather loafers, no laces to cause me only more grief to tie.

Having organised my dress, I lingered only long enough unplug my mobile and place it in my pocket before picking up my card case, some bank notes and my loose change before departing. I left my bedroom closing the door with exaggerated care quietly behind me, the hall was empty and the whole house still, with a brooding deserted silence, this quietude broken only by the steady rhythmic ticking of the old, long case clock standing against the far wall. As I passed the coat stand, I reached down my Barbour jacket; after all, I was going to the country. Although Peebles might be fishing territory I doubted whether it was shooting country, well not of the sporting kind anyway.

I unlocked, opened and closed the front door, again with exaggerated care, and as I lurched (and by the way lurched is an all too accurate description of my attempt at walking) down the first flight of steps. Remembering that I had not checked my mobile for messages I took it out of the inside pocket of my jacket. A simple enough action you might think but one that almost lead me to my downfall, literally. Taking my attention from the chosen task of descending the stairs caused me to lose balance and I only just managed to save myself from pitching forward by grabbing the hand rail with a flailing hand, and painfully grabbing it at that.

I had not, until that moment, fully realised that in my present somewhat reduced state I could not walk and undertake any other task no matter how trivial. I could walk and that was that so I replaced the mobile in my pocket and concentrated on the task in hand: the safe completion of my griefless navigation of the second flight of steps.

I reached the passage without further excitement and successfully managed to get to the outside stair door, which I opened. It seemed to me that it had become a great deal heavier since yesterday morning and seemed much less yielding than it had on that occasion. I decided on the balance of probability that I was not cut out for the rough and tumble of a physical life. Private investigation was a demanding employment that was not for me, a latter day Jim Rockford I was not! Nevertheless, in the words of the old adage, having set my hand to the plough, I felt I was honour bound to at least finish the furrow. Still since the proverb said nothing about the whole field, maybe I'd settle for just the furrow.

It had not really registered that my ablutions and dressing antics had taken a great deal longer than normal, until I noticed on a clock of estate agents I was passing, that the dial showed almost seven thirty; my how time flies when you are enjoying yourself. I continued walking down towards Holy Corner in less than a normal manner and a lady I passed looked askance at me as though she thought that I was Pete the Pervert. Holy Corner is so-called, incidentally, because it is at the junction where four roads meet, and there is a church on each of the corners. These stand as a testament to our Victorian ancestor's' desire for religious diversity and variety.

As I was about to pass a bus stop, I glanced back and saw on oncoming bus, so I joined the queue of early morning workers who were all fully iPodded and locked by their ears to some other world. I joined their almost zombie-like progress on board. I alighted at the West End and true to form the Golden Arches were shining out beacon-like, the ever-welcoming allure of McDonald's gently beckoned me and as many another would be passer-by into its comforting fast-food zone.

I'm always curious as what it is they put in their breakfast offerings that cause me to come back again and again. It was as if I was some unreformed, or perhaps unreformable junkie. I order my usual fix, a Double Sausage Egg McMuffin meal and on being asked what would I like to drink, I swithered but settled for fruit juice. There you go just past seven thirty and I am on my way to five a day. For good measure I order a large black coffee as well. The one thing about McDonald's is that it's no sooner ordered than it's there; here was a company who certainly put the fast in fast food.

I lingered over the coffee and waited till eight o'clock before ringing Billy's number. As I did, I noticed with some annoyance, that I had failed in my confused and befuddled state of yesterday evening to put the thing on charge and the damn thing's battery was now not just low, but almost non-existent. I fervently prayed that it would last long enough to call Billy because, as with almost every other mobile owner not only was this my phone, it was also my phone book. To keep a separate paper record nowadays seemed completely pointless, well that is until now…

The number rang out and I considered ringing off and trying again before the answering machine could click in with its offer to leave a recorded message. As my finger hovered over the cancel button a sleepy voice answered.

"My good God Sandy, I thought you would be dead by now, or at the very least dead to the world. Incidentally, how did you avoid your fate? How did you dodge being sacrificed by your mother to appease the earnest bridge-playing residents of Morningside?"

"And a good morning to you William. Listen, I'll be quick as I'm pretty short on battery life. Do you fancy a trip to the country? Down to the borders way, this morning? Have to talk to a policeman about a gypsy?"

"Yup sure."

His voice now attentive,

"Where are you?"

"McDonald's at the West End."

"Okay tell you what, give me say, about half an hour and I will pick you up in Charlotte Square. Can you be in front of the old church-type building thing? You know the one, the one that threatened to become the leaning church of Edinburgh."

Billy was always vague about landmarks in his native city. Unless of course it was a pub because under these circumstances he could be highly specific, in fact, he could be meticulously accurate.

"You mean St George or rather West Register House? Half an hour it is."

"Right."

With word of agreement he was gone. I switched the phone off as a precaution, finished my coffee and hobbled out of the restaurant and made towards the proposed meeting point. I turned into Hope Street and then into Charlotte Square; a magnificent masterpiece of the Kirkcaldy born and well-respected Edinburgh architect, Robert Adam. It's an architectural tour de force that never fails to uplift and gladden the heart and, on this spring morning with the buds on the trees opening, it looked at its best.

This square was the western termination of the Edinburgh's first New Town designed by the later highly impecunious, James Craig. His street plan incidentally was entitled 'A plan for his Majesty's' Capitol of North Britain'. At that historical period it had become fashionable to refer to Scotland, perhaps somewhat disparagingly, as North Britain. I could just near the wails of anguish from the SNP activists bristling with injured pride as we rename the Scottish Parliament the North British Parliament.

Adam died somewhat unexpectedly, least of all by him, and his architectural practice was carried on by his personal assistant and last architect to the King in Scotland, one Robert Reid who changed some of Adam's plans and designs; as it turned out not always for the better.

I crossed the road, carefully and slowly, on the lookout for either a Porsche sans number plate or more mundanely a careering runaway stolen pizza delivery motorbike, but at that time in a Saturday morning the road was quiet, almost unnaturally quiet. I made my way to our rendezvous and sat down on the church's steps and awaited Billy's arrival.

This building was one of those that Reid chose to remodel. In this case, in response to a request from the clients, he adapted Adam's original plan reducing the projected building cost by some £10,000 to bring the scheme in at £27,500. I once estimated for an inquisitive client that cost to be a sum not much short of four million pounds, current value.

This budget-cutting exercise inevitably led to shortcuts, in its construction. These shortcuts led in turn, some hundred and sixty years later to the churches prominent dome starting to shift and torqued out of true. Reid, it appeared, had apparently underestimated the depth and composition of the foundations required to support the load. In fact it was found that some of the founds had been bulked up with wood rather than stone; whether this owed to bad supervision or deliberate cost-cutting could only be guessed at.

Such was the extent of the possible damage caused by the movement of the dome that the net result was that the cost to repair to this listed structure was too much for the congregation or the church to meet. In addition, perhaps more significantly, God seemed particularly unwilling to intervene, thus it was saved by the nation for the nation. The trouble is when you allow those who worship only Mammon to rescue a house of God, there is a price to be paid and internally we paid that price. What must have been a spectacular internal space has now been hidden by its subdivision caused by the insertion of mezzanine floors.

As I sat there, looking out across the Square's central private garden with its statue to Prince Albert the Prince Consort, it seemed more than just a little incongruous that only some forty-eight hours, just two days earlier, my troubles had started on the other side of this elegant Georgian square. Talk about life being a series of concentric circles; unsolved murders it seemed cast long shadows.

Chapter 24
In Which I Journey to the Country

The tooting of a car horn interrupted my thoughts and as I glanced down at the street kerb I could see Billy's pride and joy, an MGB GT, its British racing green, highly polished paintwork glinting in the spring morning sun.

Complete with a waving driver, "Hey, dreamer boy, wakey, wakey; the Reivers are up and about and the border lands beckon."

I eased myself up, not without obvious difficulty, and as always in these situations, these troubles were the source of great hilarity and general amusement to the non-inflicted witnessing the struggles of the inflicted. In a voice redolent of mock solicitude he shouted, "Come on old fellow, take it easy. You're not as young as you used to be. That's it, easy as she goes, careful now, try not to make matters worse."

These words were accompanied by the hint of a snigger. He opened the driver's door and got out.

"Okay, easy does it, Uncle Billy is here to help you Granddad."

With that he came round the car, opened the passenger door and doffed his non-existent, imaginary hat reminiscent of some Edwardian chauffeur or some oleaginous, dinner suited, cinema manager of the Fifties.

I felt it only proper to acknowledge his proffered help in the right spirit, "Thank you my man. If you could just take my arm, I will see if I can get in this rat trap of a vehicle you have."

Whilst I am the first to agree that this type of British designed, British built, sports car has lovely clean lines and is, as it were, a style icon. Nonetheless I often feel that even the most dedicated sports car enthusiasts couldn't claim with any conviction, that they were easy to get in and out of. Particularly if you were in my case temporarily, hors de combat. Add to this the undeniable detail that they were designed for an immediate post-war, ration book, dietary regulated, body frame rather than that which now I was now attempting to bring on board.

"That you, sir. Nicely tucked in, oh just one other thing before we depart, sir…" he paused and looked in what he obviously thought was a quizzical manner.

"I'm terribly afraid sir; we have no place for your Zimmer."

This was followed by the shutting of the passenger door, the snigger giving way to uncontrolled laughter, "So tell me, oh injured one, where is it exactly that we're going? When you called you said the Borders. Could you possibly be a little more specific maybe, narrow down the destination just a little?"

"Peebles, the town of Peebles is our intended destination; to be precise the police station in that pleasant little place."

He started the engine, engaged first and let in the clutch and we moved smoothly into motion.

"Okay, Peebles it is."

He swung the car round the square picking up traffic as we went down South Charlotte Street, briefly onto Princes Street then, hanging a left past the Church of St John's and onto Lothian Road. We were headed in the direction I had journey from an hour ago. Leaving Morningside behind we went up through Fairmilehead and passed the artificial ski slope at Hillend and joined the Peebles road, the A710, just before Easter Howgate.

If Scotland does have an endemic transport infrastructure management problem it's that it has, not only very few miles of road given over to motorway, but it also has a lack, amounting to a veritable dearth, of dual carriageways. Thus this A road was single carriageway along its length and was, in English terms more of a B than an A road.

In the north of Scotland the major historic road building programs had been undertaken by General Wade's all-conquering English redcoats. This after the disastrous affair of the forty-five, the crushing defeat at Culloden Field, the flight in the heather of Bonnie Prince Charlie, followed by the killing times. These killing times, were a period of blood-letting which at that stage were seen as a natural consequence, an inevitable corollary to what had in essence been a civil war: the lowlander against the highlander.

The trouble with that is as in many other episodes in Scottish history, the die-hard nationalists tend not to give you the whole facts, preferring to be in denial. They would prefer you to view the episode as Scotland throwing off the English imperialist yoke. The truth, perhaps to them the highly uncomfortable truth, is that General Wade's all conquering English redcoats' ranks were approximately fifty percent filled up with Scots and Germans. To say nothing of a fair sprinkling of mercenary iterant Irish, who over the years had shed their blood in helping build an empire for a country they professed to despise.

Truth be known there are some Scottish clans, such as the Leslies, who in fact, had won at Culloden. However, as many Scots will attest, you should never let the truth temper your anti-English bias. The truth has a way of providing glasses to enable sight to those who are blinded by prejudice.

In the words of a piece of doggerel verse that did the rounds at the time,

"If you had seen the roads he made,

You would all praise General Wade."

Mind you just like Herr Hitler's Autobahns, Wade's roads were not so much to aid the purposes of commerce and communications but were constructed for the purpose of rapidly and easily moving troops to facilitate the prosecution of a war. These lines of communication were built principally to ensure the total and utter subjugation of what the victor considered to be a dangerous and unpredictable, tribal enemy.

"Do you know where the police station is in Peebles?"

Billy's voice broke in after what I realised had been several miles of silence, each of us lost in our own thoughts.

"Not a clue, but I suppose we could look out for some chavs and ask them. It would surely be something that would feature big in their lives, on a "know your enemy basis." An acquired knowledge I would imagine."

Billy shook his head,

"Do you know, I think there is a distinct lack of any chavs in Peebles? I don't think they permit them there any more: what with the new expensive, executive style housing, I think that it is more or less, now a chav-free zone."

He had a good point. The village was now in fact a dormitory commuter town for well-heeled Edinburgh workers. This had become one of the chosen rural retreats of the 'I-do-so-prefer-the-country-darling-it's-so-non-city' type of people, who created wherever they chose to reside their own little enclaves, their own little closed off 'gated' communities. Whilst the indigenous population muttered darkly about, "They bloody incomers."

It took us forty-five minutes to complete our journey on Saturday morning quiet roads, so it was just after nine when we were rolling down the Main Street. I noticed a large imposing building set back from the road with available parking in front. I indicated to Billy, "Pull into here it's the Tontine Hotel, somebody there is sure to know where the cop shop is to be found."

He pulled the car in and coming to a halt he cut the engine, put on the hand brake and entered the building. Within a few moments he reappeared with a man in uniform, he pointed up the road and made '*turning round the corner* motions' with an outstretched arm. Billy smiled, the man returned the smile and he went back into the hotel with the air of a man who had done great service.

Billy returned to the MGB with the news, he explained as he turned the engine on, that which we sought was located at the bottom of the road across the bridge to the left, and then hard right. He also imparted that it was a newish building and that his informant had expressed his confidence that we could not possibly miss our intended destination.

Despite the hotel porter's confidence, perhaps his overconfidence in our capability to follow simple instructions or simply because we failed to turn right hard enough, we did just that. We sailed magnificently straight past our destination in blissful ignorance. Seeing a sign thanking us for driving carefully and whishing us a good journey we realised that we may just have missed our objective.

"Balls," was my companion's only comment on this error of our ways.

He turned the motor into a farmer's field entrance then reversed onto the main road. In so doing, he totally disregarded my comments as to the manoeuvres legality.

He then retraced our way back along the road and it was here we picked up a sign indicating the direction to the police station, signs I had either not noticed or had been conspicuous by their absence on the other side of the road. We took a hard left and pulled up in front of a long purpose-built modern building without visible signage which looked as though it might just be a retail outlet; a large car parking area in front appeared to give credence to that allusion. Billy brought the MG to a halt in a bay that was, if the sign was to be believed, set aside exclusively for the use of visitors not, it should be noted, for suspects' or convicted criminals and others of that ilk. He killed the ignition, pushed the gear lever to neutral pulled on the hand brake and, turning to me, he said.

"Do you need a hand out?"

I opened the door and made to rise not, it has to be said, with much success so I answered, "I hate to admit it but I think it might be for the best."

He duly obliged and soon he had me standing almost on my own two feet. As he did, he enquired,

"Do you want me to accompany you to the station?"

"Who said the old ones were not the best ones?"

Billy grinned.

"No better not, you stay with the car. Sam said that the contact was a little reticent, maybe keep the motor running just in case."

He then looked quizzical, "Sam, and who the hell is Sam? You never mentioned him before."

"We only meet last night and, I have to tell you, that he's a she. As to why I haven't mentioned it, as you recall we had other more pressing matters on hand at the time. This morning the whole matter slipped my mind;

sorry I did not intend to keep you in the dark. I will tell all over lunch or coffee, whichever comes the quicker."

I walked in through the swing doors and followed an arrow sign which pointed to 'public desk'. I rang the bell as the sign suggested, and was quickly confronted by a pimply-faced youth who wore a black shirt with a logo proclaiming him to be police. I wondered if the logo was meant to reassure errant members of the public who had strayed in thinking this might be a branch of Tesco's.

"Can I help you sir?"

"Indeed you can officer. I would like a few words with the good Sergeant McIntyre, if you please."

In response the youth scratched his chin as if at some non-existent beard, seeming surprised at its non-existence and went on, "I'm sorry sir, but our Sergeant McIntyre does not see members of the public."

"What not at all? Doesn't that make living a bit difficult for him, what with shopping and all?"

What I thought a witty retort was completely wasted on this member of the force. He simply looked at me vacantly across the counter that lay between us, much as they say in these parts like a 'coo looking o'er a dyke.' The need of further explanation was clearly indicated.

"An appointment, well actually more of an arrangement, has been made for me to speak with him by a mutual…"

I let my voice trail off, giving consideration as to the advisability of using the term colleague or friend, in conversation in this context, but eventually settled for the far more vague and less legally definitive,

"Acquaintance. It was she who kindly set up a meet for me last night."

That seemed to help things along, "And your name sir would be?"

"Gray, Alexander Gray."

He picked up a phone that was mounted on the wall and punched in a three-digit number. I could hear the ring tone followed by a muffled yes.

"Sorry to trouble you Sarge but I have a bloke here, by the name of Gray he says you know about him and have agreed to talk to him."

A pause whilst he listened to the response, "Yes Sarge I have told him that but he says that the meeting was arranged by a mutual acquaintance."

Another pause presumably to take further guidance, "I'll ask."

Then putting his hand across the mouthpiece he enquired,

"What's the name of the other party concerned sir?"

"Oh sorry, yes of course, her name is Sam and she works at the collator's office at Fettes Regional HQ in Edinburgh."

A nod then into the receiver.

"He says someone called Sam who he says works in the collator's office at Fettes."

Another pause, then almost coming to attention in an almost reverential tone, "Would the Sam you are talking about be Chief Inspector Samantha Campbell?"

Although the rank had taken me by surprise I nodded my vigorously in agreement, "Yes, that's the lady in question."

He relayed the information then as in confirmation, "Right, understood, interview room two it is."

He replaced the receiver thoughtfully on its suspended cradle and after a moment's reflection he said, "Right Mr. Gray, Sergeant McIntyre will see you now."

The speaker gave a heavy and an almost surprised inflection on the word will as if this was a moment he thought he would never live to see. This was a moment indeed to be fully documented and recorded for posterity in the annals of the Peebles nick.

Chapter 25
In Which I Learn About Travelling People

"Right Mr. Gray, if you would just care to follow me I will take you through."

The constable lifted a flap on the public counter and allowed me to enter. He carefully replaced it and I followed him into the netherworld of the police station, affording me a criminal-eye's view of the interior.

I followed him down a long corridor which, by my reckoning, must be taking us to the back of the building. When we turned a corner, there was a sign which proclaimed that it was straight ahead for the interview suites.

The words 'interview suite' conjured up in my mind a setting for some kind of late night chat show. That said I could only imagine what might be the subjects of the kind of late night chats that went on within the walls of these rooms.

He led me to a dark painted door which bore the simple legend, interview room two. My guide produced a key and unlocked the door; you obviously can't be too careful in police stations, ostensibly rife with would-be petty thieves, everywhere. He ushered me inside, led me to a desk in the centre of the room and pulled out a chair on its far side and motioned to me to sit. My seating duly accomplished, his duty duly discharged, he bade me goodbye with the added assurance that the good sergeant would be with me very soon.

After a short period the door opened and a man of medium height with close cropped, and by close I mean almost to the wood, steel grey hair. He did not so much enter the room, as insinuate himself into it.

He hesitated, the pause it seemed almost involuntarily, as was the covert over his shoulder look. Happy and satisfied apparently, that enemy action was not about to creep on him and catch him unawares, unguarded, he shut the door and walked across to the interview desk on the opposite side to which I was seated.

I was intrigued by the sergeant's behaviour despite the fact that I had been pre-warned. Still on his guard, before settling himself in the seat opposite, he glanced enquiringly round the room as though in the shadowy corners some listener was lurking. Presumably the eavesdropper was disguised cunningly as a chair, the only additional piece of furniture in the room.

At last outwardly satisfied that the chair was what it appeared, a chair, and that the room had no sinister occupants, except of course yours truly, he decided to take a seat. He looked me firmly in the eye, a practiced look meant to strike fear and terror into the heart and soul of the criminal classes, and by association, me as well. It followed that the criminal classes must be different from members of the public, as the youth whom I first met had, I recalled, assured me that the good sergeant did not speak to members of the public.

"Mr. Gray is it?"

His voice had a booming quality which completely belied the relative size of his frame. I also picked up on a Welsh lilt. Welsh McIntyre's well there you go, whatever next; an English Murphy, perhaps.

"Indeed," I started.

"Mr. Gray it is."

His gaze was unwavering and to be frank, more than a little intimidating, I suppose that what it was meant to be.

"And you want to know something about gypsies, travelling people?"

His manner seemed genuine, his tone questioning.

"And I want to know something about travelling people, gypsies, correct."

I paused then went on, "That is I want to know something about gypsies, other than they no longer seem to make pegs and mend pots and pans, but some of their number have taken to stealing motor cars and causing trouble."

"The truth is Mr. Gray they never did sell pegs. It was like these old ex-servicemen that used to sell matches in the inter-war period. It was just a convenient device, a ruse if you like, to get round the requirements of the law on begging. To be perfectly frank these people have always been considered a nuisance by somebody or other."

Here was a man warming to his subject.

"The trouble with the modern day gypsy, or if you like the modern day travelling folk, is that they are more of a problem in our now heavily urbanized society than their ancestors were in our more rural past. The whole nuance factor is exacerbated by their speed of travel. Add to the mix their code of honour, producing a ring of silence to outsiders and their 'here today gone tomorrow' existence and it suits any criminal element amongst them down to the ground.

We have come a long way from Borrows' "Romany Rye" with its dreamy overtones; a time when highly decorated caravans, pulled by the horse brass-adorned piebald ponies, travelling in small bands strolled along the byways of old England. They almost blended in with the countryside or at least gave it a spurious romantic feel."

Strange, all my life and this is the first time I encountered a literary policeman.

"The advent of the modern super caravan pulled, not by a gently clip clopping old Dobbin, but by a transit van, has more or less destroyed the romantic allusion forever. If there is one thing that people in general cannot stand it's having their allusions shattered. So, when it was goodbye gypsy Palalengro with violin and bandanna, and hullo white van man, with baseball cap and larcenous intentions, it was goodbye to all our easy-going memories of yesterday, and hullo to all the harsh realities of today."

He stopped, although the foregoing had been a well-rehearsed but deep-felt speech but before I could comment he went on,

"As to the particular lot you are looking for, they are indeed a pain in the proverbial bum, heavens are they a pain. They knew just how long it would take us to obtain the initial eviction warrant and just how to defend it. They of course, knew their rights, which they fully exercised during the time it took us to obtain the final writ."

Without waiting for an acknowledgement or comment he ploughed on,

"It's like some bloody elaborate game where both sides know the rules off by heart. Both sides know the playing time and both sides know what the final score will be, but play the game out anyway. It's much as some complicated ritual where everyone knows their role and everyone know what the ending would be but somehow or other could not resist enacting the whole damned thing one more time."

He sounded more sad and reflective rather than angry. Here was indeed an unusually, in my experience, eloquent member of the constabulary. All of which prompted my question, "But why the car thefts? I mean is this part of their normal modus operandi, for that matter did they steal the cars in the sense of taking to keep or did they just borrow them?"

The sergeant looked mildly disapproving "Borrowing, you have to understand Mr. Gray, without the owner's consent is theft. But, I take your point. All of the cars recovered from the Park and Ride did turn out to be stolen. Although, the travellers denied their involvement, it was coincidence, a massive coincidence that all the cars should find their way to their encampment."

His first lecture in Scottish jurisprudence over, he went on, "So, we in the force, were asked to believe that all of Edinburgh's joyriders, while we're on the subject, a wholly inappropriate term, for the offence of taking and driving away, were drawn by a mysterious force to this one place. That the cars were there and the travelling people were there, was all we could reasonably prove. Nevertheless, they did move on after our raid, pretty sharpish and with a minimum of fuss."

Having receiving his second homily I gauged it time for an interjection in an attempt to keep him focused on the particular rather than the general.

"Is this how these particular families spend their lives travelling around the United Kingdom causing trouble as they go? Making free with peoples' property, joyriding in cars, getting involved in petty theft and generally being a pain in the arse to the rate paying, law abiding public."

"No, not with the old families or rather not with the elders, the old, of the old families; they just want to dodge along making some sort of living as they go. No, it's the young ones, it's the would-be jack the lads. If they have anything in common with our home grown city ne'r do wells, it is that they think the world owes them a living.

Whereas the oldies, they no longer receive the respect from the young that they gave to their elders. The gypsy travelling culture the whole thing, well it's in decay and who knows, the decay might be terminal. Nevertheless, I'll tell you this; if it does die out, die out completely that is and there are no more travelling families, there will be very few mourners at that particular funeral."

Well, my attempt to put the conversation back on my exact problem, was not as successful as it could have been but as they say try, try again,

"No, what I meant is, is there anything more to this car stealing. Anything perhaps, well, am I seeing the big picture? Is there, I don't know, is there something more sinister?"

He looked as though he was sitting up and paying attention, "I mean for instance: the theft and swapping of number plates isn't that, not a bit odd, well actually very odd? Were any of the other cars that you recovered in a similar state of plate deprivation?"

I had obviously, as I had with Sam, caught his attention. It appeared that this was something he did not know about. You begin to worry more than a little about police intelligence. In this case more in general than in particular.

Faced with a blank expression across the table from me, I again retold the judiciously edited story about the hit and run, the Porsche, and my tracing of a completely innocent, yet recently stolen vehicle.

"That is strange, because this has not been flagged up to me as being a feature of the case, but I could check and maybe come back to you."

I gave him my business card.

"What on earth is the point of stealing the number plates anyway?"

He smiled,

"To that I can give you an explanation."

He adopted the look of the great all-knowing, about to enlighten the great all-ignorant.

"These thieves are clever and they know three things. One, the plates are current, two, they can be sure the stolen cars are clean and, three since they are still being used by their legal owners, the car is not a write-off, so in a cursory examination, unless someone runs a computer check, the chances of them getting away with it are stacked in the favour of said felons."

He exuded self-satisfaction at an explanation well argued, but at least he was now back on track, my track,

"Okay. I see that, but what I really need to know now is, have you any idea where they might be, where they have moved onto? This roving band of vagabonds."

"That Mr. Gray is as they say the sixty-four thousand dollar question. They in fact, could be many places or none."

"But what would be your best guess Sergeant?"

Again the thoughtful expression,

"We'll my best worst guess would be that they would be heading down through Dumfriesshire, probably between there and Kirkcudbrightshire. There are plenty of fairs and things going on in that part of the world in May. You know the sort of thing, so-called craft fairs, assorted tree hugging events and if there is such a thing dancing round the maypoles Scottish-style. They won't be back up Edinburgh way till the early autumn; it'll' be towards the end of October, a visit to the capital is a biennial treat for them as it is for capital."

He hesitated again, looked round the room, another searching of the corners, bloody hell, this must be some pension he was working up to. Once again satisfied that there was, to paraphrase John Buchan no 'listener by the threshold', he went on, "I suppose I might just be able to firm up that intelligence, if I'm given some time, maybe I could be a bit more definitive."

He looked at the clock on the wall above and behind my head, presumably placed there so as the interrogator could judge the length of the interview, and by extension, the waning stamina of the interrogatee.

He peered, screwing up his eyes, almost as though he was short-sighted, but as he spoke I realised he was, in fact, calculating time.

"It's almost… ten thirty so… come back about in, say an hour and a half, and I will see what I can do."

Another break, this time though for effect,

"Remember, no promises okay?"

I inclined my head in acknowledgement.

"Understood, Sergeant, twelve o'clock it is. I look forward to our next meeting. Thank you for all your help, it is really appreciated."

Chapter 27
In Which I Receive a Warning

Thinking the interview over I rose, but as I did so Sergeant McIntyre looked at me with an almost concerned expression and gestured to me to sit back down by a staying motion of his hand, "The leading family of your group is called Maxwell and Ma Maxwell's big son Davie is the apple of his mother's eye and for her he can do no wrong. Although she could be politely described as 'the bully of the washhouse,' she is, granted by her own standards, relatively law-abiding. Her darling big boy on the other hand is in an entirely different league, he is one seriously bad bastard, who has been in and out of trouble ever since his mother stored the proceeds of her shoplifting outings under the mattress of his pram. We should have done him for receiving there and then and maybe that might have been an end to it."

This last remark seemed to amuse him and he continued, "He now has a criminal record as long as Leith Walk and a narrowly missed conviction for murder. The murder charge was overthrown by the intervention of his step brother wee Wullie, the runt of the pack, and the word pack, Mr. Gray is a completely accurate description of the social groupings these people live in. Wullie gave his brother an alibi, incidentally a perjured alibi, but it was bought, hook line and bloody sinker, by those dosey numpties an Edinburgh High Court jury. They brought in the usual 'Scottish cop out' verdict of not proven. The panel was probably stuffed with, oh so genteel, bleeding heart liberals."

I had to say this was masterly summing up of a certain strata of Edinburgh society.

"So, Mr. Gray, if you are still considering getting involved, then I would advise you to tread carefully. Tread carefully, speak softly and carry a big stick."

With that valedictory warning we both rose and the good sergeant guided me back along the long corridor leading to the public office and daylight. We exchanged the stand pleasantries and I left the police station realizing that I had just been well and truly warned. As I walked back towards the car, I was left wondering if the dire warning had been delivered in lieu of the standard 'no vigilantes required' lecture that had so forcibly been delivered by Sam the night before or out of genuine concern.

The sun was doing its best to warm the air and Billy was sitting almost as I had left him.

"Let you go then?" he quipped.

"So where to now? Back to old Reekie or what?"

I considered for a moment,

"No. Let's go back to the hotel, to the Tontine and I will bring you bang up to date as to exactly where we are with things."

"Your wish is my command oh master!"

He turned the key, pressed the self-starter and the engine burst energetically into life. We backed out of the parking space, out of the police station perimeter and retraced our earlier journey back along the road, across the bridge and re-entered Main Street. We parked up in one of the spaces thoughtfully provided by a caring management for the use of potential customers at the front of the Tontine.

After Billy reprised his 'help the cripple out of the car' routine we mounted the steps and as we went through the door, we were greeted by Billy's erstwhile pathfinder. He enquired as to whether or not we had found the police station and we answered in the positive. Our questioner seemed genuinely pleased that his comprehensive directions had guided us to our desired destination. We failed to mention (in defence of our own credibility) that, excellent those these directions had been, we only achieved our objective at the second chance.

We asked for coffee for two. He pointed to the sparsely populated lounge on the right and departed with the assurance that he would return with our order in a jiffy.

We took a seat in the room indicated and I embarked on a précis of my morning's meeting; as I was reaching the end of my narration, the jiffy apparently being up, the porter loomed large. He bore a silverish tray, on which there was a silverish coffee pot, matching cream and sugar, two china cups and an assortment of biscuits, some of which were wrapped in silverish paper.

He smiled, he poured, he smiled and he left, with an excessively cheery, "Enjoy."

Clearly, here was an employee that had been on one too many customer service courses.

Billy sipped his coffee, unwrapped a biscuit, settled back in his chair and commented, "So, if I can be allowed to sum up the situation so far. You have been warned you have to be wary of Ma Maxwell, and in particular of her burglarious and possibly murderous, but much-loved son Big Davie. Then just as you think that your cup is full and running over, you are further advised to keep your eyes open and be on our guard against, Big Davie's treacherous younger runt of the litter, half-brother, Wee Wullie. You are having a laugh aren't you,

you are taking the proverbial, you know what, Ma Maxwell indeed. The next thing you will be telling me is they are running a bootlegging business, moonshine for sale and hooch on draught, suppliers of poteen to the gentry; thus creating a whole new meaning to the phrase 'bring your own bottle.'"

I had to admit the whole scenario did sound a bit far-fetched. Maybe it would have sounded more convincing if Billy had heard it himself from the horse's mouth: the highly cautious Sergeant Macintyre. So I said nothing in rebuttal.

"Oh, come on Sandy for God's sake, let's try to stay on the same page, and try to stay real. What on earth can these people have to do with your old man's murder? What on earth could your late father and this bunch of criminals possibly have in common? Where's the connection, the missing link? You are just not thinking straight. What you're doing is allowing the grieving process to interfere with your thinking process; you are simply not making sense."

He did have a point. Where was the common factor? Perhaps it was the cold logic of his words that put me on the defensive,

"Well, when you lay it out the way you just have, you could be right. But only if you ignore the rest of what has happened. A hoodie-clad assassin coming at me out of the darkness, roaring out of the night on a motorbike trying to run me down. Does that make sense to you? A man offers to let me have my late father's notebook which he left behind at his last place of work. And what happens when he tries to deliver it, he's not only knocked down but knocked down and killed. Does that make sense to you?"

Billy simply looked at me, his face expressionless, so I continued,

"Then the driver of the car that ran him down having done so, instead of high tailing from the scene of the crime, calmly exits his car to search the body. Having found what he was looking for he gets back in his car and leaves with the package intended for me: dad's notebook. Does that make sense to you? Oh and one last thing, one last connection, one last missing link, the registration plate of the fatal blow-delivering car is a stolen plate and the theft of the car that bore the plate is linked to this Maxwell clan through their proximity to, and possible involvement in the events at the Park and Ride. Does that make bloody sense to you either?"

Billy remained impassive, trying to be the voice of reason,

"Alright, alright I'll grant you that some strange things have happened, but when all's said and done it could all be purely coincidence."

His words in that moment, were for me too reasonable, I felt momentarily angry, I broke in,

"'Some strange things have happened', well there's the understatement of the year. Is my father's corpse being found sprawled over a cannon on Calton Hill covered by your strange things, or does this come under 'purely coincidence'? Does that make sense? Do you not find this strange; do you not find this more than my allowing grief to interfere with my ability to reason?"

The anger dissipated as quickly as it had come as I saw Billy raise his hand in mock surrender,

"Sorry Billy, sorry momentary loss of perspective. I didn't mean to take it out on you. You of all people don't deserve that."

He smiled another one of his knowing smiles,

"As I was saying, that is before I was so rudely interrupted by Mr. Grumpy from Morningside, so some strange things have happened and you could be right that perhaps it's a bit more than coincidence. That said, if we are going to make any progress in this matter then you have to be a little less subjective and a little more objective. Let's start by looking at what we actually know. What we can say as fact is that your father was murdered which seems to have led to a strange sequence of events that you are convinced, somehow are linked to his death. Whilst there is some evidence to connect the death and the subsequent happenings, what we don't know is the why? Added to that, we also are in the dark as to the who. What we have to work out is who the damned enemy is, and why he is taking offensive action against you."

He broke off as if waiting for a response from me; there being none, he ventured a direct question,

"Let's start with last night, who knew you were meeting with this woman, this Sam did you say? Who did you tell either directly or accidentally?"

"Ah! Charlie's contact, yes, it is Sam., She works for the boys in blue, down at Fettes Regional HQ in the collator's office. Mind you from what I have subsequently gathered, especially from the response of the duty policeman at Peebles station, she is the collator's office."

Billy self-evidently considered he was on a roll,

"So, this Sam knew where and when you were meeting but who else?"

I gave the question a moment's thought.

"Well you did, after all if it wasn't for your fortuitous intervention by performing your knight in shining armour routine I may not have lived to tell the tale."

He shook his head as if dismissively,

"Let's assume, just for argument's sake that I knew nothing about it and let's assume I was just an innocent bystander, so who else?"

"Well I suppose her, Sam that is, might have mentioned it to one of her work colleagues but how many policemen do you know harbour homicidal tendencies to members of the public they have never met?"

Billy's smile reappeared,

"Let me just rephrase that question in view of your less-than-disinterested attitude to our local Bobbies. How many policemen harbour homicidal tendencies to members of the public they have never met?"

His smile broadened,

"More than you would think. However, let's put, again for the sake of argument, any stray maverick policemen aside, who one else?"

I played back in my mind the events of the previous evening,

"Well, assuming that I was not overheard by the barman at the Oxford, and further assuming that he is not in on the whole thing and is reporting to some evil mastermind. The only other person who knew anything of my movements, apart from those already mentioned was Charles."

"Charles...?"

"Yes, I'm not sure if you ever met. He is an acquaintance of mine from Uni days. Charles Montague-Mackenzie; he's the person that put me on to Sam."

Billy seemed surprised and almost taken aback as though a certain light had been shed in the darkness.

"So, Charles Montague-Mackenzie you say."

He lingered on the name as though weighing up and possibly checking it, as it were, in the balance.

"So, who we have so far is double-barrelled Charles, or possibly a keen eared barman in the pay of Mr. Big. These two are the only possibilities, and nobody else. Now, are you sure?"

As requested I went back into replay, again recounting the journey of the previous evening, "Yes, that's it just those two, no one else."

"Sandy, think; are you one hundred per cent sure? What about your acquaintance, your would-be informant, the one that was run over, this fellow, Macbeth, was it? Do you know how many people knew of his arrangement to meet with you?"

I centred the replay on the events surrounding our fatal meeting trying to refocus, "Yes, it was Macbeth but as to who knew well, self-evidently he did and of course, and if they were listening in, the person on my switchboard. Frankly I cannot believe my receptionist Agnes, bless her, has hidden murderous intentions towards, again as in the case of the local constabulary, relatively unknown people."

Billy considered what I had related for a moment then went on, "So to recap, in the matter of the first little problem, we have two possible but highly improbable suspects to your rendezvous in Stockbridge. In the matter of the second little problem, the Charlotte Square meet, we again have two possible suspects one highly improbable and the other passed over. My conclusion old son, for what it's worth, is if what you say is the truth, the complete truth, and then clearly, you Alexander are doing all this to yourself."

He smile poured another cup of coffee sat back in his chair and gazed skywards with the air of a man well satisfied with his efforts at reasoning,

"As a matter of academic interest, when did Charles Montague-Mackenzie re-enter our lives anyway?"

"Charles em, well... oh, that was in the aftermath of the Macbeth incident. I was in Whigams wine bar attempting to comfort the lovely Cammy..."

My voice trailed off as my thoughts suddenly coalesced.

"I ran into Charles at Whigams wine bar, where I was consoling the gorgeous Cammy. He made an appearance, out of the blue. I haven't seen him for years; he had as they say just blown in from the US of A."

In the following silence Billy prompted, "Who the hell is Cammy? Where did she just spring from?"

"Who indeed, Sweet William, well may you ask. I have just worked out your link – the connection you sought between the two incidents, I know the common factor. Jesus, have I been slow."

Chapter 28
When I See a Little Light

Billy's face showed a mixture of expectation and impatience and he repeated his previous comment, "but who the hell is Cammy?"

In the eagerness of my revelation, I side-stepped the question,

"Cammy knew in advance about Macbeth meeting with me at Ma Scott's. She also knew where and when I was bound on my outing to Duddingston Village and my later assignation yesterday evening."

Billy made a slow down gesture,

"Okay, let's take this one step at a time. Firstly, who the hell is this Cammy and secondly where exactly does she fit in?"

"Cammy or I suppose to be more formal, Camilla, is employed in the same office as the late lamented James Macbeth. She is some sort of personal assistant; some type of office manager. They both worked for the Weldon Hospice charity that's the people who have purchased the Old Edinburgh Hospital for the Incurables. Which they then converted into a state of the art palliative day care centre facility. That's the one up at Newington, the one which was used in recent time as a geriatric facility."

Billy looked interested but still puzzled.

"This is the company that the old man had been doing the audit for – it was a sort of tidying up exercise – to provide an asset register prior to final handover. The building had been decommissioned and a final price agreed with the health board so he was there crossing the t's and dotting the i's. This was my father's last audit. As you know before he finalized it he upped and popped his clogs or, perhaps in reverence of his passing, it would be more accurate to say he upped and popped his handmade brogues."

"Right with you, so far, but how does she appear in the frame for last night's 'escapades in the dark?' What's' her connection?"

Billy's tone sounded a shade sceptical, obviously further convincing was in order.

"She and Charles were dining last night when I phoned to see if he could be of any further help with the local force. To be truthful since they met they seem to have been joined at the hip. When we were on the phone I overheard him speaking to her and reference the purpose of our lunchtime meeting and my visit to Duddingston. So between pillow talk and a little tête-à-tête that they would certainly have indulged over a romantic dinner by candlelight…"

Billy's expression showed that scepticism was replaced by puzzlement, "Wait a minute, let me catch up, surely you have missed something out. I still don't get it. How come this woman is suddenly hooked up with old Charles? According to you he is only back in town for two bloody minutes and he is at it, like some randy bloody rabbit, seeking out the female of the species as though he were on heat."

Billy was sounding a bit censorious like a 'wee free' minster.

I explained about the tearful scene in her office that had followed the revelation of her unfortunate colleague

Macbeth's sudden death and my efforts at consolation. I told him about the wine bar and how he, Charles, had appeared on the scene, enter stage right as some white knight on an equally white charger. Then how he had wrapped her in his cloak of charm and had swept her away with a promise to a transport her to a world without tears.

This explanation had whetted my companion's interest, so I went on, "To be very truthful I think being on heat is a permanent state of mind with Charles. Having said that, maybe it wasn't just Charles's charm, or his ever-gleaming platinum card, which caused her to fall hook line and sinker for his merchant banker's allure. Perhaps, there was more to her motives, more than being swept off her feet by our knight errant. There is something else here, something more than immediately meets the eye, Billy my boy!"

"Agreed, but does this takes us any further down the road to a solution?"

I heard him, but leaving the question unanswered, I ploughed on, "What about poor old Charles? What a blow it would be to his ego if it turned out that Camilla had not immediately and readily fell deeply and madly in lust with him. What if she had not fallen for, what he considers his obvious and plentiful charms?"

Then recalling the unanswered question, "What if, Billy... what if, she has taken our favourite merchant banker to her bed, simply because he was an old friend of mine and this friendship meant she could keep a close watch on yours truly? I wonder if this is true, will his ego ever overcome a blow such as this?"

Billy laughed.

"I think Billy, it'll only take as long as it takes for his next conquest to acquiesce to his lecherous advances and allow herself to be persuaded to slide between his no-doubt black silk sheets."

"Silk sheets. Sandy, do you really think he has black silk sheets?"

"Good God, of course. No self-respecting serial seducer will ever be caught without a pair and in his case they are probably monikered with a full set of initials, top and bottom."

We both laughed, as much I think out of the relief of progress made as our speculations on the composition of the material of my old friend's bed linen.

"So what do we do now? Where do we go from here?"

"Well Billy, I think it's time for a leisurely stroll. Let's have some of that health-inducing, fresh Borders air; you never know, it might just aid our thinking process. I am not due back to the cop shop for about forty-five minutes so and the good Sergeant McIntyre is not one to hurry."

We finished the coffee. I asked for the bill which I duly paid and paused only to put the receipted bill in my wallet, in a truly accountant-like way. All evidence of expenditure kept and filed away, just in case. This done, we strolled out of the doors and onto the high street.

We spent a quiet half an hour uneventfully strolling along the streets and backstreets of Peebles without coming to any firm decision on where to go from here. The chosen time having arrived, we returned to the police station at the pre-appointed time.

I entered and as previously, rang the bell where it said so to do, and was confronted by the same pimply-faced youth as before. He nodded and with the assurance that he would tell Sergeant McIntyre that I was here departed without further comment.

This time, untroubled, I had leisure to glance round and noticed, as in many public waiting rooms, the walls were adorned with gratuitously obvious advice. The advice was principally about locking your car and putting your valuables in the boot and one felt that if you failed to take the suggested elementary precautions then you may have to live with the consequences. These consequences, if I correctly, interpreted the tenor of the message would be your own dammed fault.

However, amongst the plethora of advice to the unwary, the least helpful was a reminder to always extinguish your cigarette before becoming comatose and succumbing to sleep in a drunken stupor in front of your telly. Presumably, having consumed your twelfth pint and before drifting off to a well-earned rest this picture was meant to flash into your mind. Thus jolting you from your alcohol-fuelled nodding off and back into immediate lucidity of thought and action.

My further speculation on public information posters was interrupted by the arrival of the Sergeant himself. The Sergeant had presumably decided to forsake his lair, deep in the bowels of the station, and make a rare appearance at the public counter. He scrutinised the room thoroughly and, having satisfied himself that we were on our own, he spoke to me in a would-be conspiratorial fashion.

"Right Mr Gray, as promised I have something a little more definite for you. The lot you are after left Aberdeen some two weeks ago and are now on the western leg of their return journey south. If this journey is to plan and they have not run into any unforeseen difficulties they will have swung across to Stirling, then down. That being the case, I estimate that they would be fetching up near or about Moffat this coming week.

If they are running true to previous years they will be going on to Stranraer and on the ferry bound for the Irish Republic, for the big summer solstice do in County Wicklow. They normally arrive a few days before the equinox which is, of course, the twenty first of June."

I listened, straightened up, then thanked him and was about to take my leave when he again summoned me to stay in an even more conspiratorial fashion.

"Remember what I told you earlier, these people could prove extremely dangerous; particularly if they suspect that you think that they are up to no good, or even worse that you might be on to them. As I told you these people play for keeps understand?"

I reassured him that I did fully understand the danger and that I would proceed with care and after being duly re-warned I was allowed to take my leave. When I reached the car Billy had already started the engine and as I got back into my seat, with, what I was pleased to notice was with much less pain – an advert for the curative properties of the good Borders air-he asked, "Back to town, is it sir?"

I nodded agreement.

"Yup, back to Edinburgh it is, to a late lunch and a long confidential heart to heart with Charlie boy. I think it's time to clear the air."

He slipped the car into gear and we completed the return journey in comparative silence, apart from the occasional expletive undeleted as Billy commented on the relative driving skills, or relative lack of driving skills, of some, if not all of his fellow drivers.

As we crested the hill and rolled back down into Fairmilehead, I took out my mobile and rang Charles's mobile number. There was no answer and, as it went onto the answering announcement, I shut it off, only for my own phone to ring almost immediately.

"Looking for me Alexander old chum?"

Charles's familiar hearty voice sounded in my ear.

"Charles good afternoon, I most certainly am. I need to have a few words with you if possible?"

"Of course, certainly when and where would suit you?"

"I think I'd prefer it to be sooner rather than later, so as soon as suits you will do."

There was a pause for thought and then, "Have you had lunch yet?"

I replied in the negative.

"Okay, neither have I, so why don't we meet at that fish food restaurant on the Shore at Leith. You know the one; it's got a lighthouse on top? How long before you can make it?"

"We're just coming up to the lights at the bottom of Morningside. I can be with you in say, twenty minutes or so will that do?"

"No problems. I'll be there before you and secure a table. See you soon."

"Thanks Charles, oh and can you make it for three? I have Billy with me."

"No problemo old chum, ciao."

With that there was a click and he was gone. I relayed the gist of my conversation and our intended destination to Billy, whose only comment was,

"Fish, I hate fish."

Mimicking, with I have to say a certain degree of accuracy including the dropped h, an advert of a bygone era.

Cross town traffic was light for a Saturday so we arrived at the Shore in just a little under the projected time of arrival. We parked the car on the quayside and made our way to the restaurant. As we entered we were approached by an eager and expectant waiter. Glancing beyond him into the interior of the restaurant, I noticed Charles ensconced at a corner table with a bottle of wine in a silver bucket chilling quietly away, whilst he sipped what had to be his statutory G&T.

I waved in acknowledgement and the waiter, picking up on the situation, ushered us to the table. He hovered, so I looked at Billy and made drinking motions.

"Just fizzy water for me, that will do fine thanks."

I turned to the waiter.

"And for me have you a large bottle of Pellegrino? That would do fine."

He nodded, presented us both with broad sheet menus and departed to collect our chosen tipple.

Charles glanced up at me squinting, and then with a wry smile he said, "You look as if you have been in the wars, old chum. Did we have rough night last night?"

"Charles, Charles, do you know you're absolutely right, rough it was. Mind you rough, not in the over imbibing of alcohol sense, more in the almost being run down and totalled sense."

"Run down, you Alexander? Surely you jest. Who on earth would want to run down a pleasant mild-mannered Edinburgh accountant? Been fiddling the odd client or two's books rather than auditing them perhaps."

"Well..."

I broke off as I was interrupted by the waiter, who appeared with a large bottle of the ordered mineral water and two ice-filled glasses. He asked if I wished him to pour and if we were ready to order. Being mid-story I responded,

"No thank you, that's alright, I will pour for myself. Eh, no, not yet, give us five minutes and then we will be ready to order, thank you."

The waiter sidled off in that particular, singular way that waiter's do; something they learn whilst in training mode perhaps.

"Well, the attempted hit and run, that's just what I wanted to talk to you about."

Charles to his credit, looked at me somewhat incredulously, "Sorry you want to talk to me about an attempted hit and run?"

Again to his credit, his voice conveyed the incredulity of his look, "This is a joke isn't it? What have I to do with it? Do you imagine I'm a member of some... oh I don't know some...some assassination bureau?"

"Do you know, Charles I don't think you are, but I think that you know someone who knows someone who is?" I said.

Chapter 29
In Which a Meeting is Called

Charles's face was the proverbial picture. His expression betraying his attempt to come to terms with his struggle, between disbelief and curiosity. The hesitancy of his answer showed his mind failing to process the concept.

"You think... that I know... someone who knows someone who is...?"

His voice trailed off, into silence,

So in attempt to move things along I ventured, "Yes, that is exactly what I think. You are friendly, very friendly, with someone who is, in the words of a private detective of yesteryear, in league with the ungodly."

"When you say someone, do you have a specific someone in mind?"

"The someone I have in mind is Camilla."

"Camilla!"

If anything, this appeared to have increased his incredulity.

With a certain imperfection of timing, unless of course he was trying to build up the dramatic impact, the waiter arrived to take our order. Gauging that the one thing Charles needed at this juncture was thinking time, I looked up, smiled at our member of serving staff and with an 'ah right' I plumped for one of the specials of the day.

"I'll have the venison pâté and the smoked haddock linguini, what about you Charles, you fancy the same?"

He nodded agreement in an almost automatic distracted fashion.

"And the same again what for that gentleman, I indicated Charles, and that leaves you, what would you like William?"

He waited; it seemed to me as a man torn by the desire for a quick decision, and his complete dislike of fish. Actually, to call it complete was not quite the truth, when visiting the chippie he did have a favourite fish and it began with S and it was called a single.

"Pâté and the warm chicken Caesar salad, that'll do for me."

Oh the lengths that a Piscean abhorrence would lead you. That was almost, if not quite, the vegetarian option.

"Well that was damned close. You almost plumped for the rabbit food of the day. I would never have let you live it down."

Billy chuckled and the waiter, his task achieved, left clutching the order and conveying back to the kitchens for fulfilment.

Charles took a pull of his gin and, looking round in a conspiratorial fashion nearly in a Sergeant Macintyre mode and in a low and subdued voice, said, "Cammy, are you sure? I mean that seems, well to say the least of it, a little far-fetched. Are you sure, and I mean really sure or is this just some sort of accounting perversion, are you perhaps adding two and two and making five?"

He seemed like the proverbial drowning man clutching for the equally proverbial straw. His insecurity was palpable and it was Billy who interposed,

"Charles, you and I both know or, at least we should know, that adding two and two and making five is just not Sandy's kind of arithmetic. I'm sure all these years trying to follow audit trails knocked that kind of inaccuracy clean out of him. This is not an accusation we've snatched out of the blue. We have talked the whole matter through, and, well do you know, we can find no other answer."

Charles gave a wan smile. "Last night our chum here had a brush with death's winged charity, or rather, in this case, death's more terrestrial, two wheeled and more conventionally engine-powered conveyance. Try as we might, we can ascertain only two people who knew directly, for certain, of our man here's whereabouts exactly night and they were…"

Bill paused for effect, as though he was compering an awards ceremony, "Yourself Charles, and, of course, we cannot forget the lovely Sam."

I interrupted Billy taking up the narrative.

"Sam, we reckon we can scratch from the list for the obvious reasons, because she is, even on slight acquaintance a career policeperson, and is therefore not likely to sacrifice her, already promising present and no doubt glittering future, to get herself involved in dirty work at the crossroads.

Which old son, leaves you unless, unlike the leopard you have decided to change your spots, a change I frankly would find unlikely, to say nothing of unconvincing. I mean I know you have a full, Catholic group of friends and varied acquaintances and I have no doubt amongst that in that lot there are the odd ball or two, but not, I feel, someone who has murderous intentions on a complete stranger. That is of course unless you can tell me different."

Charles slowly shook his head.

"So you okay with my thinking process so far?"

He nodded agreement in an almost resigned manner and said, "Yes, I'm with you so far."

"Well, if we rule out both of you as being those who were involved directly then we have to rule in anybody who knew indirectly, who knew as it were, second hand. So if again we repeat the exercise and rule out Sam from the equation – something I am sure you will agree with – then that I'm afraid Charles that leaves only you."

At this juncture, the waiter who did seem to have the knack for dramatic timing arrived with the pâté, napkin-wrapped fresh warm toast, and small ramekins filled with butter, which he distributed with well-rehearsed facility and departed.

I re-commenced my narrative,

"So, as I just said, that leaves you Charles, and only you. Did you tell anyone, anyone at all?"

The whole matter seemed to have left Charles somewhat speechless. His only response was a shake of his head in apparent denial.

"So that's a no. Then I have to ask you, are you one hundred per cent sure. For instance did you perhaps in a post-coital afterglow, after the 'I love you' and the 'that was great', perchance make mention of something along the lines of 'you never guess what Sandy wanted me to do for him when I meet him for lunch?"

At that question, Charles sat up and took notice.

"Later, in the evening, did you perhaps, when excusing yourself for making a phone call when your table was ready for dinner, make some remark to your companion as to why the call? Did you then go on to converse more freely under the influence of candlelight sweet music and the flowing champers, Veuve Clicquot yellow label no less?"

These revelatory enquires seemed to be giving him pause for thought. He made an effort to re-gather his wits and even managed a hint of a forced smile. Then conceded, "Well, yes, I suppose I may have mentioned something about lunch, some I don't know, loose pillow talk. Yes and later again I suppose I may have mentioned the purpose of your pre-dinner phone call and why it had been so urgent, and why I had to make subsequent phone calls."

Billy put down his knife which he was about to use to smear his toast with pâté.

"And?"

"And what?" replied Charles.

"And did she use her phone?"

"Well not that I noticed, but she did leave the table, she said, to go and powder her nose."

"Powder her nose you say? I suspect in this particular case, with her mobile." Billy commented as he re-addressed his attentions to his pate.

I was about to follow suit when Charles decided to go on the offensive, "I hear what you both say, and to be truthful you make a good case albeit a prima facie one. So, are you saying that Cammy is passing on information to some shady person or persons unknown, gathered from me, about your movements? For God's sake, I don't wish to be disrespectful Alexander but whom on earth would take even a passing interest in the whereabouts of a middle aged, middle income, over-the-hill accountant?"

It never fails to amaze me that people who say they don't want to be impertinent frequently go on to be exactly that. Charles bore a belligerent stubborn expression – the look I supposed of the suddenly disillusioned – bearing nothing but ill will to he who performed the disillusionment, "Really my friend, is that your considered opinion? Can I just mention that there is sitting across the table from you a middle aged, middle income, over-the-hill accountant who is giving serious thought to this description you have given of him? His serious thought is that he can see no reason why he shouldn't rise from his seat and smack an aging Casanova with fading charms, sitting across the table from him."

To his credit his countenance changed to one who is abashed, he said almost apologetically, "Incidentally, and purely to set the record straight, the candlelight was supplied by an energy saving bulb and the music was anything but sweet."

"Well thank you for the correction however, as whether your very own Mata Hari is involved in anything shady well the answer just has to be yes; add in the previous incident and it does, as they say, seem to put her name in the frame."

Charles had regained his puzzled, frowning look which was threatening to become a permanent feature and said,

"Add in the previous incident you said. What previous incident?"

I explained, giving a précis of Macbeth's intended rendezvous with me and the unintended long journey he embarked on. This accidental voyage was one that took him from this mortal realm, from a broad earthly city street to an even broader heavenly highway. I ended my narrative with my efforts at grief counselling and how they naturally involved a wine bar, and alcohol.

"Then, of course, like a bolt from the blue, you arrived on the scene to better my efforts: to personally take over the comforting of the bereaved and the giving of solace to the bereft and friendless."

"Christ, Sandy you make it sound as though you're rehearsing a submission to be delivered to the Holy Father in defence of Charles's claim for beatification, prior to the ultimate, his well-deserved canonization as the blessed Saint Charles," broke in a pâté-mouthed, totally unsympathetic Billy. So I decided to join in and lighten the mood, "Do you know William; I have to agree that the 'Blessed Saint Charles' has a nice ring to it: Patron Saint of Merchant Bankers. Duly appointed as Protector, Defender and Guardian of waifs and strays, provided that is, that they are young, female and good looking?"

Charles obviously had decided to go with the flow, it was time as it were, to simply do exactly that, "You bloody two, what a pair you are, you're almost bloody incorrigible. You're like some sort of double act. You should do some sort of show on the festival fringe. I'm sure it would be a sell-out."

"Yeah man, sounds good to me, something like Billy meets Sandy or Gray and Grayer?" quipped Billy.

"No, not really what I had in mind for you was, well nearer the truth. I was thinking more along the lines of dumb and dumber," was Charles's riposte.

The' whole interchange helped to lessen the tension and, following Billy's example, we started and finished our starters in companionable silence. It was therefore, not until our ever-efficient waiter had cleared away the starters and served the main course and Charles had tasted and fully approved his Chablis which had been gently chilling, that Charles turned his attention to us both.

"Right gentleman, exactly how do you propose we play it from here? What do you want me to do? Do you for instance want me to confront her with your, or perhaps now, our suspicions and see if somehow or other we can have her tell us some, if not all, of the truth? I have to say to be completely frank with you, based on my albeit short acquaintance, she doesn't seem to be the type to break down in floods of tears or dissolve in a fit of the vapours."

"No, no agreed. I don't think we should make any precipitous moves. If we are right these are highly dangerous people and they are obviously playing for high stakes. I just wish we knew what they bloody well were. If I'm correct then they have already killed twice, both my father and Macbeth. Not only that they tried for the hat trick – the proverbial three in a row – with me but failed. This, I think will have to be a case of softly, softly catchee monkey. So Charles the big question is, when will you two meet again?"

Charles put down his glass.

"Do you know Alexander, that question sounded like a Shakespearean quote?"

"If it does it's highly inappropriate as it's from Macbeth, so in plain English when is your next lover's tryst?" I amended.

"I'm meeting Cammy tonight, in fact we've arranged to meet up for a few drinks and then, for a change of scene, we thought we might try a little Chinese cuisine. Go somewhere for a taste of the distant Orient; a savour of the mysterious east."

"Easy there boy, Charles you sound like a blooming advert. It's us you are talking to not some new would-be conquest," chimed in Billy.

"Don't be so hard on him. It's not his fault he has a vivid imagination," I chipped in with my tuppence worth.

"Imagination aside and back to business for a moment, where and when are you meeting for these few drinks? I ask because, if possible, I would like to engineer a casual meeting, a sort of 'oh what a surprise, fancy meeting you here', type of thing."

Charles started to look conspiratorial again, but managed an, "Understood."

I had the terrible feeling he was going on to say, over and out, and although he did hesitate he went on…

"We're due to meet at seven o'clock this evening in Madogs on George Street; you know the place? It's downstairs."

I smiled with reminiscences of my father's tales of Edinburgh in the Swinging Sixties,

"Oh yes, I know where you are. It was, according to father, the late lamented Princess Margaret's favourite Edinburgh watering hole, who could possibly forget. Seven o'clock. It's' a date."

Chapter 30
In Which My Mother Sheds Some Light

Our plans laid and our evening arrangements firmed up we finished lunch, settled up and went our separate ways with promises to meet later. Billy and I went in Billy's car whilst Charles left in his usual in a black cab.

"Right Sandy, where to? Back home for you, for an afternoon snooze and a bit of rest and recuperation?" Billy asked.

"Well, no if you have the time, maybe you could drop me at the police station and we will see if we can head off another possible crisis situation with dear mama."

He nodded and pulled away and queried, "I take it it's the police station at St Leonard's we are going to?"

"Well yes, I suppose that's the one that now serves Morningside; for the life of me cannot think of one that's nearer."

Some ten minutes later and we were driving up the Pleasance towards St Leonard's Street. This particular police station is a modern affair and to be truthful, if it wasn't for the blue lamp outside, announcing police you could easily mistake it for a modern housing development.

It appears in modern times there is a tendency, as in this case, to put police stations down side streets where no one can find them. So, when we have a falling crime rate in the city, it's not so much that there are less crimes being committed, it's just that the victims cannot find anywhere to report the damned theft or other felonious act. Billy pulled in just before my destination, "Do you want me to wait or will you be alright on your own? I would imagine after the practice you had this morning, you should be quite used to going into cop shops on your lonesome."

"William, you are absolutely right. I'll fly solo on this one; I shall beard the beast in his den without fear or trepidation. If you come in with me they might just suspect collusion and we can't have that. Afterwards' a stroll across the Meadows; who knows it might just do me the world of good."

As I extricated myself, again with no great ease, from his infernal machine Billy signalled to me he would like a word, so I walked round to the driver's side. Billy rolled down his window,

"So Sandy, remember what we agreed the other night. Keep it vague, don't be specific, and don't give them anything they can check up on. Keep it general and I have remembered to fix it with Davie."

"Fix it with Davie, Davie who?" I asked.

"Davie, the taxi driver from the other night, remember?" he replied almost despairingly.

"The taxi driver, Davie of course sorry it's just…"

"Yes, I know, a lot has happened and you are not becoming any younger."

I touched his shoulder and as I turned away to go towards the entrance to the police station, I was momentarily arrested by his parting words:

"Oh and Sandy, do me a favour; please look both ways when you cross the road and from time to time also behind you as well. That I feel would be not only a good but possibly a lifesaving precaution. Ring me whenever you can and let me know how the meeting with Cammy went. Have a good night and do try to go early to bed."

I assured him that I would follow his advice and he pulled gently into the traffic turned down Rankeillor Street, and quickly disappeared from sight.

I roused myself and entered the building, following the arrows to the public desk. It occurred to me that the police were very fond of their arrows. I entered a room which, as with the one in Peebles had its walls adorned, perhaps littered would be a better word, by the same banal posters warning you of the blatantly obvious. The only difference was this reception felt as if it was designed to intimidate, rather than to welcome. Planned, it appeared, to discourage the beleaguered citizen from seeking advice and possibly redress for wrongdoing.

The counter was manned or, perhaps in acknowledgement to modern speech forms, peopled by a civilian who appeared to giving directions to a confused-looking individual with a rucksack and large suitcase. The man behind the counter appeared to be closely consulting an A to Z-type publication whilst omitting a noise which to him was presumably meant to suggest mild puzzlement.

Suddenly his eureka moment arrived and relieved, he turned the map to the enquirer who looked on with interest. Then our substitute policeman, with much gesturing, demonstrated the correct series of rights and lefts that would be required to be taken for the weary traveller to reach his required destination complete with his encumbering luggage.

After repeating in a slow deliberate fashion the steps to be taken, as if speaking to a none-too-bright child, the enquirer eventually saw the light and worked out the direction in which his goal lay. Then, accompanied with almost effusive thanks, he shouldered his rucksack, lifted his case and departed, going joyfully on his way. This left the floor to me. The man behind the counter looked enquiringly at me.

"Good afternoon, my name is Alexander Gray and I reside in Morningside Road. I am given to understand from my mother that someone called last night at my address wishing to have words with me, so I'm presuming that someone from the constabulary urgently wishes to talk with me."

The man behind the counter looked to me as though he might be someone to whom not just giving directions was a puzzle, but to whom the whole of his life was a puzzle. But he ventured, "What would that be regarding sir? Was there some incident? Were you perhaps involved in some accident?"

When I heard this reply I could not help but marvel at how accurately this almost stock character was written and portrayed in cop shows.

"It could be to do with an affray at the Edinburgh Royal Infirmary the other evening," I suggested tentatively.

Affray, for God's sake, I just realised that I had lapsed into some policeease. I realised I was beginning to sound as though I was enacting a part in a cop show.

"An affray you say sir?"

Now here was a man who recognised a technical term; police speak, when he heard it.

"Right sir, if you would just care to take a seat, I will ask the duty sergeant and find out how you can help us."

With that he was gone and, to paraphrase the words of a poet read in my schooldays known for lurking in a graveyard in Stoke Poges, 'leaving the world if not quite to darkness, but definitely to me.'"

The clock on the wall showed a lapse of ten minutes before my little helper returned, his former quizzical look replaced with one more bordering on the harassed.

"I've talked with the duty sergeant and he informs me that the officers concerned are not on duty till later on today, but he says if you would be good enough to make a statement now then he can have an officer take it down. This would save us from having to make another visit to your residence or you having to come back here."

"Sure, let's go to it," I replied.

The civilian officer again disappeared to be replaced in a short order by a non-civilian officer, a fresh-faced policeman of middle age, the three silver stripes on his right arm denoting his rank. He conducted me out of the door across the well-lit entrance atrium to a drab interview room.

After the statutory legal preamble, he asked me to give my statement, a true account of the facts of the matter of the incident that had occurred at the etc, etc. I related to him the approved version of events as agreed with Billy and our 'star witness', his taxi-owning mate. I told of my trip and the heavy fall I had suffered when leaving the Oxford Bar and thus my presence for treatment at the Royal Infirmary. I went on to explain how I had abandoned the whole project in the aftermath of the chaos following the attempted drugs robbery.

The statement-taker nodded knowingly and confirmed that it had been 'a hell of a night' and that literally dozens of officers had attended the scene. Conveniently enough my facial bruises and my slightly limping gait acquired in my brushes with danger the previous evening added verisimilitude to my tale. This to the extent that the sergeant vouchsafed the personal thought that I looked as though I had had a heavy fall and added that it looked to him to have been a painful affair. I said that it had indeed been somewhat sore, but on the plus side nothing was broken, and I was beginning to improve slowly. I added the obligatory remark that I had not even had a lot to drink, just a couple of pints, and we parted. He was apparently satisfied with the truth of my version of events borne out by my scars and bruises and I was satisfied in a lie well told and the thought of no repeat performance with my dear mama.

I left the police station, crossed St Leonard's Street looking, as Billy had cautioned, carefully both ways, then cut along Rankeillor Street across Clerk Street, and along Melville Drive. I then cut across Bruntisfield Links with its free pitch and putt course; the land granted to the city in perpetuity by the last Scottish-only Monarch James II and I or as he was known in the land of his birth, Jamie the Saxt.

Then I skirted what had been Edinburgh's women's only hospital, our very own Garret-Anderson. To ensure no London metropolitan one-upmanship, or maybe more appropriately one-upwomanship, this city's clinic also sported a double-barrelled title Jex-Blake. In addition, the similarity did not end there as both founders had been southern English, both with suffragette inclinations and both female medical pioneers. This infirmary is however, now tastefully converted into upmarket flats. Ostensibly it would seem that here at least, women to women medical treatment had been consigned to the 'medical waste only' bin of history.

I then walked through the incredibly neat streets of the exclusive Grange district, emerging at Holy Corner. I strolled over the hill, and on reaching the main door to my flat, with what had become an almost automatic reaction, I looked over my shoulder before entering the common stair. I surmounted the internal staircase then, with some little difficulty, I succeeded in opening the door and entered the flat.

I shouted a hullo into the void, but all was quiet, all was silent, as silent it occurred to me, as the proverbial grave.

I looked at my watch and suddenly felt extremely weary so I decided that what was called for was a lie down and possibly a short nap. I walked along the darkened hall and into my bedroom, taking off my outer clothes. Before slipping under the duvet I set the portable alarm clock in its green morocco leather case, which lay on the bedside table, for seven o'clock. I laid my aching head on the pillow and drifted swiftly away into a pain-free land of nod.

In the end I had no need of the alarm as I was suddenly roused from slumber by the strange and disturbing feeling that someone was in the room. I surfaced almost unwillingly from sleep and as I opened my eyes I was almightily relieved to find the intruder was not a sinister assassin intent on finishing an incomplete job, but my mother.

Such was the suddenness of my awakening that I seemed to have startled her. She took an involuntary step back with something resembling fear in her eyes. As I sat up the duvet slipped down and as she looked at my naked upper torso with disbelief she put her hand to her mouth smothering a gasp.

Her face showed the dichotomy in which she found herself. On the one hand revulsion at the injuries and on the other her desire to comfort her injured child but maternal instinct won out. Recovering herself she moved to the bedside and sat down. She spoke in a voice, which for her, was as near to tears as she would ever allow herself to come, "Oh Alexander, Alexander good God boy, what on earth have you been doing? How on earth did this happen to you?"

Then with a look as if the thought appalled her, a gradual realisation began to form and crystallize and my mother continued more tentatively,

"Were you like this last night, when, I mean, were you like this, well when I was…"

"When you insisted on berating me and treating me like a sh…"

I broke off perhaps that was not quite fair, as she replied, "Well how was I to know? You didn't tell me, you gave me no warning."

She had a point but I still had some residual disgruntlement,

"You never gave me a blooming chance. You treated me like something the cat had dragged in. Yes mother dear, you are absolutely right, I failed to pre-warn you. But much as it pains me, to be fair you had had a shock. I thought the last thing you needed was another knock on the door and it's the police again, with God knows what tidings. You've had your fair share of bad news recently, and well, it was dark and you weren't to know and so I decided to keep the injuries to myself."

My mother looked sympathetic, shaking her head she said,

"Oh dear, dear, Alexander sometimes you can be just the same as your dear father."

"Stubborn," I interjected.

"No, not that, what I had in mind was considerate and, well sometimes understanding actually," she replied with just a tinge of sadness in her voice.

"So what is this all about? How earth did you manage to get yourself into that state? I'll bet that Billy's at the bottom of it somewhere. He was always trouble that boy. I never knew why you took up with him. Your father never liked him."

I flatly refused to rise to that bait, so instead I decided that I would explain how I had been reluctantly drawn into this affair and how I had unknowingly placed myself in a position of danger. I also told how Billy -that 'boy that was always in trouble' – came timeously to my rescue and went on to summarize my investigations so far. I made light of the dangers; too much nitty gritty and too much gory detail was, I felt, something I could spare her. When I finished what I thought had been a masterpiece of precis' she, completely ignoring my single-handed crusade for justice, said in an off-hand, matter of fact way,

"So why not leave it to the police? Alexander they after all, are the ones that are trained and equipped to deal with this matter, let alone being very well paid on top to do it."

Her reply I must admit almost took me aback, but I managed to retort,

"Yes mother, it as you say, but can't you see, until I became involved nothing had happened at all. There was no investigation, the police were not doing what they had, apparently according to you, been trained to do and, equipped to do, and on top, paid to do. The enquiry had run out of steam, the whole thing was like a clockwork toy that had run down and no one can find the key to rewind the damn thing. The boys in blue were only too happy to let their so-called investigations, unlike my father, die a natural death."

My words or perhaps the force of their delivery seemed to have hit home. Even so, her agreement was reluctant, "Oh I don't know Alexander, I just don't know. Maybe just maybe you could be right. I suppose. Just it's I..."

She hesitated and momentarily she looked as though she might just lose control of her emotions, but such a loss of command, she would view as being a serious lapse of taste. She steeled herself and the feeling seemed to pass. She mastered her emotions and went on,

"It's just that I don't want; well, to lose both of you."

With that said she sniffed and turned her head away, "Mother you have my solemn promise that I will try my damndest to stay in one piece. I know I have asked you this often previously but before it all happened, previous to the murder, and I know this is old ground but, is there anything you can remember? That is anything at all, anything father might have said, might have hinted at, or even might have let slip. To be truthful I'm at the stage that, well, well, I'm prepared to grasp at straws."

She appeared to consider the matter before speaking, "No nothing, not a thing. Like father, like son; he was as you – as discreet as the grave – and as unforthcoming about his clients affairs. So I'm sorry, as before, I can recall nothing amiss, no dark secret, I have, I believe the expression is, no fresh leads, no new lines of enquiry, for you to follow."

She touched my arm gently in a gesture of compassion, and rose from the bed. Before straightening she leant forward and allowed her lips to touch my brow, not so much a kiss more of a gentle peck. Her maternal duties discharged she moved away and made to leave the room, however, she paused in the doorway, turned round and looked back at me. She took a couple of steps back into the room,

"Do you know Alexander I have just this moment recalled there is one thing. I don't see it's important but, do you remember I told you in the days before it all happened that your father was not quite himself. He seemed to be disturbed, worried almost obsessed with something? It's just come back to me this minute that, well, something he said when I asked him about a phone call he had made one evening just before dinner. What sticks in my mind was that the whole thing was odd because as you know, like you he was not a man to bring affairs of the office into the home…"

She paused as if struggling to recall the exact memory.

"Yes, go on, a phone call you said," I urged, almost pleaded.

"I went into his study to tell him that dinner would be five minutes and I found him on the phone, and I realised by the sound of the conversation I heard that it was a business matter."

She paused again as though the remembrance was painful.

"You're absolutely right that was highly unusual, so to whom mother, to whom, was he speaking, do you know?"

Her gaze seemed to focus and she answered, "Yes, he was speaking to that Weldon man, the man that he was doing some work, for you know the one? You must have finalized it after…"

This opening a window on the past was not, I suddenly realised, an altogether easy matter for my mother. So I swiftly offered confirmation, "Yes, I know the one. Weldon's charity was the concern that father was doing a final audit and asset register for at the old Hospital for the Incurables. The building is the subject of a transfer agreement between his charity and the Health Board. Yes, I know who you mean."

She looked somehow relieved at my confirmation, and continued, "That's right, this Weldon character runs a Charitable Trust that's setting up the new hospice. Your father told me that the reason for the phone call was that something had been bothering him. That something he apparently felt couldn't wait; something he wanted to have clarified that night."

"Did he say what this something was that was bothering him?"

My mother shook her head empathically, "No, he was vague, as though he was lost in his own thoughts. When I asked him all he said was it was strange, and when I asked what was strange? He replied it was strange because he thought they should have been real."

Chapter 31
In Which I Keep an Appointment

With that, for a second time, my mother turned to go, but my next words caused her to again pause and turn back.

"So what I wonder *should have been real*? To the best of your recollection is that exactly what he said?"

My mother's expression had changed and her look was of someone who vaguely regretted saying anything at all. She regarded herself as someone who was now involved, now somehow complicit in the whole affair. The look of vagueness of regret was replaced again, with one of hesitancy as though she was stepping back from commitment.

"Mother for God's sake, this isn't some bloody childhood game we're playing. Please look at me; look at what my attempts to get to the truth of my father's death have cost me."

She made to turn her head away.

"No, damn you, take a good long look and remember that this was the best outcome from last night. This is not what, whoever is worried about me and what I might or might not have found out, had in mind for me. This believe me mother dear, was not his outcome of choice. If he had had his way you would be looking out your little black number. You know the one; it goes with your Victorian mourning brooch and your rope of pearls. Then you would have dear old Mrs. Watson put on more funeral hams and distribute the dry Amontillado to the mourners."

She looked at me, her face a mixture of imagined fear and repressed anger, "Alexander, do you know you can be so cruel at times, so cruel."

Then collecting herself she went on, heavily emphasizing her words, "What he said was exactly what I just told you. He said they should be real. He said he simply could not understand why on earth they were not."

The anger was gone, as a look of enlightenment flitted across her face

"No, no, wait minute, no, that's not quite right. What he actually said was it was not real and, when he checked none of the others were either."

She stopped as if summoning up some muse of recollection, to check her remembering was correct this time…

Then I interjected impatiently.

"And that was it, was that all he said, no other details you might have, well perhaps let slip your mind?"

Ominously her imperious look was retuning.

"No. That is all he said. After our conversation we both left his study. I went to the kitchen to check how the dinner was coming along and your father went to the drawing room to pour the drinks. After that we simply let the matter drop, just as I wish you would. Can I go now, have I your permission to withdraw? Is this interrogation over? Have you all the details you want? Can I now be excused?"

She pursed her lips in that way, that annoying way, in that God-how-it-pisses-me-off way, and without another word she left my bedroom.

"Let it drop, let it drop, mother for heaven's sake. Mother for heaven's bloody sake, how in the world would you suggest I let it drop?" I found myself shouting at my closed bedroom door. She had done it, she had won again. I checked the clock just in time to cancel the alarm. I raised myself from the bed a shade too quickly for my body's ease and well-being. I slumped painfully back onto the bed wincing at the waves of pain. I managed make most of my involuntary expletive, almost deleted. The nap had not been the best idea I had had that particular day.

I tried the manoeuvre again, this time more gently, more gingerly and having carried out a couple of tentative stretches. I again rose this time with a degree of success and made my stiff-legged way to the en suite.

An hour later I was showered, powdered, dressed, in a marginally less painful state and in the back of a swift-black city-bound. Edinburgh is in some ways an oddity, as the city centre at night remains vibrant. It's a place where residences exist, cheek by jowl, with commerce; chic apartments side by side, with places of entertainment, eateries and hostelries. The city in the evening is not some business-opolis that lies quiet and still after banking hours. A time when the ledgers are closed, shut safe in the knowledge of accounts having been balanced.

Mind you, after the problems of 2008 a year not of just a Black Monday or equally Black Friday leading to in turn a whole black week or month or year or two. This was the year of the Big Bang for the Bank of Scotland and the RBS et al, the year when Sir Fred the Shred became plain Fred. The year when the myth of Scot's thrift and prudence had been shown to be exactly that, incidentally that's exactly what rest of the world had already suspected. Perhaps this was a case of the ledgers being closed but the accounts not being balanced.

"Madogs mate," the voice of the taxi driver almost barked at me. I thanked him, paid him off, alighted with some difficulty, and descended the steps to this fine example of Edinburgh's many and varied watering holes

The bar was reasonably full for the time of night, but I had no difficulty picking, or a better word might be shuffling, my way to the bar. Before ordering I glanced around me and picked out Charles. He was sitting at a corner table accompanied by the gorgeous long-limbed, well-bred Camilla. He gestured me over,

"Alexander, what brings you here old man?"

"Oh, I just fancied coming uptown for a spot of dinner. I am not flavour of the week with my mother so I thought I might try one of the Italian's in Hanover Street."

Restaurants in Edinburgh have a tendency, for whatever reason, to favour the cluster effect, so with eateries where there was one, in time there would be many. Perhaps restaurants, like people, suffered from loneliness.

"So I thought this would be the perfect place to pop in for a couple of drinks first."

First contact made, first lie told, all according to plan.

"Well it's good to see you my boy. You remember Camilla off course."

"Oh, indeed, once seen never forgotten. Good evening Camilla. I hope you are well?"

In response to my enquiry she smiled, she smiled very prettily indeed.

Charles gestured to an empty chair at his table,

"Take a seat old man; you look like you could do with one. You look as though you have been in the wars. What would you like to drink a pint is it, of some sort of exotic lager?"

I nodded my acceptance of his offer, "Yup, okay, one effervescing pint of Hoffmeister-spandanbrau type thing coming right up."

I took the indicated seat and as I did so, Camilla cautiously turned her carefully made-up face towards me. She favoured me with a dazzling smile. Whilst I examined her expression, I noted that her look changed, to one of concern.

"My heavens Sandy, Charles is absolutely right you do look as though you do look as though you have been in the wars. Oh you poor thing, does it hurt?"

Poor thing, does it hurt, indeed I thought. It's all thanks to you and your intelligence gathering activities, you treacherous bitch. But I bit back the retort and left it parked fully formed in the back of my mind settling for a less vituperative response, "Do you know Camilla…?"

Before I could finish she broke in, "Oh, Cammy please, everyone calls me that, I told you, remember?"

Before I could continue Charles returned, a foaming pint in hand. She turned her attention to my returning friend,

"Charlie I was just saying to Sandy, as you did, he really does looks as though he has been in the wars don't you think darling?"

So it's Charlie is it, and it's darling is it…?

"And I was about to say to Cammy…"

As Charles placed my pint down on the table he flashed me a worried look as though he feared that I was about to abandon our pre-ordained plan, as if, suddenly, I had forgotten our lunchtime plotting session.

I smiled back at him in what I hoped was a reassuring way and said, "And I was about to say to Cammy…"

I paused to emphasise the use of the diminutive,

"To Cammy that, 'you do look as though you have been in the wars' is what everyone says; I just long for another expression of condolence."

Charles face betrayed his look of relief, and he went on in a voice heavy with bonhomie, "You mean you'd prefer something such as, 'you look as though you have been dragged through a hedge backwards', that sort of thing?"

"You have it Charles, although actually, I was thinking more along the lines, of a snappy retort something like 'you should see the other chap.'"

This elicited a braying laugh from Camilla. She had obviously never heard this expression before, evidently not a type of joke that circulates in her more elite circles.

"So Sandy, tell me how does the other fellow look then?" Cammy enquired curiously.

"Oh, he's perfect, not a scratch on him, I was the one that lost."

This caused renewed mirth signalled by a repeat of the jarring noise of her laughter. This was followed by the inevitable question,

"But what really happened to you?"

"I was almost involved in a road traffic accident, unfortunately in avoiding it I seemed to have caused a lot of wear and tear to various parts of my anatomy."

She looked suitably shocked and appalled, but repeated, "Oh you poor thing."

I sipped my pint and smiled graciously, but then in a bid to get our meeting back on track I decided to move the conversation along, "Do you know, come to think of it, it's perhaps fortuitous that I ran into you? I have been meaning to phone you to make an appointment to see your boss?"

Second lie told, all according to plan.

"You mean Hugh?" a smiling Cammy asked.

"Yes that's the fellow. I could really do with a face-to-face with him."

Although the vacuous smile lingered, it looked as though it was a façade, behind which, mentally she had 'come on guard.'

"About anything…"

She allowed her voice to fade away slightly presumably for effect.

"Anything important, anything urgent that is?" she queried.

"Well that depends on how you define important. Put it this way it certainly is to me. I have just one or two matters that I think that the Chairman of Trustees should be made aware of."

Third lie told, all according to plan,

Camilla frowned and then offered, "But Hugh isn't the Chairman of the Trustees, for that matter he is not even a trustee."

I clearly showed a puzzled, to say nothing of a dumfounded, expression.

Because she continued, "Oh I am sorry you didn't know, well, of course judging by your expression you obviously didn't know."

She was enjoying this. Third lie told, but not all according to plan, but I pressed on, "I thought it was called the Hugh Weldon Hospice Trust?"

Cammy smiled again almost pityingly. "No, it's his mother who runs the whole thing. She is the sole trustee and it's her charity. Well to be more accurate it's her late husband who set it up, he was Hugh Weldon thus the name of the charity. She took it over early in her widowhood. Her son Hughie baby merely runs the office and the day to day affairs. To be brutally honest he is just, well, he is no more than a glorified but well paid office boy."

Although she could not possibly discern it, this news began to raise the clouds of uncertainty and confusion from my mind. At last, at long bloody last I could begin to see what this whole thing might be about. Mind you although I could see the why I could not as yet see the what or more importantly, most importantly, the who. That said, third lie told, and all was according to plan after all. I was aware that she was still speaking.

"When I say he runs things on a day to day basis, he only does so for trivial, unimportant things, because mummy, the widow Weldon, Adeline by name, would you believe, is a control freak. Not only that but Adeline, mummy dear has a boyfriend. When I say boyfriend, I mean exactly that, he is at least twenty-five years younger than her; he is called Richard Amiss, known to the staff by the name of Tricky Dickey. Adeline met him when she was on a holiday in Venice. He was the holiday rep for the company she was travelling with, but now he has hit the big time. His lover appointed him as a non-executive Administrative Director of the Weldon Trust, with a company credit card, and a Range Rover. Any decision other than buying the paper clips or balancing the petty cash falls strictly within the lovely Richard's' domain."

Enter another suspect stage right; I thought. In an attempt at clarification I responded,

"But Hugh, he is still the front man I mean the person who I should speak to initially. When you're back in the office on Monday, could you perhaps arrange an appointment for me? If you could then give me a buzz at the office, my number should be in your copydex."

She nodded her head but looked mystified.

"Sorry, by copydex I meant your contacts file."

I corrected forgetting momentarily that copydex were things of the past. Although, in my own case the recent past.

"Yes, Hugh I suppose he is your first port of call. If you want to get to Richard, to lover boy, the easiest way is through Hugh. Mind you Sandy, it will have to be early on in the week as he is leaving mid-week to take an early holiday."

"A Spring break; is he going somewhere nice, somewhere in the sun perhaps?"

"No, he's motoring down south, down to Dumfries. He is booked on a ferry."

"Catching a ferry, from where?"

Cammy thought for a moment, and then answered with what was more of a question than a statement, "Not sure could it be Cairnryan?"

So I responded hopefully helpfully, with a question of my own, "Is he perchance sailing to Ireland?"

"Yes, that's right I think he mentioned he intended going to some sort of folk festival."

"Attending a folk festival in Ireland?"

A question posed more to myself than to Cammy, mindful that I had begun to sound like some sort of human auto prompt. Nevertheless, she gave a confirmatory reply, "Correct, it's some sort of new age hippy celebration of the summer solstices. He showed me it on the internet, it's held in a place called Glendalough, that's in County Wicklow, in the Mountain National Park."

Chapter 32
In Which Things Become Much Clearer

"Glendalough in County Wicklow," I murmured, again more to myself than to the others.

"Well, well 'das wildvogel' the wild birds, the wild birds are gathering."

"Pardon, Sandy what was that you said?" enquired Charles, interrupting my thoughts.

"Oh nothing, nothing my old friend just talking to myself."

I took a long draught from my glass and replaced it on the table, then enquired,

"Can I get either of you another perhaps?" I asked, of them both, it was Cammy however, who replied,

"No, thanks all the same but I think it's time we made a move don't you Charles. We don't want to be late for Roy and Fiona, you know how edgy she becomes if people are late for one of her dinners."

Judging by Charles's expression he apparently didn't or perhaps, he simply just did not care.

As if to underline the urgency of their departure she arose and set about straightening her dress, whilst endeavouring to put a full stop to our conversation, "Sandy, I'll give you a ring on Monday morning as soon as I can tie Hughie down to a time and place for you to have a meeting. In the meantime, I do hope you enjoy your Italian meal."

I said I hoped that I would, and with that she moved to the door.

Charles caught in a state of indecision by the abruptness of their departure seemed to be unsure of his best course of action and paused to enquiry almost in a whisper,

"Hope you obtained the information you wanted. From what I heard I just can't see how this gets you any nearer a solution. Are you still positive that Cammy is involved in this in some way or other?"

I looked up at him from where I sat, and I saw clearly in his face the signs of his indecision. He turned his head towards the door on being summoned to 'hurry up' by his dinner date, but his vacillation was still evident. So in attempt at reassurance I replied in the same conspiratorial undertone, "You better go Charles your friend is growing impatient and, yes, I gleaned the information I needed, well at least part of it."

On receiving yet another exhortation from Cammy 'can we please go?' he made to move away but, delivered, a single word Parthian shot,

"And?"

To the unspoken part of his question I could give no reassurance, "Right up to her neck, sorry old chum, but she's in it, right up to her pretty neck."

Without further comment, Charles left in the wake of his by now, impatient to be gone, lover.

I drained my glass, went to the bar and ordered another one. Returning to my seat I set my pint down on the table, sat back and tried to sift through the things that Cammy had told me. Possibly more importantly the things she had left out. So, what I supposed we have here is an interesting case study of Hugh. Hugh the up till recently dutiful son, Hugh who thought himself the apple of his mother's eye, Hugh the heir apparent, Hugh who now found he had in effect been sidelined by a cuckoo in the nest, Richard. So I conjectured, as a result of this perceived slight, this alienation of his affections, Hugh thought to himself why not look around for a little sideline; a scheme to maybe make myself a bit of extra cash. Not just for the money but for one in the eye for mummy's lover boy. This he had no doubt would be a sweet revenge for his replacement in the bosom of his mother's affections. The only trouble was although I was damned sure he had found his lucrative little sideline, I still could just not work out what the hell it was.

I sat there for a while reviewing my options whilst the tide of early evening drinkers ebbed and flowed around me. Then, still undecided on my course of action, I checked my watch, finished the drink and left the bar. I climbed the stair and, regaining street level, I realised that my appetite had seemingly left me. I was still considering my options, which no longer included food, when I noted a cruising taxi with its 'for hire' sign illuminated. Purely on a whim I engaged it and told the driver to take me to Salisbury Place. That was street where Weldon's Hospice Trust was giving its final cosmetic touches to the old Incurables Hospital. This work was being undertaken in anticipation of a grand opening with attendant local worthies who always in their wake brought their own statutory collection of assorted hangers on. All the necessary pomp and ceremony followed by free-flowing wine and efficiently delivered canapés. Everything in fact, considered an essential precursor to any charitably funded medical clinic's inauguration before opening its doors to admit, across its expensive threshold, its first intake of unfortunates.

I paid the taxi off and with no plan in mind I approached the darkened building, and mounted the steps to the imposing front entrance doors. A quick movement of the door handle indicated that they were locked. Nothing ventured, nothing gained and having come this far I decided to have a look round. I spotted a small side window next to the door, moving close to the glass I peered into the gloomy interior beyond. As I stared I could just make out, somewhere in the inner recesses, a light. Believing that where there was light there was hope; well at least if not hope, a person, I gently knocked on the door. On receiving no answer I knocked again this time a little louder and then as I glanced though my 'window on the interior' I saw a flickering light appear, moving towards me. As I continued to look I made out a figure emerging from the interior which, as it came closer, firmed into a stooped grey-haired man carrying a torch.

Approaching the window he eyed me quizzically. I signalled to him to wait then I took my card case from an internal pocket and selecting one I placed it flat against the window pane for him to read. He shone his torch at the written legend which he inspected closely regarding it through thick-lensed glasses. Seemingly reassured by what he read he opened the door and enquired as to how he could help. I explained who I was and that my late father had been working here prior his unfortunate and tragic demise.

"Gray, of course I place the name now sir," he said. "Your father would sometimes work here late on. On these occasions I used to nip out to the café across the road to buy him a coffee."

Then he added almost as an afterthought. Evidently not wishing to be seen as speaking ill of the dead,

"He bought one for me as well, of course. Considerate like that, your late father, he was a proper gent."

A proper gent; how much the old man would have liked that description, a proper gent, yes that was my father.

"Yes, that was my dad. I was just well... I was passing and I... just wanted to have a look and see how things had turned out, purely out of interest, well... to be truthful that and a bit of nosiness."

"Oh I see sir, just out of interest."

His words were delivered with what I thought was a strange look, I took me a while to catch on, but then I realised the look was not as much a strange one as rather one of barely restrained anticipation. I gave my watch an almost theatrical look and enquired,

"Is that the time, right yes I would love a coffee – that would be great. I take mine black no sugar, and please of course, have a cup yourself."

He nodded his acquiescence with some unsuppressed enthusiasm, but with some exaggerated hesitation, he moved towards the doors.

"Wait. Let me give you some cash," I offered, signalling that I had received the message loud and clear.

"They do nice toasties there as well, they have a full selection."

There was an almost pleading tone in his voice. Here was man who had no intention of looking a gift horse in the mouth or, for that matter looking in any other orifice either.

"Do you know that sounds just the thing, maybe a ham and cheese or ham and tomato, something like that would do the job? Naturally feel free to join me, if you would care to?"

He eagerly nodded his assent. I supplied a twenty pound note and after pausing to put the entrance hall lights on he was gone. He disappeared with all the appearance of a man on a mission; a man who would brook no interference with the task in hand. Here was a perfect example of the hunter-gatherer in action.

Left to my own devices I looked around me and then, like a moth to the light drawn, I strolled towards the partially-lit interior. Ahead of me lay a heavy, tall door standing partly ajar, through which a subdued light was leaking. I pushed it open and found myself in a grand high-ceilinged chamber. It had suspended from the ceiling an ornate partially light chandelier, from whose rays I could just make out an elaborately corniced ceiling leading down to dark oak wood panelling. Above the wainscoting, on the walls to the left and right, hanging from the picture rail were black lacquered boards mounted in heavy gilded, highly decorated ornate frames. The en-framed panels bore, written in the sign-painters' best gold leaf copperplate, the names and the amount of the donations of the munificent and open-handed late Victorian patrons whose generous donations built this Edinburgh Hospital for the Incurables.

Perhaps all this altruistic giving was not as selfless as at first sight it may seem. I could not help but think that there might just be a hidden agenda to this philanthropy. Were these patrons perhaps hoping that by the very act of their charitable generosity, an all-seeing, all-merciful omnipotent God, would in lieu of these emoluments freely given, excuse their giver's the misfortune of having to use this splendid institution they had so nobly endowed.

I allowed my gaze to move around the room where it was drawn by a large oil painting hanging above an enormous marble fireplace. This was a splendid ornate object which, by modern taste, was outrageously over the top, with its heavy intricate carvings and its blue and white Doulton Dutch-style tiles complete with, in the grate, a superb pair of wrought iron fire dogs.

The portrait was a masterpiece of the painter's art and from this distance it looked unmistakably to be the work of the court painter to George III, Sir Allan Ramsay, or at the very least a product of his studio. The subject of the picture was the likeness of an extremely earnest, po-faced and seriously rotund clerical gent with a snowy white Geneva band; so snowy and pristine did it look that it might have been fresh out of the band box.

My artistic musings and wonderings were interrupted by the return of my new friend, complete with, as promised, two large containers of steaming coffee and two paper bags, presumably containing the promised tasty toasties.

"Oh, there you are. This was the Trustees Board Room – they meet once a month apparently, to go over the accounts – it's very grand isn't it? Come to think of it, do you know that's just where I once saw your father standing, in the same spot as you were, looking up at the picture the same one as you were."

"Really? Do you mean the one that's hanging above the fireplace?"

"Yes, that's the one and that was just shortly before his death; that was oh, I suppose it must have been the week before."

My interest sharpened.

"And did he say anything about the painting; did he say why he was interested?"

"Well not as such, not in so many words, he asked me for a ladder so he could look at it more closely."

He paused in a way that was obviously meant for me to prompt him; to continue presumably he wanted to generate some climax. So I duly obliged, "And did you?"

Succinct but apparently sufficient, as he looked at me in what he apparently considered was a more conspiratorial manner and went on in a tone of voice to match, "Indeed I did. I gave him the big extension job and he clambered up like a good 'un regardless of his age. He was up there hardly any time at all, just a couple of minutes or so, and then when he came back down he was smiling."

My new friend was obviously enjoying telling his tale; this he clearly regarded was his fifteen minutes of fame. Why not indulge him I thought, and gave him the unasked for prompt, "So, he was smiling. When he came back down did he express any opinion did he say anything, anything at all, to go with or perhaps explain the smile?"

This question brought a look of satisfaction to my narrator's face, "He said to me 'do you know Colin' – that's my name sir – he said 'Colin it's just as I suspected all along. It's really good to know that one's judgment sometimes is right.'"

Colin now looked as they he had reached, if not his journey's, at least his story's end. But I, as the tiring boxer who felt one more punch might do it, tried one more time. I tried for that vital clue, which might make the whole thing clear.

"So, that was it, he did not say anything else; he didn't explain what his judgment was right about?"

"No, he just patted me on the back, and gave me a fiver. I put the ladders away then I went and brought the coffees as usual. Are you ready for yours now?"

He thrust a cup and a package towards me.

I took the proffered food and drink, Colin signalled me to follow him back out of the council chamber. He led me into the hall, but not back towards the interior from which he had emerged, but in the direction of the front door. I began to think of him as some grand high Victorian patriarch addressing a fallen woman servant, was going to ask me to leave and tell me never to darken his door step again.

However, just as we were about to exit to the greater, outer world beyond, he took a sharp right and I dutifully followed. He led me behind an ornate marbled Ionic pillar where there was a concealed door. When opened, I saw that it led to a cast iron spiral staircase leading upwards. Again I followed, albeit in my case encountering some little difficulty, navigating the corkscrewing steeply pitched stairs. Having with some little relief regained level going I found myself in a long poorly-lit passageway. Colin walked about half way down the corridor before he turned sharp left and entered through a wooden door that bore a sign, in gold lettering, which read "Porter's Lodge."

Immediately inside the door was an imposing ebonized hat and umbrella stand. Beyond it, and running the whole length of the wall, was an enormous green baize-covered board, furnished with brass hooks, here were hung numerous well-labelled keys. The collection included some of a vintage, of a bygone era, dark and large, others of a more modern time, shiny and compact. Above the key board, running along the roof were a series of wire cables, each cable separated and terminated on the top of one of a series of spring-mounted bells attached to a brown lacquered wood panel on the wall. Underneath each bell again in gold leaf lettering was the location of the ringer, descriptions such as "Matron's Office" "Senior Physician's Office" and the chilling legend "Morgue." This engendered lurid visions in my mind, probably brought about by watching too many Hammer Horror films in my misspent youth.

Whilst I had been orientating myself and fully taking in my new surroundings, Colin had seated himself at a long deal table around which were several bent-wood chairs. I pulled one up and joined him. He unwrapped his toastie, opened his coffee container and, pointing up at the summoning system of yesteryear he confided, "You see the real trouble with the bell system in this place was that there were so many bloody bells. If more than one rang at the same time it wasn't always easy to see which one it was who was wanting the poor old porters. Apparently they considered introducing one of those electric box systems, you know the ones. They had little windows where the call sign stays visible till it was cancelled by the caller, but by the time they made their mind up the modern world in the shape of the intercom had arrived."

Following Colin's example I unwrapped my toastie, de-lidded my coffee and, feeling it was somehow important to keep the dialogue flowing, stated my agreement, "Yes, I can see how it might just have been a little confusing. I suppose the staff of the time had some hierarchy of summoner some medical pecking order. I assume they answered whoever they considered the most important first."

"Oh, indeed. I used to know an elderly chap; he's passed over now, who worked here before the war. We both used to drink in a pub, in fact it's roughly the same vintage as this place; it's called Leslie's Bar just down the road from here, down Causewayside on the left. What he told me was that the person they always answered first was the Matron because the successive holders of that, then elevated post, apparently ran this place with a rod of iron."

For whatever reason, my mind strayed back into my Walter Mitty mode. This time however, not to thoughts of nights of the living dead, and Sir Christopher Lee somnambulating, portraying the mummy with a curse. More in my mind, was dear old Hattie Jacques, in heavily starched apron lusting after the ever-effete Kenneth Williams who was shouting, "Oh matron, do control yourself!"

I returned to the here and now and, opening my bag, I extracted my toastie which turned out to be ham and tomato. This I consumed, as did Colin, in companionable silence. Having finished my repast I took a sip of the coffee and, as it were drawing a bow at a venture I said, "Still got access to the ladder?"

Colin stopped mid-sip, "The ladder?" was the questioning reply.

"Yes, the extending one you allowed my father to use?"

"Well...yes."

The first word was noticeably attenuated, as if it had slowly dawned on the speaker that he realised where this was leading. With this realization came a smile and another enquiry, "I suppose you now want to borrow it as well?"

Well obviously, I thought, but said,

"Curiosity runs in the family: inquisitive father, inquisitive son."

Colin's look was that of a man, torn apparently between the possible consequences of being caught and that, the most innocent of human vices, simple but overwhelming curiosity. I felt that what was needed here was to discourage the former- the fear – and bolster the latter – the inquisitiveness. I reasoned that a little carrot dangling was what was called for,

"Colin, what if I was to say, make a small donation to the coffee fund, just a gesture you understand to compensate you for your trouble; to pay for your time."

I saw he was slithering, so time for the coupe de grâce,

"And, of course, if there is any trouble, I will take full responsibility. My company is after all the auditor of record for this project. It would be quite simple for me to make up some official reason for my visit, some cover story that would explain I am here in an official capacity."

I felt that now was the time to match words with action so as I spoke the last words I laid fifty pounds unostentatiously on the deal table. Before I could blink the money was gone and Colin was on his feet and making for the door. Evidently when correctly motivated he was a man of decision.

"Come on then, if it's a closer look you want a closer look is what you'll get. That much at least I'll help you do, let's be getting to it, shall we?"

Colin rose, went through the door and I followed him along the passage and back to the staircase. As I descended the stairs I was surprised to find the expectation of an important revelation seemed to have taken away my aches and pains. I was surprised to find myself almost springing down the cast iron steps. We reached the bottom and as we remerged into the entrance hall, Colin suggested,

"You go through to the old Council Chamber; the centre chandelier light control is the top switch immediately on the left of the door. I will join you there as soon as I find the ladder – I'll be with you in a jiffy."

I did as I was bidden and went back into the room, finding the light switch in the place I had been told. I flicked it down, filling the room with a harsh light. True to his word Colin arrived with the promised extension ladder neatly balanced on his shoulder. He placed it on the ground near the wall; putting his foot on the bottom rung he disengaged the whole folded additional section. He then raised the second set of rungs and pushed them up until the ladder reached its optimum height, at which point he set to engaging the locking mechanism. Colin, with a competence born of much usage, swung the whole erection clear and leant it against the wall just under the painting. He checked the assembled structure, by shaking it vigorously, then having assured himself that it was secure he turned to me,

"There you are Mr. Gray, up you go then I'll keep my foot on the bottom to stop it slipping."

Colin's last words came out more as a command than a request. So doing as I was bidden, I ascended. As I climbed it occurred to me, not for the first time, just how flimsy and wobbly these extending ladders are. There must surely be, I felt, what with our now almost omnipresent, to say nothing of omnipotent, Health and Safety culture, some sort of ban on these self-assembly means of ascent. Apart from anything else Colin had been a little cavalier about the whole thing, he hadn't even bothered to check whether I had been on the appropriate training course for using them.

Halfway up the second set of steps my eyes drew level with the bottom of an ornate gilt frame. In the centre of the frame's bottom edge was a gilt name plate with neat black lettering, it read 'the reverend James Wilson by Sir Allan Ramsay'. Underneath this description was an undecipherable date. I risked climbing up another few rungs and as my eyes drew level with the bottom of the canvas of the painting, I saw what my father had seen. I now knew what he had known, but unlike him I now knew, not only the why, I also knew the what.

Chapter 33
In Which I Review the Situation

Although the picture had been heavily lacquered to give it, at a distance, the appearance of age, close to you could see this was not an original work of art. This was a copy, probably a print on canvas, a fake, so this was the scam. Someone and Hugh Weldon the thwarted son seemed to be, as they say, the name in the frame, and had hit on a scheme to remove original works of art and replace them with artificially aged counterfeit copies. This was of course, to cover their disappearance from an inquisitive auditor completing the transfer of assets register; my late father. These original works of art had presumably either been purchased or donated to the infirmary, and left here by the former trustees. When this hospital was eventually absorbed into the National Health system these paintings had simply been disregarded as mere wall ornaments or mere dust gatherers.

Presumably no one from NHS – that great uncurious bureaucratic body – was sufficiently concerned about works of art, not at least when a well-funded charity had offered to relieve them of the burden of this now out of date old-fashioned hospital. They had simply jumped at the chance and handed the whole thing, lock, stock and barrel to the Weldon Trust.

The health service in its desire to cut costs and meet targets, had simply taken the decision to rid themselves of the responsibility for this the unglamorous side of medicine, with its associated horrendous staffing costs. In effect, they had simply cut and run. No doubt they were glad to dissociate themselves from this building, which in its way was a chilling reminder to the medical profession, as in its way it was a monument in fact to their failure.

However, enter our Hugh; a man on the lookout for a money raising scheme. He was the somebody in the Trust who had an eye to the main chance. He was the somebody in the Trust who had seen through the dust and grime and saw not just a collection of assorted old paintings but highly expensive works of art. The other question that came to mind of course was if he was the prime mover in this scheme was he in it alone, or did he have an accomplice. Someone on the lookout for his interest, someone for instance who worked closely with him, someone perhaps whose no doubt expensive background had included exposure to the finer things in life, including the works of celebrated painters, someone such as, Camilla. Come to think of it, it maybe not just paintings. There would have been other objects d'art given in lieu of cash, that the gold leafed recorded donations that surrounded me bore witness to. These products of the sculptor and painter's talent, donated to assuage the guilty conscience, or in memory of a loved one whose misfortune it had been to have been an inmate. This, no doubt in the relief felt, to someone else who had lifted the burden from their shoulders.

"You alright up there?" came Colin's voice, intruding on my ponderings.

"Yes thanks, fine. I'm just coming down but I'll be damned if I can see what dear father was getting so enervated about. Everything seems in order up here not a sign of what set the old boy off."

This I felt, was not the time for 'show and tell' and this was not a time of revelation. This was a time of hold your tongue, this was time of caution, a time of let's walk before we run, I counselled myself.

"Oh."

Was the only reply, delivered with an inflection of disappointment. Presumably his curiosity having been sufficiently roused, he was now seeking something more concrete, something more definite to ensure assuagement of aroused interest.

I descended the ladder and helped Colin drop and secure the upper section into the lower. Hoping to bring the matter to a close, and in preparation for making an orderly exit I said,

"Well thank you for all your help Colin, sorry we drew a blank. Mind you I suppose it was a long shot. Anyway, better be making tracks and many thanks for the coffee and food – it was great."

Colin smiled wanly, but he was evidently pleased at being acknowledged as the host with the most. Nevertheless, he seemed to be disappointed on my behalf so he said, apparently in an effort to console, "I'm really sorry you did not have more luck with your problem, particularly after all the trouble you have been to, and can I also say how sorry I am about your fathers passing."

Passing was obviously dear old Colin's favourite euphemism for death, but, acknowledging his obvious sincerity I responded with, "Me too. Discovering what the old boy had found might have helped a bit, but there you are. It wasn't to be. Though to be truthful, I think you went to more trouble than me, so thank you again for all your help."

Colin smiled in an almost sheepish manner, here was a man who evidently did like his efforts to be not only acknowledged but fulsomely praised.

"My pleasure, anytime. It's' been good to have met you."

As I made to leave I was suddenly struck by an afterthought,

"Oh Colin, just one other thing before I go, have you been the night watchman here for long?"

"No, I've only been here a couple of months. I got this job at about the same time as your father started his audit, that would be, oh, just about the time of the formal handover to the Weldon Trust. In fact it was the Trust that employed me."

"Right I see. Not so long then. What about during the day? Who looks after the premises then?"

Colin looked thoughtful.

"Well of course there are workmen coming and going during the day, painters, carpet fitters that sort of tradesman. There is also of course a foreman; he signs for deliveries, does time sheets, work allocation and keeps an eye on the subcontractors, but there is no actual security guard, as such."

Interesting, I thought and said, "What about you Colin? What hours do you work?"

"I do six at night till six in the morning, seven days a week," Colin replied.

"God, that's long hours. A twelve-hour shift is no joke, doesn't give you much time for a social life eh?"

He frowned.

"No, you're right, but it's a short term contract to cover the handover period, until the hospice is up and running. It's good money and I can afford to have the rest of the year off."

So there was method in his apparent madness. I went on, "Well if you put it like that, at least you have a goal in mind. Do the assorted tradespeople work normal hours?"

"Oh yes, they are here on site eight till five Monday to Thursday and eight till four on a Friday."

So there were convenient windows of opportunity at either end of the working day and at the weekends, for those with larceny in mind.

"Thanks, that's very interesting. One last question and I'll leave you alone. I don't suppose you know what the security arrangements were before your arrival?"

Colin's thoughtful look returned,

"From what I gathered they had one of these mobile operators, one of these companies that make visits at prearranged times of the night. I understand they have a sort of schedule of tariffs' and you can pick the frequency that would suit your needs best. The type of cover chosen would no doubt be dependant your budget. What you can afford, balanced against the value of what you have to guard."

How interesting I thought, if one had a mind to you could arrange your security visits round your burglarious requirements.

"But no static guard, no man on the spot, no Colin for that matter?"

"No not to the best of my knowledge, well not that I know of any way."

With that we shook hands in that solemn, almost ritualistic, way that men do and I took my leave of my new little helper, with less in the pocket but more in the motive bank than when I arrived. Progress was at last being made I thought. At last the darkness was lifting and the dawn, I hoped, was about to break and I hoped even more that it would not turn out to be a false dawn.

On leaving I turned right, remembering to look both ways as I headed for the well-lit area of Newington. At the end of the street I turned left, achieving Clerk Street and I walked towards the city centre. This is an area of town that is well-populated by students, thus it is well served with takeaways from many ethnic origins. It is also fully supplied with grocers formerly hailing mainly from the subcontinent, but joined in recent times by these of an eastern European origin, and of course pubs aplenty, of indigenous origin.

The day had left me drained and despite my afternoon nap, or perhaps because of it and its traumatic conclusion, I decided not to fight my tiredness but to give in and have an early night. I paused only long enough to use a hole in the wall machine to top up my funds which had suffered depletion from my donation to the coffee fund. Actually, now I thought about it, it occurred to me that I had also failed to receive a refund for my coffee and toastie purchase. One way or the other this was becoming an expensive night out. Spying a passing cab I hailed it and in a positive effort at cutting my losses I gave the cabbie directions straight back to the flat.

I exited the cab, again exercising the now well-rehearsed caution. I entered through the street door, surmounted the stairs and let myself into the flat. As I stood in the hall all was still but I could just discern a little light coming from under the door of the drawing room. I quietly moved to the partly opened door where I could hear the faint strains of some classical composer, but not at sufficient volume to make out whom.

I heard no greeting so assumed that my mother had nodded off in her chair. I followed that old adage, the one that advises you to let sleeping, possibly irascible, parents lie. I crossed to the dining room, flicked on the light and went to the silver drinks tray on the well-polished sideboard. I lifted an upturned a cut crystal tumbler and placed it down on the surface, then lifting and de-stoppering a matching decanter I poured myself a healthy measure of brandy. Healthy that is by my standards not healthy by the new 'have you counted the alcohol units in that drink, if not visit us on our drinks aware website', which can be found at health-freak-zealots-are-us.co.uk

I went back across the hall and entered my bedroom. Traversing the space I went to the drum table that sits in the bay window. I sampled the brandy and let the velvety warmth trickle down my throat, putting the glass down on the leather surface I leant across the table and drew the heavy brocade curtains. With my free hand, and at the same time, I located the control on the table lamp and depressed the rocker switch. The bulb lit up shedding a restrained corona of light enough to send the darkness to the coroners of the room, keeping the shadows at bay without dismissing them completely. The light provided was sufficient to illumine the table.

I shed my jacket, placing it on the back of the balloon-backed chair on which I sat down thoughtfully. Now it was time to marshal the facts, time to think about all that I had learned that night. Time to think of how exactly Hugh, and his possible partner in crime fitted in to the scheme of things. Time to work out how they had arranged to have the paintings copied, then how they had arranged to replace the originals with their so well produced fakes. Add to this, in all probability that they he had no doubt pulled a similar switch with other precious objects, sculptures or the odd good piece of furniture or two. Then as each substitution was complete an arranged vehicle arrives in one of the windows of opportunity and spirits the originals away and no one is any the bloody wiser.

Unless of course, you happened to be an elderly Chartered Accountant, with an eye for detail and a working knowledge of object d'art. Or you were someone who could distinguish between an original and a good copy; between figures cast in bronze and those cast in spelter. Unless of course that is, you happened to be my father. As I sat there I realised that for the first time since the funeral, that tears were forming behind my eyes and as I blinked to clear my blurring vision I could feel them gently running down my cheeks. God dad, god I miss you.

Scotland's favourite poet Robert Burns wrote a poem with, it has it be said not the snappiest of titles, called 'To a Mouse, on Turning Her Up in Her Nest with the Plough', but it does have an oft-quoted line 'The best laid plans of mice and men gang aft agley'. In this particular case, an extremely apposite quote as the plans went agley when the incurious Macbeth found and attempted to pass my father's notebook on to me. No wonder the perceptive action, no wonder he had to go. What was certain was that the list of suspects in the matter was not a long one. What was also certain was the full extent of the enterprise would not now perhaps ever come to light as the original schedules of assets, just as my father's carefully complied notes had by now, in all probability, been disposed of. No doubt consumed by an ever-cleansing fire or unceremoniously flushed down an ever-convenient toilet.

I now knew why, and I also now knew for what, my father's life and that of a, would be acquaintance had been cruelly taken. It amounted to nothing more than basest of human desires greed!

I sipped again at the brandy; the remaining pieces of the jigsaw were at last all falling into place. The cars, for instance, were removed by our travelling friend, that's why they had been stolen, not for joyriding. They had not been purloined on an impulse; they had bloodily well been stolen to order. They needed them to transport the goods from the hospital to the Park and Ride for onward transmission to the point of sale. No point risking their own vans. A big white van being loaded up in the middle of the night might just look a tad suspicious. Whereas the casually parked private car discreetly loaded would not be in any way remarkable.

With the works of art removed and the fakes in their place, this was the perfect crime because no one knew it had been committed. This was a felony that rang no alarm bells, because no one knew there was a reason to ring the damned things. This was an almost perfect crime and up till my father's snooping, a victimless one.

For heaven's sake, they even knew the security company's guards' schedule of timed visits; what a sweet set up they had. Then suddenly all this meticulous planning put at risk by the interference of an over-curious, interfering old man.

I felt again the tears pricking and welling behind my eyes, once more felt I felt them hotly coursing down my cheeks, but this time I somehow felt deep despair. I felt my feeling of loss and I heard myself shouting at the top of my voice, shouting into the void, shouting to anyone or no one.

"Oh for God's sake why didn't you tell someone why didn't you tell me, or even better why did you not leave well alone, you stupid, stupid stubborn…. Sadly-missed old man."

Chapter 34
In Which I Keep a Business Appointment

Three more top ups of France's best, eased away the aches and pains both physical and mental. However, before turning in I decided the advice of the thrice married Mary, Queen of Scots' which I felt might just suit my present situation, when she said, 'No more tears; I will think upon a revenge.' I then went to bed and to sleep resting and waiting for repose to come to me. I awoke late on Sunday to find the house as it had been the night before – still and quiet – but unlike last evening the house was also empty. The vacant house meant that mother had taken herself off to church, this was located at the bottom of Morningside Road in Nile Grove thus within easy walking distance.

There she would be singing hymns sacred to the Lord, in between making snide comments to her cronies on the attire of her fellow worshippers. In fact it was the same thing that happened every Sunday morning in various denominations all over Great Britain and, as far as I knew all over the world, all to the accompaniment of organ music played with varying degrees of competency.

I went to the kitchen, put two scoops of coffee and the requisite quantity of water in the electric percolator and set on. Whilst it made reassuring gurgley noises I toasted a couple of slices of bread. Sundays are usually an uneventful day in my life and this particular one was no different. I phoned Billy before lunch and brought him up to speed on what I had discovered last evening at the old hospital and my encounters of the first kind with Colin. After an almost taciturn lunch during which the conversation turned out to be as strained as the carrots, I escaped with the Sunday Telegraph to my room and stayed there until day became night.

As I struggled with last crossword clue (ten down), I heard movement in the hall just outside my bedroom door. I opened it to find my mother titivating her hair and examining her appearance in a looking glass which hung on the wall adjacent to my door. She glanced in my direction and gave me a stilted and somewhat hesitant 'goodbye' followed by the information that she would probably not be back till late. As she departed she reassured me that there was plenty to eat in the refrigerator if I wanted supper; it's supper on Sundays because of the late lunch, all other days it's dinner. A difference, a distinction, a detail not to be ever forgotten by my mother and one she obviously felt that needed constant reinforcement. I considered myself duly re-educated but as the evening played out, I spurned further food in favour of alcohol and an early night.

Monday morning found me at the office bright and early and waiting with some excitement. I felt a bit like a child who had been made a promise to be taken to the zoo. I sat at my desk almost anticipating the promised phone call from Camilla; The call she had promised to make on Saturday night with a time for an appointment to meet with her employer, her co-conspirator the deeply in the mire, Hugh.

At exactly ten o'clock the phone rang and I answered. The familiar voice on the other end said,

"I'm putting you through to Mr. Gray, now caller," then came a click.

"Alexander Gray speaking,"

Then an even more familiar voice, that of the lovely Camilla.

"Oh Sandy, how formal and businesslike you sound."

"Cammy, how good of you to call so promptly."

"You know me Sandy; I do like to keep a promise."

I was smiling as she went on, "Can you make two o'clock?"

I paused for effect, not wanting to show the eagerness that I felt. But there was no way I was going to put off this particular meeting. In attempt not to betray my keenness, I queried, "Two o'clock today, I take it?"

She concurred.

"That sounds fine thank you. It's a date. I'll see you then first thing this afternoon."

I replaced the receiver, happy in the knowledge that at last things were underway. A knock sounded on the door heralding the arrival of my morning coffee. I glanced up but the cup-bearer was not someone I knew.

"Where is Miss Wilson?" I enquired of my refreshment bringer.

"Oh, it's her mother.' She's' been taken ill so Miss Wilson won't be in today. My name is Rhona and I'm from the agency. Mr. Ingram phoned first thing to have someone to come in and help out."

Her mother's ill I thought. Well there's a surprise. I had never seen her as a dutiful daughter, in fact, I had never really thought of her as someone's offspring at all. If I had thought about it, it was more along the lines of an early example of cloning, sorry about that, Dolly, the sheep that is!

"Well thank you, erm, Rhona. Has anyone said how long she is expected to be way for, do you know?"

I must admit to feeling somewhat inadequate, bordering on the stupid, asking about a long time trusted employee's domestic situation from a recently engaged temp, but the thought of going over all the details with the pedantic Mr. Tommy Ingram, our revered cashier was far, far too much for me to cope with at this time in the morning. It was especially far too much for me to cope with at this time, on this morning, but my temp answered without equivocation.

"Mr. Ingram seems to think she might be off for a few days, possibly the whole week."

I made the expected conventional response, a series of 'oh dear noises' and thanked her; she placed the coffee minus I noted, the traditional accompaniment of biscuits, on the desk and departed. The rest of the seemingly endless morning I spent going over, or rather attempting to go over, a series of audit accounts and as the clock crept round to one o'clock I was surprised to find I was hungry. I phoned down to reception and asked if someone could go out to the local delicatessen and pick me up a sandwich for lunch.

When it arrived borne by Rhona, it turned out to be Pastrami on rye because that was the Monday special, had it been Tuesday it would have been Italian ham and red onion chutney on a panini', I was informed by my new temp. The things you learn when you trust your' catering arrangement to a relative stranger. Accompanied with a glass of fruit juice this constituted lunch, virtuous, by any standards I thought. Anxious not to be late for my meeting and with the bracket clock on my office mantelpiece showing one forty-five, and allowing myself fifteen minutes for the journey, I set off for The Weldon Charity Hospice offices.

I crossed Charlotte Square, looking both ways, and was down the basement stairs and through their front door by one fifty-five. As I entered Camilla was seated behind her desk and treated me to one of her radiant 'look at me aren't' I a stunner?' smiles.

"Sandy, prompt as I could have predicted. Just come through Hugh is expecting you."

She rose from her desk pausing only to pick up a smart card, then walked across the room to a door in the wall behind her. She swiped the card through a mechanism and the door released, she held it open and I went through. It turned out to be a connecting door leading to a short passage from which two further doors apparently opened. Cammy indicated with her hand,

"It's the one on the right. Hugh is expecting you, just go straight in."

I did as I was bidden but observed the courtesy of knocking on the highly varnished multi-panelled door before entering. The room was well lit as the ground falls sharply away at the rear of the properties built on the northern side of Charlotte Square. Thus what is basement level at the front is more like normal ground level at the back. Glorified office boy or not, Hugh's office was expensively and extensively furnished, he sat behind a well-polished flame mahogany Victorian partners desk complete with all the fittings, including a sliver double-well ink stand. There were discreet recessed art deco wall lights strategically placed around the walls which were hung with a set of hunting prints. Hugh looked up from that essential, must-have for the up and coming would-be executive, a top of the range laptop. A special toy that mummy had bought to make Hugh's playpen for grown-ups all the more pleasing.

He rose from behind his well-proportioned desk,

"Good afternoon, I don't think we have meet my name is Weldon; Hugh Weldon."

He came from behind the desk, and walked across the best Axminster towards me. He was, I guessed, in his early thirties and already running, or more accurately sprinting, to fat. He extended a flabby hand in a manner that made me question whether I was meant to shake it or kiss it. I plumped for the former and grasped the proffered limb in the approved manner and shook it. His grip was surprisingly firm.

"And good afternoon to you, my name is Gray, Sandy Gray, of Gray and Co. CA's I believe you met with my late father?"

He signalled to a circular rose wood conference table which stood in the corner of the room. As I moved in the direction indicated he answered,

"I have, yes indeed he came to visit me so that I could give him the instructions for the audit to compile the asset register he was carrying out for me, before I had the Trust sign off on our deal with the NHS. A sort of crossing the t's' and dotting the i's' exercise."

We both sat down at the large well-polished conference table. In the centre the statutory chased silver tray upon which sat a cut crystal water ewer, silver collared and a stylish thermos. Next to which was a crystal bowl similarly sliver collared with assorted sugar, sweeteners and sachets of whitener. In addition, there were cut crystal glasses and fine china cups and saucers; no signs of mummy cutting corners here. As I sat down Hugh enquired, "Can I offer you some coffee or perhaps a glass of water?"

"No thank you. I have just had my lunch."

"I will have one myself if you will excuse me."

Politeness itself, which I reciprocated by making an acquiescence motion with my hand and he poured himself a cup of black coffee. Then seemingly believing that bland is best he inquired, "Camilla tells me that you have a matter of some urgency you wish to discuss with me. She said that not only was the matter urgent but important, something she hinted that affects the running of the Trust."

He sipped cautiously as though wary of the temperature of the liquid.

"Camilla has briefed you correctly, Hugh. The matter I want to converse with you about is the content of my late father's phone call to you. The one he made last autumn, late last autumn."

He almost spluttered into his cup, as I went on, "To refresh your memory I believe that the conversation that he had with you was the conversation when he told you of his suspicions that someone was defrauding the Trust, someone was ripping you off '*big style*'."

As if to give him time to recover his sang-froid he slowly and deliberately put his cup back in the saucer and turned and bestowed a smiling countenance towards me. The impact of the initial shock having passed, he seemed to have regained some of his poise some of his equanimity. However, as he replied, the tentativeness in his voice betrayed his inner tension,

"A phone call from you father, late autumn last year did you say?"

He paused momentarily as if for effect, then he went casually or perhaps over casually,

"Do you know I really can't recall that at all, no, no definitely not? I think, as I said, the only time your father and I spoke was that first time for the briefing. I'm afraid someone has misinformed you old boy."

"Do you know Hugh; you don't mind me calling you Hugh do you? It's just as though, I feel that I know you."

He smiled and nodded his head, apparently well satisfied with a lie well told.

"Fine, well it's like this, there is something I would like to share with you Hugh, because you see in the last few days I have been through a lot and to be blunt, you don't mind me being blunt with you do you?"

I went on before he could reply, "You see I'm having trouble with my patience it's... well it's, shall we say, at a very low ebb. The fact is it's at a point where when I hear downright bloody lies, it's more than likely to drop to a point where it will not be able to stop me becoming, well, becoming shall we say a tad unpredictable. Do you understand me old boy?"

I sat up in my seat and fronted up to him across the table, "So Hugh I am going to ask you once again: my father spoke to you one evening late last year and told you of his suspicions that someone was defrauding your, or rather your mothers, charity do you remember that conversation. Does that ring a bell with you old boy?"

Hugh, god bless him, looked torn between lying and wondering what the immediate consequences of such mendacity might be.

"If it will help you to decide I loved my father so I'm prepared to go the extra mile for sake of his memory. I cared for him to the extent that I am willing to die to find his murderer and thus the natural corollary follows that is of course, I would be willing to kill to see justice done. That drastic action may of course not be necessary but it goes without saying that I'm prepared to kill and I'm prepared to break a few bones in pursuit of truth and justice. Do you understand where I am coming from old boy?"

I noticed his gaze flick to the desk as he looked round him for a way of escape, thinking its bulk between us might be a good thing. So when he made his move I was there before him. I was out of my seat and round the side of the table blocking his escape route, as he was rising out of his chair. As I advanced towards him, he almost cringed back into seat, the colour draining from his face.

"Okay, okay there's no need for rough stuff."

His tone was almost pleading.

"Well let's hear what you have to say and depending on the answers I hear will depend whether or not there we will be any of the rough stuff, old boy."

There was a thin bead of perspiration forming along his forehead. He nodded repeatedly and almost mechanically, much in the way that dog does in the insurance adverts. Then, as if the realization of his parlous situation dawned on him, he decided that the conciliatory route might be the path of least resistance. So he opted for an admission, "Right, yes I did speak to your late father. Yes, yes right he told me that he suspected, no, no that's not right, he told me he *knew* that certain works of art, valuable pieces had been substituted and that someone, a certain someone, was robbing the Trust blind."

He paused, as if the confession having run its course had not only been good for his soul but hopefully had been good for my temper. He looked at me as if I was some sort of father confessor about to give him four Hail Mary's and grant him full absolution.

"Go on and then what?"

He looked almost disappointed, no Hail Mary's, no absolution just a continuation of the inquisition, but went on,

"Well, I confided your father's suspicions to Richard – that is Richard Amiss – do you know who he is?"

I looked down at him, "Yes, I know not only who he is, but what he is, he's' the real muscle in this company. However, I'm reliably informed he's not so much the power behind your mother's throne, more the power between your mother's sheets."

He made to rise from his seat the colour rushing back to his cheeks, then with his fists tightly clenched he slammed them down on the table, rattling the expensive crockery. The anger within him flaring like a fire, catching and blazing.

I pushed him rudely back into his seat where I witnessed a genuine collapse of a genuine stout party. The rage flared briefly and as quickly as it rose, it fell. His face took on a haunted look; his head dropped, his chins touching his chest. Then as his tears started to, not just run, but flood down his fleshy cheeks he began to sob rhythmically and rock gently to and fro. I waited, not knowing quite what to do; I had come prepared for conflict and was faced with abject and total surrender. I felt hopeless and helpless. Suddenly the sobbing abated, and he almost blurted out.

"It all went wrong when mother met her oh so pretty toy boy. Before that, everything was fine; I had her and she had me, we had each other and we didn't need anybody else. We were happy. We made father's dream of a Trust a reality. We made his charity something to be proud of. We were helping the less fortunate, our hospices were allowing people to have dignity in death, and best of all, we were happy. Then that stupid old woman allowed this damned gigolo to turn her head. It's true you know there really is no fool, like an old fool."

As he finished the sentence, with a convulsion his chest heaved and the tears returned. Oh God in heaven, I really had been cast in the role of a father confessor and what I was hearing was bordering on incest, as dear old Sir Walter said 'oh what a tangled web we weave.' Then with a schoolboy snivel he continued his liturgy, "Then along comes bloody Prince Charming with his perfect tan, his perfect teeth and his perfect bloody manners, with not a hair out of place and the whole world is turned upside down. Would you believe he's young enough for her not only to be my mother, but his as well. Do you know he is even working on her? He wants mummy to ask me to go, to be fired, to be made to leave.

He wants me out of his life, out of his house, it's not his bloody house, it's my house, my family home and he wants me gone; he wants me to become some Stalinist non-person. This bastard, this bloody cuckoo in the nest wants to roll me like some poor unfortunate egg out of his nest."

The tears came again but this time like a weakening storm front, only briefly and waning, then with an effort of self-will he went on, "When I met with Richard, I told him the full extent of what your father had found out. I also told him it was my certain feeling that your father felt it was his duty to report his findings to the police. Richard said that I should do nothing; he would handle everything. *Sit tight,* he said, *sit tight Hugh, and Richard would make it all go away.*"

I felt my anger rising again as I spoke, "You do know that meeting where you so casually confided in your would-be new stepfather, was tantamount to signing my father's death warrant?"

Hugh's haunted look returned, and he stammered out, "You can't blame me. All I did was pass on the information, nothing more. For God's sake I have nothing to do with your father's death; I did nothing I tell you, nothing."

"No, that's right Hugh you did nothing. When immediate action was needed you did nothing. Do you know what, Hugh, old boy I do blame you even if it's for doing nothing. I hold you to account and I am rendering that account payable forthwith. I'm asking you to settle it now, do you understand, it needs to be settled this very minute. So where can I find this Richard?"

The haunted look remained as he disclosed, "Well the last I saw of him he was at the house with mummy, they were playing happy families: she Mrs. Gullible the Merry Widow and he Master Smoothie the con man's son."

I moved back from the table in a gesture of de-escalation,

"That being the case I think we should find where he is now. I personally want to know Richard's current whereabouts, and I want to know, like now. So why not pick up the phone and find out Master Smoothie's up-to-date location?"

He visibly seemed to give himself a shake; he had patently recovered some of his courage as when he spoke it was in a petulant tone, "Okay, alright, God what an impatient person you are."

I moved to one side to allow Hugh unimpeded access to his desk. He picked up the receiver and hit the speed dial. I could faintly hear the number ringing at the other end.

"Mother, good afternoon, can I speak to lover boy? No mother I will not be more polite about your toy boy. Where is Mr. Wonderful? Listen closely mother dearest this is a matter of some urgency; you see I'm with a man who, if he doesn't find out the whereabouts of your paramour within the next few minutes, is going to break both my arms. Which mother is just, I suspect, merely for starters!'"

The information I had just given Hugh had apparently lead him to consider that the tables were turning, which lead him in turn to have confidence to believe that he now held a stronger hand. The knowledge that lover boy had been well and truly rumbled and was about to land in the septic tank, had given a boost to his courage. Hugh was someone who believed that knowledge was power and that belief, obviously emboldened him. This was instanced by way he had just spoken to his mother. This was, I suspect, not in line with the recent manner of his filial conversation style.

"No mother, I am not exaggerating. I need to know and I need to know at this very moment or your baby boy's continued existence in one piece is looking less and less likely. My continued wholeness is now totally dependent on your answer."

He stopped apparent listening to his mother then he almost shouted down the phone, "Well, if he's' not there, where the hell is he mother? For God's sake, this is no bloody joke, I have told you this is serious and believe me and when I say serious I mean very, very serious."

He paused, seemingly awaiting a reply, then as none appeared to be forthcoming and as if overtaken by frustration, he seemed to have another thought, "The real problem here mother is, this doesn't concern only you and me. If this thing, this problem that Richard has involved us in gets out it could well, it could involve the good name of the Trust. The trouble with mud is, if you throw enough of it, some always sticks, it might be…"

He stopped abruptly. Even from where I was standing I could hear the reason why, for issuing from the earpiece of the phone was a banshee-like wailing. Obviously in extremis like mother like son.

"Calm down, mother will you please calm down. Just tell me where he is and I will come home right away. We can have a nice cup of tea and we can have a nice long chat, just like the old days, just you and me, and no nasty outsider no nasty man there, to come between us."

There was a pause as the bawling died back then he went on, "Yes, I have got that. Yes, and did he say when he was coming back? Oh, he was vague, was he? Yes, and I think I know the reason for the vagueness. No mother I shall be home within the hour. Relax, think good thoughts and I will be back before you know it. Of course, if that's what you want, of course I'll bring in a nice cake for us both."

He replaced the receiver slowly and thoughtfully and then turned to face me, his courage now ebbing back, "Well, it seems that after all, your visit has been a good thing for me. With any luck I might be able to draw down the curtain on this recent farrago of nonsense. You Sandy, despite your bad-tempered behaviour, would appear to have done me a good turn and since one deserves another, Tricky Dickey has bolted for it and has just left the house. Now that my dear mother knows that his departure is not of a temporary nature, as you may have heard, she has been left distraught, poor thing."

So, dear distraught mother was it now? What happened I wondered to the stupid old woman who had completely ruined his life? It never fails to amaze me how things can change in the mere beating of a heart.

"Lover boy has apparently left town to keep, what he said, was a business appointment. He left my mother's house about half an hour ago. He received a call on his mobile and she thinks she heard him mention something about a Kings Rock. Mothers told me she only heard a part of the conversation, as he walked out into the conservatory after he took the call. But she is sure, well almost sure she overheard him say something about Dumfries. Oh, and one other thing, she's certain she heard him mention a time, she says before he rung off he said he would be they would meet at 6 o'clock."

Chapter 35
In Which We Journey and Arrive

"King's Rock and Dumfries she said? Well I suppose it's something to go on, it's little enough, not much but better than nothing."

I took out my mobile only to find that here in this Georgian basement there was no signal.

"Can I borrow your phone Hugh?"

He made a nodding gesture with his head. Then taking the further away of his two phones he lifted the receiver and handed it to me.

"Use this one it's a direct line so no possibilities of inquisitive little ears eavesdropping on your conversation."

So saying, he turned the instrument towards me. I dialled Billy's; number like my own it was one of the very few I knew off by heart. It rang and then rang. Please, please be in Billy, please be in. It rang and rang and then a voice answered. It had a mechanical, metallic tone; it was of course the answer-phone. I was thinking about leaving a message when I heard his voice on the line.

"Hullo, who's this?"

"Billy, Billy thank God. It's me, Sandy."

"Sorry, I didn't recognise the number, so I was a little reluctant to pick up; I thought it might be one of these damned sales calls. But in the end simple old-fashioned curiosity got the better of me, come to think of it, it's as well I'm not a bloody cat. What can I do for you this fine afternoon, Alexander?"

I went on ignoring the usual pleasantries, "Billy, have you got your car with you today, sorry I mean is it handy, is it nearby?"

"Yes and yes, it's in the underground car park just round the corner from the office," he confirmed.

"That's great. Can you pick me up? I'm at the Weldon Trust Office on the north side of Charlotte Square?"

As I spoke I noticed Hugh frantically signalling to me, so I said,

"Hold on a moment Billy, give me a minute will you?"

I took the receiver from my ear,

"What is the problem Hugh?"

Hugh, put his fingers to his lips in the universal sign for silence, and with a speed that belied his bulk he moved to and flung open the door. He looked up the passage and seemingly satisfied that we were not being overheard he closed the door and moved back into the room, and said to me,

"I have found recently you can't be too careful in this place. If you are wishing to go out without a fuss and without being observed by…"

He pointed in the general direction of the reception area.

Catching on I replied, "Oh I see. Leaving without the knowledge of that treacherous little, but lovely, informer Camilla do you mean?"

"Exactly. I could not have put it better myself. So why not come with me and I will take you out the back way. Our car park backs onto St Colme Street just down there."

He motioned to the window of his office "I have never been sure of that made up bitch on reception since the day that Richard employed her. I've never trusted her as far as I could throw her. I've always suspected she was in this right up to her pretty little neck. But I have never been able to prove anything against either of them. She is the oh so charming, Mr. Amiss's special project, his hobby, a hobby incidentally that keeps him out of the house three nights a week. Without definite proof, I thought it best to say nothing to mother, in case she thought I was just acting out of jealousy. That and the feeling that if mummy knew it would have broken her heart, but now the whole thing is out in the open, I will simply have to be cruel to be kind."

He looked as though being cruel to be kind was right up his street. Poor old mummy I thought. Minus her young ardent lover, but plus her young pious son. I put the receiver back up to my ear, "Sorry about that Billy can you make that St Colme Street; yes, St Colme Street is the continuation of Queen Street, okay? Got it? Good, what, about fifteen minutes? Yes, that will be absolutely perfect."

I replaced the receiver.

"Thank you for that Hugh. So if you're ready shall we exit swiftly stage left, out the back door?"

He again nodded his agreement. We left the room, entered the passage and took the second door, the one which adjoined his office door. This entrance took us down a flight of steep steps, illuminated by a single wall light. When we reached the bottom he opened a substantial, heavy old-fashioned external door and we emerged into what must have been originally the garden and coach park of the property. The horses and the conveyances they pulled now being a distant memory, the area had been converted for use of horseless carriages. It was neatly tarmacked with clearly marked parking bays. We strolled companionably together stopping at a sliver-coloured Mini Cooper, almost as though we had been lifetime friends. Then, taking his car key from his pocket, he looked at me with an earnest expression and said almost resignedly, "Well this is mine, I'd better be off and see what I can salvage from the wreckage; see if I can save the happy home."

He held my gaze and went on, the resignation replaced by regret, "I was supposed to go away this week to Erin's green isle. A little holiday on my own, away from it all, off to Ireland to attend a folk festival. It's one of my few vices: a quiet pint of the black stuff, draught Guinness and a listening to few sentimental ballads. But... I don't suppose she'll let me get away now."

On the whole he seemed to be at ease or at least reconciled to his fate. I did think that this whole affair and Hugh's involvement or rather his non-involvement had, at least, given me back faith in coincidence.

"Do you know?" Hugh went on, "Do you know Sandy Gray; on balance I am happy to trade a Celtic away day for a return of the status quo?"

That somewhat rueful comment delivered, in the manner of the final words of a funerary address, he opened his car door and with a regretful sort of wave he drove away.

I walked to the bottom of the car park and exited onto the street. As I did so I glanced round and saw the disappearing taillights of the Mini vanishing to the west. As I watched, I heard a gentle toot; as Weldon left, Billy arrived. I bent down, opened the door and lowered myself into his car.

"Good afternoon; car for Gray. What's up, where's the fire?" was his cheery greeting, my response was less so.

"How much petrol do you have in the tank and do you have a decent up-to-date road map in the car?"

Billy looked at me with some curiosity and replied, "Oh and good afternoon to you, Billy, it's really good to see you and by the way many thank you's for coming to pick me up so promptly. The answers, incidentally, to your less-than-polite enquiries are, there is about a quarter of a tank and no, I don't. And if I'm allowed a question of my own?"

He paused then went on without waiting for a reply, "Why do you need to know the answers to these questions?"

I just had to smile,

"Sorry about the formalities unobserved. Good afternoon William. It's really good to see you and thank you very much for coming so quickly. The answer to your question is because as dear old Holmes would say 'The game's afoot' and you are the nearest thing I can have to a trusty Watson and you have the closest thing to a Hansom carriage."

"Well Sandy since you appear to be in an expansive mood would you mind telling me where the game is afoot?" he enquired.

"Dumfriesshire-ish, but I'm too not sure at this stage exactly where."

His curiosity was being replaced with doubt as he asked,

"Is this some sort of remake of Treasure Hunt? If so can I point out this is a car not a bloody helicopter. And you, my friend, are neither as agile nor as good looking as either Anneka or Annabel."

"And you Billy are no Kenneth Kendal. But yes, we are on a hunt and we are looking in a manner of speaking for treasure."

"Right, so what are your orders, Great One?"

"Let's start by making for Penicuik, there is a superstore on the main road where we can refuel and buy the desired map in the shop. By the way, we have to be where we have to be, by six, and if your dashboard clock is correct, it's gone half two already. So shall we?"

Billy nodded pressed the starter button and wheeled the car round and headed for Queen Street, the Mound and all points south. As we drove I filled Billy in on the salient details of my meeting with Hugh, his capitulation and confession, Richard's flight from justice, and dear mummy's recalled but scant details of a partly overheard conversation. He signalled his taking in of the information and then after a moment's thought he queried,

"Isn't it time you started to share all your little secrets with others?"

"What others had you in mind, Billy?"

"Well, there's these people, they wear black uniforms and hats with a chequered band and they chase crooks for a living. I don't know... someone such as the police perhaps."

I responded sharply,

"Contact the people that do it for a living! For God's sake, you are starting to sound like my damned mother. Added to which you, of all people, recommending that I go to your most un-favourite people – the police."

As I spoke we were stopped at a red light, which allowed Billy to take both hands off the steering wheel, turning to me he made the sign of a cross. Then he retorted with reasonableness, "No I think that's taking the whole thing too far! Sound like your mother indeed! You really know how to hurt a man. Well if not the police direct, what about via Charles and his copper friend?"

The lights changed so he engaged first gear and let in the clutch and we crossed out of Hanover Street and up the Mound. This street runs up a steep hill that was created by the dumping of two million cartloads of soil and stones excavated whilst digging out the foundations for the buildings, from the creation of the first Georgian New Town. All that intricate traffic flow planning, all those august learned bodies, and Edinburgh's main traffic artery north to south was built on a spoil heap. No wonder people treat so called town planners with some well-founded suspicions.

"Yes, point taken; you just could be right."

I took out my mobile, clicked on to the directory, scrolled down to the required number and pressed the green phone symbol. As I put it to my ear I heard Charles's drawling tones issuing a greeting,

"Charles hi, yup I'm feeling a bit better and thanks for Saturday's accidentally-on-purpose meeting. Look, I have something to tell you. Something, which you might feel you want to pass on to Samantha. Something that the police might be interested in. Something they might want to act on."

I paused, allowing the message to register then went on, "I don't want to do it myself as she might not approve of the action I'm about to take. For me this matter had a very personal start and I want it to have a very personal end."

Then as I spoke, Charles listened. I recalled the whole story, warts and all, pulling no punches. When I finished there was an almost ominous silence on the other end of the call.

"Are you still there? Charles, did you hear what I said? Look I'm sorry about Cammy and everything but I can't change the facts, I can't dress them up. I can only relate them to you."

Then as if with a great effort of self-will he said, "Yes, thank you I heard it all. You're right, I will be in touch with Sam and let her know the story so far. You will keep me posted and let me know when and if you have eventually worked where on earth you're going? Be careful, and Alexander one other thing, you might need help from someone."

Here we go again, another person giving me that same advice. This was becoming a bore, so I retorted somewhat resignedly, "Yes, Charles I know. Don't' tell me I might need help from someone who is employed to catch criminals, yes thank you, I have had that very suggestion made to me before."

"Right but just, well just go carefully, these people as you can well attest have not taken any prisoners so far."

I thanked him with a promise that full information would be shared with all, that is, when I had worked the dammed thing out. By the time I finished the call, we were rolling out of Edinburgh's suburbs and heading into the once small conurbation of Penicuik; a town now swollen by the ranks of Edinburgh commuters on the lookout, the hunt, for more reasonably priced housing. Tesco's appeared on our left and we drew into the store's related adjoining garage.

As we pulled up I said,

"You fill it up, I will settle up. When you're full give me a wave."

Billy nodded and we both exited the car, he to the shiny pump, me to what I hoped was a well-stocked shop. As I entered, I noticed between the chilled cabinet and the newspaper shelve there was a small display of publications which included a limited selection of road atlases.

From the restricted range I choose a hardback edition entitled 'The Truckers Guide' as it seemed the most comprehensive and seemed to provide the largest map area. The fact that, in addition it offered an exclusive guide to Britain's best greasy spoons did not in any way, affect my decision to select this particular volume. I also picked up a couple of bottles of chilled sparkling water and noticing Billy's exaggerated thumbs up sign, I moved to the desk and after assuring the pleasant girl behind the counter that I did not have a club card I paid for the petrol and the journey's necessities and re-joined Billy in the MGB.

He restarted the car and we were of down the John Street, and turning left along the Carlops Road, past the High School and in no time we were through Nine Mile Burn, a small hamlet, not a stretch of water. Soon we were progressing down a hill into the picturesque village of Carlops. As we pulled up the hill out of the village, as always, I was intrigued by the signpost that showed that if we cared to turn left we would be on the road to Lamancha. I was always left wondering if I'd ever meet a man that came from there?

However, putting the thoughts of Don Quixote, that comic gallant figure of Cervantes novel aside, I opened my recently purchased 'The Truckers Guide'. I consulted the opening page, which showed an illustration of Great Britain, the various map sections numbered and choose the Dumfriesshire section and looked at it for anything resembling Weldon's mother's recollection. Kings Rock, where are you, come to Daddy, come to Daddy. Billy decelerated as we entered the village of Dolphinton, a long straggling settlement built, somewhat oddly, on only one side of the road. As he changed down the gears he leant over and asked, "Making any progress there? Tell me what exactly are you looking for? You weren't less than definitive earlier."

"Billy, sorry old son, I'll try to be a bit more definitive. As I mentioned, dear Hugh's darling mama overheard a phone conversation that Richard took. To be more accurate she earwigged part of a conversation. But whatever it was about, it was sufficiently alarming to him to cause him to make a sharp exit immediately after."

"Yeah got you; I listened when you were bringing Charles up to date," he replied.

"Good, well according to the little she heard Richard is going to a meeting presumably with his confederates and the rendezvous is at, or at least she thinks what she heard is, it's at a place is called the Kings Rock."

"The Kings Rock, did you say? Um, no I can honestly say I have never heard of it in my entire puff. But as you know the things I don't know are legion. The Kings Rock, are you sure it's not something that, well sounds like *a* kings rock?"

With that thought he changed up and we were again on the open and somewhat twisty road and heading towards Abingdon and Carlisle. As he did so the import of what he had said sunk in, "Billy it's your turn to be less than definitive. What do you mean by *a* kings name? What difference does the indefinite article make?"

He swung the car into another bend and responded,

"No, no it's really anything to do with the indefinite article or for that matter the definite article, what I mean is, what if it's something along the lines of a monarch's name. Something such as, I don't know, a bit like Duncan's Rock or Kenneth's block or Charles's boulder or something like that."

"Right Billy, with you."

With that I re-examined the open page of my road atlas.

Then almost immediately I went on,

"Or perhaps, Bruce's Stone,"

Billy nodded as we decelerated on entry to yet another village, and agreed, "Yes, something like that."

I immediately responded,

"No, no I mean exactly that. There is a Bruce's Stone and it's located apparently, in a place called, would you believe, Clatteringshaws Forest?"

Billy changed down as we took a sharp bend leading to a narrow bridge, before enquiring, "Clatteringshaws Forest, can't say I've ever heard of it. Where on earth is it anyway? Are we on the right road?"

I re-consulted the map before replying, "Its North of Dumfries and yes we are on the right road. When we get through Abingdon turn off, and look for signs for Elvanfoot; follow them and we will take it from there."

Turning to me Billy grinned, "Well done Sherlock. Do you know I now really believe the game's afoot; I'll just whip up the horses, whilst you pass on the information to dear old Charles for onward transmission to the boys in blue? May I remind you that even Holmes needed a Lestrade or a Gregson on the odd occasion, even if was just to show off to. For us I think that this might just be our odd occasion."

He smiled and accelerated. I made the call as promised. Charles had his feelings now more under control. The affair with Camilla had obviously cut deep, perhaps for once in his life he was the one who thought, or perhaps hoped, that this was the real thing. As no doubt many of the women with whom he had affairs with in the past had thought or hoped, but for them, the wedding bells stubbornly refused to ring. As in the present case, these affairs had all had ended, with a final revelation, the reality of falsehood, and final abandonment and hurt.

He said that Sam had been issued a general warning to the Dumfriesshire local Bobbies. He added that she also advised in the strongest possible terms that I should observe absolute caution. I promised that I would exercise exactly that, and reminded him of the six o'clock deadline. He acknowledged my reassurances and rang off.

We tracked through Abingdon and took an exit from a roundabout that curved under the motorway at Elvanfoot. Here the landscape completely changed; gone were the leafy lanes down which we had travelled from Edinburgh, here we were in moorland sweeping away as far as the eye could see.

This was a landscape peopled, or rather animaled, by oddly incurious sheep, chewing the cud and gazing placidly as we drove carefully by. This cautious driving observed in response to hand-painted signs warning passing drivers to beware of the lambs. It has to be said these signs did not underestimate the possible danger, as a skittishly unpredictable lot of lambs they were.

Should you have read the book 'The Thirty-Nine Steps' by John Buchan rather than just having seen the cinema versions, then you would know this is the hero of that novel, Richard Hannay's, real territory. Not the highlands, as it is portrayed in the films, but this part of the smaller yet equally rugged lowlands. It was here in these hills and glens he was pursued by the lawful seekers of his custody- the police – and by the unlawful seekers of his custody – the members of a sinister organization known as the Black Stone. As the road curved we found ourselves at the top of what looked like a giant helter skelter, a precipitous theme park ride, the ground seeming to drop away. To the right of us sheer cliffs soared skywards whereas to the left the land simply fell away over an almost vertical drop down to a long glen lying in a hollow hundreds of feet beneath the wheels of the car. We descended the corkscrew-like road carefully, Billy having selected a low gear. As we took a particularly bad bend ahead there lay a waterfall, a cataract of water leaping from the craggy face of the cliff dropping some fifty feet splashing, foaming and frothing as it bounced and almost danced off the rugged surface.

"The Grey Mare's Tail' that's what the waterfall you are looking is called. Mr. Gray meet a female horse's rear hairy appendage."

I smiled and as I glanced back and down, I could see that at the head of the glen stood a substantial cottage surrounded by sheep-holding enclosures and assorted outbuildings. I said almost to myself, "Oh my God, what a damned awful, desolate place to live. Imagine what it must be like in bad weather, not just in the bleak midwinter, more in the bleak start, mid and finish winter."

"Ah, Sandy but what price for solitude and peace and quiet?" interjected a somewhat reflective Billy, to which I retorted,

"Ah, Billy but what price warmth and a convenient all day and all night opening supermarket round the corner?"

The scenery was now filled with the hills and the glens: the land like a massive green canvas unfolding in front of us, here was a landscape on the grand scale but uncannily, I noticed an entire absence of trees.

After some twenty odd minutes of the rural country we reached the reasonably large village of Thornhill. It was not till we were through it and on the other side, that I suddenly realised we were on the wrong road completely.

"Sorry Billy, old son, I'm afraid were on the wrong road. Can you turn her round and go back to Thornhill I seemed to have missed the turn off somewhere."

He grunted his vocal disapproval of my poor map reading skills, but then said that he would find a turning place. This he did when we turned the next corner as on the right there was a large roadside dump containing road grit, presumably for use on icy roads. However, at this time of the year it was seriously depleted thus affording us plenty of room to swing round and return in the direction from whence we had just come. Second time round we picked up the signs for the villages of Penpunt and Moniaive. As luck would have it at the very start of the village.

I nudged Billy, pointing at the road sign and, as we took the required turn, there sitting on a dry stone dyke that fringed the road was a fat, jovial-looking child, with a vacant expression, consuming a large ice cream cone. I mentioned this apparition to my companion, "There you go, you see, this *is* a proper rural community, they even seem to have a village idiot."

Billy nodded acknowledgement, "Do you know Sandy; sometimes you can be so cruel."

Obedient to my directions we found ourselves back on the correct road. I checked the dashboard clock. It showed four forty-five. Time was, as they, say certainly marching, if not quick marching on.

Penpunt was a small place, more of a hamlet than a village, but nevertheless on its main street, outside the church stood its statutory war memorial. That long gone Great War had cast its tentacles so wide and so far that the causalities of that bitter and bloody conflict had spread even to this quiet rural backwater. This backwater situated on a back road between nowhere and nowhere.

We had no sooner entered this community than we had left it. Some minutes later we were in the larger settlement of Moniaive and a stranger place, in a way, I have ever seen because it has a serious lack of pavements. The front doors of the cottages and houses simply opened straight onto the road. Obviously the denizens of this particular village had to take great care when leaving, or for that matter entering, their properties. This made the matters of egress and ingress highly problematic to say nothing of downright dangerous. Here was a health and safety nightmare in the making.

So amazed was I with the thorough absence of pavements, that once again I allowed us to overshoot our correct turning. However, after a bit of tricky manoeuvring, much admired by passing locals, a grunting William put us back on the true and narrow path to our destination, spinning the wheel and taking the car into a tight left turn at the town centre and setting course for St John's Town of Dalry.

En route we passed through a large wooded area called, apparently, Corriedoo which seemed to have enough Christmas trees to supply the whole country. According to Billy this was a place to note well, for a return visit later in the year.

As we cleared though St John's Town of Dalry we picked up signs for the forestry commission and for Clatteringshaws Forest. Here the road zigzagged wildly and unpredictably, some of the turns violently spiralling against the camber of the road, causing Billy to go up and down the gears as, according to me, a demon but according to him like a whore's drawers.

Then the zigzagging without warning ceased and seeing the road ahead now straight and level Billy accelerated. To the extent we flashed past a sign which announced Forestry Commission Clatteringshaws Forest. Before we had time to respond and react we were past it. However, no sooner than we had time to think about turning back, another sign announced Clatteringshaws Forest public car park, shop and picnic area two hundred yards ahead, "Look Billy, on the right. That's' us."

I pointed to the sign. Billy acknowledged, nodded his head and flicked on his indicator. We turned into a deserted car park and he drove the MG to the farthest corner of the hardstanding, parking up as near as you could take a car to the pedestrian exit. He killed the engine and we both alighted from the car.

We looked round before heading for the exit from the car park. Here we were confronted by a finger post that bore several legends. These informed that to the to the right lay the shop, the picnic area, the toilets, the Iron Age Roundhouse, and at one mile distance, that which we had journeyed to find, our desired destination: Bruce's Stone.

Chapter 36
In Which I See It Through

I passed Billy a bottle of water I had brought from the car, from which he took a quick slug, before handing it back. As he did I enquired,

"What time do you have?"

"Five to six, and it's time we were moving, so shall we?" was his terse reply.

We took the path in the direction as indicated by the sign, passing the shop and the toilets; both were firmly shut and shuttered. No place here apparently for the famished or the incontinent, to further accentuate this deserted theme, the picnic area was completely deserted. We carried on, coming to a path constructed from rough granite chips which are best walked on with thick-soled hiking boots, town shoes as I encountered this surface I realised, regretfully just do not do the job. We hobbled on past a tent-like structure, constructed of bent and woven thin tree branches, clearly as advertised, this was your actual Iron Age Roundhouse.

The land all around was very boggy with little streamlets criss-crossing the ground, joining and swelling bigger streams that pushed their way out to a stretch of water on our left, this presumably being Clatteringshaws Loch. A measure of how wet a winter it had been could be gauged by the fact that many of the shore-clinging bushes and trees were growing, no longer from the land, but were peeping out from the gentle lapping waves of the loch.

We crossed through a rustic wicket gate and entered the forest. Here there were tall Douglas firs, their high growing dense foliage immediately creating a skyward canopy and severely curtailing the light beneath. The path became widen out to the extent that it was now wide enough, in fact, to allow vehicular access. As we breasted a small rise, we saw down on the left in a clearing between the trees were parked a dirty white transit van and beside it – well cry hallelujah – the mysterious death dealing disappearing Porsche. I also noticed snaking away to the right a wide but rough metalled track, the entrance to the slip road we had failed to notice quickly enough to take on our initial approach.

The trees to our left gave way to give us another wonderful view across the loch which proved to be a seriously large body of water. A signpost assured us that we were on the right road and confided in what was clearly meant to be an encouragement to keep going, now that we were only half a mile from our destination. This royally connected stone was obviously a place of some significant pilgrimage in the 'season'. I stopped and moving closer to Billy, half whispered.

"Right Billy, time I think as they say in Scots to ca canny."

"Ca canny, you have," was his only reply. But I did notice his face was completely relaxed, almost expressionless as though he knew there was danger, not only knew but he welcomed it, almost it seemed relished it.

Further down the track we came to another clearing and there, big and bright and shiny, stood a Land Rover Discovery; top of the range sports model of course. It stood testament to the exact definition of a big boy's toy. That particular big boy was the big boy I was seeking,

Tricky Dickey and if the toy was here, therefore the toy's owner would not be far away. So my suspicions had been right and dear old Mrs. Weldon had overheard the conversation correctly. To paraphrase the words of a long-gone radio comic "Hail, hail the gang really was all here."

We continued to follow the path and our rate of progress was encouraged with another sign. This one indicated that we were now only one hundred and fifty metres from Bruce's Stone.

I turned to my companion and in another half-whisper I said in an attempt to lighten the situation, "Christ we've only come quarter of a mile and bloody hell we've gone all metric."

Billy gave a rueful smile and said, in an equally low voice, "That's these damned Eurocrats, they get everywhere with their continental measures."

Then touching my shoulder in an apparent gesture of caution he continued, his voice almost trailing off,

"Right remember your advice now is the time to ca extremely canny"

The path became narrower, now only enough room for two people to walk side by side in a more or less companionable manner. The undergrowth on both sides had become much denser here, although to the right there were a few yards of rough grass distancing the vegetation from the path.

Ahead the path turned sharply away and I could discern the sound of voices carry to my ears. Billy had obviously had also heard as he signalled for us to move across the grass, to the shelter of the low bushes on the right. We both stepped off the path. The ground here was alarmingly yielding and spongy like an over-taut trampoline beneath my feet. We made our way to the tree line and crouched down. As I knelt I could feel the moisture seeping from the bracken through the knee of my trousers. I paused momentarily and then cautiously edged my way to the apex of the turn. Risking a look I saw that the voices were coming from a group of figures. There were some four or five people gathered in the near distance. They were congregated round the base of a large roughly hewn piece of rock; this presumably was the eponymous Bruce's Stone.

Judging by the exaggerated and somewhat frantic arm movements of the participants, the discussion up ahead was if not bad tempered at least highly animated. A falling out amongst thieves perhaps I thought.

"What's the plan now Sherlock? Time to make a call to Lestrade, perhaps?"

Billy's voice came, quiet and low, but insistent in my ear.

I shrugged in a non-committal way; torn between the need for action and my fascination at the scene ahead. As I continued to watch, the meeting seemed to break up and several figures broke away and turned back towards us. Billy and I, in an effort of concealment, moved deeper into the bushes. As I peered out I could see the group approaching our hiding place. The man at the front was of an enormous stature, he had the mulish look of the terminally stupid. This had to be the one and only big Davie. Behind him almost snapping on his heels with the appearance of a little terrier, came a small, slight built man with the face of a weasel. Presumably this was Davies's half-brother, the equally notorious Wullie. He certainly bore all the resemblance of the runt of the litter.

Believing discretion to be the better part of valour, we cautiously drew even further back into the bushes to allow them to pass. After a few moments I gauged if safe for another glance and saw their departing backs. As they went from my view, I reckoned it was time for us to make a move. I prodded Billy, "Right William it's time for a call to arms."

He rose and we exited from our place of concealment and stepped out onto the path. As we rounded the bend, I saw leaning on the rock, inhaling greedily from a cigarette and apparently in deep reflection, my quarry. Here standing in front of me was the man that if he had not *actually* performed the act, had at the very least ordered my father's death. This was the master puppeteer, the deadly spider in the centre of his well-spun web. I had sworn to myself before embarking on this chase that this time, it would be biblical style retribution, a life for a life, even if I had to kill Dickey myself.

The noise of our feet on the path jolted him out of his reverie, he eyed us with curiosity, and as we moved closer his inquisitiveness turned to caution. As a slow realization coalesced in his mind, it gradually dawned on him that we were not passing hikers as we were not dressed for that pursuit, thus we were not there for the view, and we were there for him. So I thought only polite to confirm his suspicions, "Good evening Mr. Amiss, you're a difficult man to catch, I trust we find you well?"

His face took on what could only be described as a hunted look. He seemed to have lost his power of speech so I went on,

"No, Mr. Amiss you are absolutely right we are not a pair of twitchers looking for the Goldcrested Tit, a rare early spring visitor. I am by way of being your Nemesis. To be fair, I am, as many a keen birdwatcher, out to do a bit of spotting and I'm in a way of speaking on to the hunt, the hunt of the Lesser Spotted Liar. Do you know I think my hunt is at an end, yes I think I have, because you Richard, you don't mind me calling you Richard do you? You Richard are who I'm looking for – you old chum are my quarry. So let me dispense with the formalities. I don't think we have met have we? I am Alexander Gray. I believe you knew of my late father."

As my words hit home Amiss's expression changed from hunted to fear. He paled under his expensive shop bought tan and pressed himself back into the rock, as though by this action, the stone could somehow absorb him and by so doing, somehow save him. Then suddenly, realizing the futility of this act and the parlous nature of his position, he pushed himself back from the rock face and as I watched his hand dropped into his trouser pocket. When it reappeared it had grown, for when it re-emerged it had a shining silver extension.

Billy was the first to react he shouted at me, "Christ, Sandy watch out he's got a bloody gun!"

At the same time as his voice broke the silence, he launched himself at Amiss. His forward impetus caused them both to smack back against the rock, Amiss's head catching a small protuberance on the side of the monolith. Then they both toppled sideways and ended up sprawled on the turf. As the bodies untangled it was Billy who rose. His former protagonist lay supine and groggy on the ground at his feet. As William regained his feet I noticed in his right hand the gun, this he had taken possession of during the brief struggle. He shrugged and turned back towards where I was standing as he approached closer I pleaded with him, "The gun, give me the gun, William please. Let me have it. He was my father, it's time William, it's time for me to even my personal score."

Billy stared at me almost disbelievingly as though he hardly knew me anymore. Now it seemed he was torn between the dictates of a long-established friendship borne out of his troubles and forged in mutual difficulties, and the dictates of the law which he knew under different circumstance I would be obedient to. He moved as if to speak, perhaps even to plead for my sanity to return but before he could make this entreaty the air was full of noise. A cacophony of sound, the shrill noise of whistles, the clamorous shouting of human voices and the loud barking of dogs, the sound of pursuit.

As the clamour rose and fell, I glanced round behind me and I could see striding up the path towards us a tall grey haired uniformed policeman. On both his shoulders, he wore epaulets with rows of treble pips, denoting his rank. As he came closer he enquired,

"Is one of you Alexander Gray?"

His voice bore a heavily-accented Border's tone, which somehow in the present situation lent a reassuring feel. I stepped forward, hand extended,

"That will be me Inspector; sorry Chief Inspector."

"Good evening Mr. Gray. I'm Munro, sir. Chief Inspector Munro and you will be Mr. Clark."

This remark made to Billy.

"And this is?"

I turned back and pointed at the semi-comatose, recumbent figure on the ground, "This Chief Inspector Munro, is Richard Amiss thief, conman and at the very least, a commissioner of murders."

"And you two are you both alright, no injuries of any kind?"

We both nodded almost in unison like a pair of marionettes.

Reassured the policeman continued,

"And what about him, what's his problem?"

"Well, he pulled…"

I started but Billy laid a restraining hand on my shoulder, cutting me short.

"What Mr. Gray means Chief Inspector is that our friend here tried to pull a fast one and tried to escape, so I felt that in the interests of justice I had to restrain him.

Unfortunately in the ensuing tussle he accidentally hit his head on the side of that rock. He will come round presently, I'm sure."

Munro's walkie talkie spluttered and burred and made general 'answer me' squawking noises. He unclipped it and clicking a switch he spoke into it.

"Munro here, over, okay, okay yes all clear here. Sorry, what was that say again? Yes indeed, that is unfortunate. What, both of them? Yes, as you say, very unfortunate indeed, but you have the van, the Porsches and the other three? Right yes, I'm with them both now and they're both safe and sound. Oh one other thing can you perhaps send up a Paramedic we have a suspect down, yes that's right down, but not out."

He flicked the radio off and replaced it in the clip on his belt. He then took off his regulation issue hat and ran a hand through his iron grey hair. Then addressing Billy and I he confessed,

"I'm afraid to say gentlemen, especially after all the trouble you've been to, that this has not turned out to be an entirely successful operation., The Maxwell brothers got away, but not I suspect or hope for long. I hear we have their vehicles and they are now on foot. That I know that's not a mode of transport the larger and older of the brother's favours. We have another squad of officers raiding their encampment on the other side, on the far shore of the loch with any luck we should have the whole gang rounded up by night fall."

He smoothed down his unruly hair and, replacing his cap went on,

"Incidentally, Mr. Gray, I would have been here sooner, but Superintendent Gallagher's message was delayed for some reason or other at regional headquarters before being relayed to the Dumfries division, and then re-relayed to the local station. Never mind sir, as they say, better late than never."

He paused as though regretting that this last thought had been a comment too far. But then went on, perhaps feeling 'in for a penny in for a pound'.

"Mind you I have no doubt the excretia will well and truly hit the fan and there'll' be one hell of a stoochie when the Super finds out about the delay. She is, I'm told, a real stickler for optimum efficiency and the timeous carrying out of assignments, ah well."

I was listening with great interest to his report, as a man, clad in almost iridescent green overalls, came up the track and joined us. Munro signed to Amiss, who was now gently moaning murmuring and making coming-round noises. The medic knelt on the turf beside him, and opening his bag of tricks he, like the Good Samaritan, set about "lavishing help and succour upon him."

"Tell me one thing Chief Inspector. Your Super, the one you mentioned, that is your Superintendent Gallagher, she wouldn't happen to be blonde and have the Christian name of Samantha would she?"

"She certainly is and she certainly does Sir. Apparently, she joined the force straight from St Andrews where she gained a double first and then enlisted in the graduate accelerated promotion programme." Then he added with a mixture of what sounded like regret and remorse, "It's a scheme that seems to work, that is, for some people. Do you happen to know her sir?"

"Oh I know more of her. We've' had the odd drink or two."

Economy with the truth I judged was in this situation, what was called for.

As I spoke there came in rapid order a brace of heavily-breathing constables, a youngish sergeant and, in a moment of pure farce a dog handler. He appeared on the scene enter stage right, being dragged along in the wake of an extremely strong and apparently self-willed German Shepherd. The dog immediately set about trying to savage the by now recovering Amiss. Munro looked vaguely astonished and annoyed and appropriately barked out an order to the dog's supervisor,

"For God's sake, Constable Jamieson, you're supposed to a bloody dog handler; currently it's more like that beast is a police handler. Will you damned well pull yourself together?"

The offending constable seemed to be uncertain, caught on the horns of a dilemma, unsure whether to acknowledge the command by using a hand in salute. But fearing that if he did, that would leave only one hand on the dogs' leash. This he calculated would be insufficient to restrain his overexcited out of control charge. So he settled for a shouted,

"I'm trying my best, Chief Inspector."

With these ironic words both dog and master were last seen disappearing into some low lying scrub going in the direction of the loch, never to be espied by me again.

Munro shook his head as if in despair. As he did so I noticed the clamour was dying down, the police presumably casting their net further afield in an attempt to ensnare the missing brothers. Serenity was returning to the rural scene. We watched with interest as Munro's constables,' under the directions of the sergeant, handcuffed and lead away a still not entirely compos mentis Amiss. The Paramedic followed and the Chief Inspector made to follow suit, stopping only long enough to ask, "Can you follow us down to the local nick? It's at Kirkmichael and we can go through the formalities: statements and that sort of thing. Where are you parked, close by?"

"Yes, not far. We're in the public car park just at the start of the forest, where the shop is."

"Great, I know where you are. Right, see you as soon as you can."

With that he was gone leaving Billy and I to our own thoughts and devices he put his arms round my shoulders in a gesture of consolation, "You and I know Sandy, it is better this way; I don't think you could have lived with the guilt. You're too damned respectable to be an executioner. Morningside people never take the law into their own hands."

Then with an exaggerated put on posh voice he went on, "It's just not done old boy!"

With that he turned and made his way to the footpath, where after a moment's hesitation I joined him and we returned together companionably back down the track to the clearing. Here Amiss's well-polished motor was being carefully winched on to a police low loader. A cheerful constable who was in charge of the vehicles' removal, confided to us, that he was taking it away to allow the forensic boys, and girls to give it the once over.

We left a man obviously happy at his work and carried on down towards the path that led us out of the forest, as we came to the first clearing I noticed that the Porsche and the transit were receiving similar treatment to the Range Rover. These removals were being supervised by the good Chief Inspector, who waved a greeting.

I acknowledged his salutation and was about to carry on, when a thought occurred to me. So I stopped and moved across the clearing towards him, "Do you know, Chief Inspector, what with all that's gone on, something has slipped my mind, something well, rather important."

He moved away from the low loader and asked, "Right Mr. Gray and what's that; what's concerning you?"

"The Porsche, whose is it?"

"It's Maxwell's younger brother, Willie's. I'm told it's his pride and joy."

I shook my head.

"And Chief Inspector, it's also his weapon of choice. You will nail the bastard won't you?"

"Oh yes, sir we will not him slip through our fingers. We will have him, I promise you, we will as you requested nail him. See you at the station."

With that Munro spun on his heel and walked away to rejoin his uplift party.

Billy touched my arm companionably, "Right old son shall we? Let's hope that this paperwork doesn't take too long because, between you and me old friend, I murder a pint."

This woke me from my reverie of revenge and retribution, "Ah Billy; murder a pint! Consider me a potential serial killer in the murdering a pint department."

We walked out of the tree cover and through the wicket gate. The view caused me to stop and reflect, "That really is a bonnie stretch of water you know, a really beautiful view."

Billy agreed with my sentiments and we moved on. As we passed the reconstruction of the Iron Age Roundhouse a figure emerged from its interior and we found our path blocked by a short stocky figure, this was unmistakably the younger Maxwell. He almost radiated menace as he spat out his words,

"Goin' to the car park pal?"

My mouth dried, speech seeming to leave me, so it was Billy who took the lead. This was his territory here, he was truly at home.

"What's it to do with you if…"

A pause, to my stretched nerves a very long pause, "I am, pal."

Our protagonist's faced twitched as if in the grip of some terrible palsy, then an almost smirking smile flashed across his features.

"You see it's like this mate, dinae you be gein me ken oany of your cheek ken we need your stevestotter like so nae mare lip geus yer car keys."

Billy looked, if anything faintly amused and settled for a monosyllabic reply,

"We."

"That's right pal, we,"

A voice boomed from behind us. As I turned, there he was as big and ugly as life: Davie. Close up he looked every bit as formidable as his reputation.

The good Sergeant Macintyre's words came back to me "Walk carefully Mr. Gray walk carefully and carry a very big stick." In my present situation it would appear that I had been lamentably remiss on two counts. I had not looked over my shoulder often enough, and had completely failed to equip myself with the necessary large lump of wood.

It also occurred to me that the Borders Police Force, in particular Dumfries's' finest, were searching high and low for our two miscreants, looking everywhere for our very own grown gruesome twosome. Whilst the guardians of law and order were scouring the countryside, the fugitives were hiding in some bloody prehistoric Wendy House. God give me strength.

It was Billy, however, once more who was the first to respond. He spun round and to my surprise he was laughing out loud "There's no chance, no chance in hell that you would get into my car, not even if your life depended on it. No, no pal, you aren't going anywhere in my car, lardy butt."

By the expression on the big man's face this was not quite the expected response, not quite what happened to him in the normal run of things. He looked as though he was about to implode and he almost shouted at Billy,

"Dinae you be getting wide we us pal now's if you want to get oot oh this in yin bloody piece you'll dae whit you're bloody well telt."

He moved, or rather he shambled towards; us threat and intimidation emanating as unhealthy miasma from his substantial bulk.

"Sandy keep your eye on the poison dwarf there, while I sort out Big Daddy here,"

Davie's forward momentum was momentarily arrested. He paused and looked, if anything genuinely puzzled. Resistance and defiance were obviously not problems he and his brother had to deal with on a regular basis.

Again Billy's voice, low, commanding and confident, sounded. I began to feel that the whole situation was beginning, from my point of view, to take on surreal overtones. It as though I was in one of my less pleasant dreams. I heard my voice.

"Billy, Billy are you alright?"

"Sit tight everything, as they say, will be cool."

This was to my ears, an over confident reply.

As if coming out of a stupor Davie started again to move towards us, "You cheeky wee git I am going to wring you're bloody stupid, scrawny wee neck, like a damned chicken. I'll teach you to be a wido pal, you bloody nae user ye I'll…"

His voice trailed off as he and I both noticed that Billy's hand had grown the same extension as the one that Amiss's had grown earlier and like Amiss's it was long and glinting.

The extension, again arrested momentarily his forward movement, but then with a mixture of fury and bravado he lunged toward Billy yelling as he came,

"Dinae be stupit ye…"

The rest of Davie's words were cut off by the crack of the revolver, its report echoing round the clearing. His forward movement again arrested as he grasped his knee, mouthing a string of expletives. As he did I could see the blood trickling through his clenched fingers?

Then I heard Billy, almost expelling the words from his mouth,

"On your dammed knees or the next one goes in your gut, and that will hurt big time, you'll be screaming for your mother before the ambulance gets here. No, don't think about trying anything; don't be any stupider than you are. Christ at this range and the size of your belly you idiot, it would more difficult to miss you, than to hit you."

His brother, wee Wullie was making a sort of whining noise and as I turned round and watched I saw he was showing signs of real agitation bordering on fear. Was this a display of genuine brotherly love and fraternal affection I wondered? When he spoke he was pleading almost begging,

"Dae what he says Davie dinae risk it mithrer would ne'r forgive me if anything happened to you."

So he was motivated not so much by brotherly love, as by a fear of motherly reprisals, an inherent fear of incurring vengeful maternal wroth.

Davie, faced with the inevitable, duly sank to his knees. I indicated to his brother to join him and with an air bordering on resignation, he joined him.

Billy keeping a careful eye on our prisoners, said to me over his shoulder, "Right, maybe Sandy, you could now summon the cavalry that is if it's not too much trouble."

I pulled out my phone and as I looked at it I noticed the message which I immediately shared with my brother-in-arms.

"Billy, it says *no signal emergency calls* only."

"Sandy, do you know my friend; I think that this situation could be termed as an emergency."

We both laughed.

Epilogue

Summer had now arrived, hot and full blown. I sat in the drawing room in my mother's flat, with the blinds half drawn against the offending morning rays. My mother looked up from her copy of the 'Scotsman' and enquired,

"So, Alexander, have you made up your mind whether to stay in Edinburgh or go on your travels' again?"

I put down my coffee cup on the ornate Late Victorian fireplace. Above on the wall, taking pride of place was a portrait executed in oils of my late and dearly missed father. Before replying to my mother's question, "Well mother I think that all things considered, I will probably stay on for a while. Now that I have caught up with old friends, it would be a shame to take off again so quickly and the firm is not yet back on course and naturally I will be required to testify at the upcoming trial."

"You know there are some of your friends that…"

"Mother please can we let it drop. Billy helped me out of an extremely tight spot and did help me find father's killer."

She looked as though she were about to suggest that he only pulled me out of a situation I would have not been in had I not had him as an acquaintance at all, but settled for, "Is Charles over everything now?"

"Yes, he's on the mend. His ego I'm sure will survive and Camilla is on remand as an accessory of Amiss. He is being charged with robbery and inciting murder, well, with her not on the scene it makes the whole thing a lot easier."

"And what of these dreadful travelling people, what's become of them?"

"The Maxwell brothers; they will not see the light of day for many a long year."

"Well that's that and now we can all get back to normal. Of course, you know Alexander you are welcome to stay here as long as you wish, after all this is your home!"

I shook my head and walked towards the door, I opened it, but before going through, I paused and looking directly at her said, "Well thank you kindly mother. However, this is your home; to me this will only ever be a house."

Fifteen love to you Alexander I thought, I smiled, I left.